CW00696508

When the
Moon
was White

When the Moon was White

JEFF PROBST

Matador
Unit E2 Airfield Business Park,
Harrison Road, Market Harborough,
Leicestershire. LE16 7UL
Tel: 0116 2792299
Email: books@troubador.co.uk
Web: www.troubador.co.uk/matador
Twitter: @matadorbooks

ISBN 978 1803132 365

British Library Cataloguing in Publication Data.
A catalogue record for this book is available from the British Library.

Printed and bound in the UK by TJ Books Limited, Padstow, Cornwall
Typeset in 11pt Minion Pro by Troubador Publishing Ltd, Leicester, UK

Matador is an imprint of Troubador Publishing Ltd

Goodmews, South Dakota

ONE
Early spring, 1965

Francine had always doubted it could happen. That a person visiting a place for the first time, could be so taken by it they would decide to return. But on her first Goodmews evening, gazing up at the moon as she stood alone on the salmon-pink pavement, bathed in the front gardens' white-flowered fragrance, she said to herself, *Yes, the moon is the moon; Goodmews's is no brighter than any other. But is there something in the way it hangs above the orangewoods? The way it reflects off the Mars-coloured cliffs?*

And I thought my heart belonged to Arizona.

Even though she'd been drawn to Goodmews by the TV programme about its moon, she soon found that the town beguiled her too. After a few disoriented walks past rows of houses along bendy streets, she got used to seeing windows and chimney stacks directly ahead. And she found herself warming to the Goodmews accent, which at first had seemed disconcertingly harsh for such a gentle-feeling place. As she listened more carefully, the discordant twang became less bitter and began to dissolve into something like a dark chocolate, that was coating a softness inside. And she liked the way that people said 'Goodmews', with the stress falling lightly on 'Good'.

She often ended up on Goodmews Way, stopping outside the scaffolded church, which reminded her of the pictures she'd seen of Gaudi's basilica in Barcelona. It struck her as Goodmews's own bandaged creature, but beneath its timeworn boards and blackened bricks, she could sense its balanced beauty.

TWO

GOODMEWS

1643 YARDS

The train trundled through another endless thicket of trees before emerging again into the open. Sam saw a small brown tourist sign staked in the ground.

WELCOME TO GOODMEWS

Below the words was a sketch of a crescent moon above a white church surrounded by scaffolding. *Bullpucky*, Sam said to himself. He disembarked and walked along Goodmews Way, checking his watch every couple of minutes, quickly getting past a place called JOHNNY'S with The Supremes' 'Baby Love' coming from inside.

A restaurant, AN-O-<u>DINE</u>, had its slogan on the door.

SAFE FOOD
FOR THE CAREFUL AT HEART (AND STOMACH)

Such malarkey. He recalled snarling at the TV a few nights before, feeling afterwards that the 'Decade of the

3

Moon' programme, which usually focused on America's Space Race, had wasted his time by featuring *this* place just because its residents felt the moon here was unusually bright.

But in the end he'd decided to recce it. It looked like it was probably small enough, naïve enough, to be the sort of place he could put his stamp on; and South Dakota wasn't all that far away.

He went up and down a few side streets, passing a furniture shop, One Nightstand. It had a *1* on it and the street name, Good Morning. Next door was LETTERBOX HEAVEN.

MAIL SLOTS
MADE TO ORDER

Sam studied the crescent-shaped letterbox that had pride of place in the window. *Is that what people in this 'moon' town want? Bent mail?*

He paused at the clock tower just outside the station. A poem, framed in orange wood and protected by glass, was affixed to the bricks at reading height.

> When the moon comes over Brooklyn
> On time with the borough clock
> 'Tis the same that saw Palmyra
> And the walls of Antioch.
> — Nathalia Crane

Give me a break.

He looked up at the clock. There were letters and dots going round in place of numbers. Instead of a one, there was a G; instead of a two, there was the letter O; and instead of a three, there was a dot. The same pattern of letters and dots went round until it got to where eleven would be, and there was an S, to complete the spelling of GOODMEWS.

What is the point – of any of this? He walked round to the other side and read the notice that someone had stuck up.

FULL MOON GAZERS!
TONIGHT 8 P.M.
14 WEST STREET
GM'S DARKEST AND NOOKIEST MOON-NOOK
ALL WELCOME

The trees blurred as the train picked up speed. At least it had only taken him half a morning. He hadn't grasped the fact from the 'Decade of the Moon' that Goodmews might be one of those phoney-feeling places that seemed to be cropping up these days, places with 'cool' clothes, as they put it, and trendy shops, even turning some into so-called community spaces. These towns trumpeted how different they were to 'the mainstream', but Sam had found in his scouting about that they were much more like each other than different to anything. He'd take the mainstream any day.

A train whistle roused him, and he woke with an image of Goodmews lodged in his mind. He wouldn't have admitted it to anyone, but the closest he could get to a picture of it, was that of an innocent town nestled below a downy fuzz of green, in a virgin valley, offering itself to him.

Could he do what he wanted with it? It clicked into place. It *was* the decade of the moon.

5

THREE

On the last morning of her visit Francine did her Orangewood Drive amble again. Even though at times she rued the fact that her knowledge of the outdoors got in the way of merely enjoying it, the simple act of walking almost always made her feel good. And as she carried up the gently rising lane, appreciating nature's gradations of shades, she thought, *Is there anything more wonderful than unabashedly walking by yourself, looking at, thinking, what you want.*

She passed a manurey-smelling field of sheep, chomping and cropping bright green pasture, enclosed in one of the low stone walls that criss-crossed the hills. She stopped to watch a lamb scratching at its face with its hind leg, seemingly in time to a bird tweeting, then looked back towards Goodmews. Would a Martian think it was home, as it ruminated on the terracotta colour of the cliffs? They looked rose madder, a washed-out red she liked experimenting with.

As she walked on, she could smell what she thought were Shasta daisies, then saw it was cows. Their black and white patches made her think of the moon – its bright rays and peaks, and the darker face of the Man. Then she smelled the pineyness, and soon the grove towered up – giant orange poles fronded with green. She went through the stile and walked in, weaving through trees on barely visible paths that were now floored in leaves as slippery as magnolia petals. *It's the sort of place*, she felt, *that you wouldn't see litter, even a banana peel.*

Off to her right the gamboge tree jumped out at her. She was surprised at how assuredly she'd found it again, but it was much shorter and thinner than most of the orangewoods and obvious with its lemon-like fruit. She circled it to confirm what she'd known the first time. It was clearly ripe enough to make extracting its colourful sap worthwhile.

She took out the hook she'd brought and screwed it as far as it would go into the tree trunk, then got out her bamboo cup from Happy Goblet Massage, hanging it so it was flush with the tree. With her penknife she made small spiral incisions in the bark, just above the cup.

She watched one milky-yellow drop fall into it. It was tangible proof of what biologists studying the area had determined: orangewoods are also found elsewhere in the world, but only here did they co-exist with gamboges.

A pine needle floated down, like a small bird treading air.

She watched for the next drop. The plodding Stones song 'I Am Waiting, I Am Waiting' came into her head. As the local Sioux had apparently once said, 'yellow pain' is what gamboges bled.

I'll come back in five minutes to see what I have.

She walked back to the path she'd come from, and continued deeper into the grove than she'd been before. A piece of paper tacked to a tree stopped her in her tracks.

THE ORANGEWOODS
TOOTHPICK BEHEMOTHS OF SILENT GRANDEUR

It looked like someone had written it with blue pen, though the words were faded; they'd no doubt run in the rain or from the grove's greenhouse moisture.

She liked what it said. It made sense. And she liked the idea of someone tacking up their take on the woods for others to happen upon. She took out her pen and a piece of paper and copied down the words.

Back at the gamboge tree, a few beads of sap glistened up at her from the bottom of the cup. 'Sap'-ling, she thought, like young sap. It would take time to fill up, months probably.

Maybe it was too close to the path to be hidden, but she'd leave it as it was – a symbol of the promise she'd made to herself to return to Goodmews one day.

FOUR

A muffled announcement confirmed that the train was approaching Goodmews, quickening Sam's pulse. The thicket thinned, and a louvre of sun opened out to a window of blue.

He grabbed his suitcases and walked into town and along Goodmews Way, stopping outside JOHNNY'S. A white-haired man stood looking out of the large front window. Sam smiled and walked in. No one else there.

'Hello, sir,' Johnny smiled.

'Hello. I'm Sam.'

'I'm Johnny. Nice to meet you.' His voice sounded raspy, unfriendly, to Sam.

'Nice to meet you too. Just to explain myself and all this baggage... I was here for a short visit a few months ago, after that programme on Goodmews?'

Johnny nodded.

'It made me curious, and the place stuck with me, and I thought I'd give it a try, at least for the summer. Do you have a minute? Could I ask you a couple of questions?'

'Sure!'

'Could we sit down?'

'Of course. I'm not busy. Would you like anything?'

'Would I like anything. Do you have any cake?'

'Cakes are coming later, I'm afraid. Biscotti?'

Sam had no idea what that was. 'No, I'm alright.'

Johnny led him to a table along the wall and sat across from him. The wooden chair was uncomfortable, the back too straight.

'So what brought you back?'

Sam shrugged. 'The place has character… it's *diff*erent. Wonderful clock, great little shops…'

'You're able to just up-sticks?'

Sam felt he could tell what Johnny meant. 'Yeah. I'm only renting. I put my stuff in storage. See how it goes.'

'Well, welcome. Do you have plans?'

'Do I have plans?' Sam's heart was suddenly pounding. He gave himself a minute to shape his answer. 'Well, I'd like to contribute something – pay my entry fee, so to speak.'

'You mean money?'

'Not necessarily, unless you think I should?'

'No no.'

'The thought I had was… Does Goodmews have its own newspaper?'

'No. Only 500 people.'

'Do you think people might want one? Would *you*?'

Johnny moved his head side to side, like the jury was out. 'Depends I suppose, what's in it. Never been one. Have you done them before?'

'Newsletters. Smaller scale. But if there are only 500 people here…'

'Well, maybe you could introduce yourself, introduce the idea. See what people say.' Johnny was onside, or at least not against the idea.

'Sounds good. I'd start with a single sheet of paper... Does anything go on here that people might want to read about?'

'Oh. Bits and pieces.'

'Not much?'

'Things do happen. We've got building works next door right now, in fact. You can see it being fitted out every day.'

Sam nodded. 'One thought I had... if people were interested... is that this "news sheet" could include residents' thoughts about the moon, like in the programme – why people feel it's special here.'

'Well,' Johnny nearly growled, 'I think the last time I heard the moon mentioned, besides that programme, was someone complaining about it shining too brightly through their window.'

Was Johnny trying to be funny? Sam smiled. 'I understand. But do you think it might be fun for people – to see their own ideas and their names in print, and seeing others'?'

'Maybe... Give it a go. The main thing is, you "come in peace"; it's a gift you'd like to give to us as a newcomer and you're seeing if it's something Goodmews wants... Would you charge for it?'

'No.'

'Fair enough. Do you have a typewriter?'

Sam nodded. His foot was in the door.

'How are you going to distribute it.'

Sam shook his head. 'I hadn't thought about that. Maybe put it on the notice board I saw somewhere?'

'Tell you what. I've got one of those new machines – a "photocopier"? – at the back. It's the only one in town besides the library but it's hardly used. I can show you how this one works. In fact, why don't you take it.'

'You sure?'

'Happy to.'

'Great. Thanks.'

'I don't know if you know, but we have something called Bank Holiday here – celebrates England.'

Sam wondered why Johnny was bringing this up. 'Don't know about that. Why do you have that?'

'Not really sure. But people's letterboxes are one of the offshoots of it. Most of the mailboxes outside homes have been removed. So you need to put your newsletter through the letterboxes, the mail slots.'

'Alright. I saw the shop. They can be odd shapes – but very inventive!'

Johnny half-nodded. 'I use a wooden spoon on Station Road to stick my menus through number 44. It's a tricky one.'

'Good to know. I'll give the café some publicity.'

'No need for that, especially now with the programme… Just give me a few copies to keep here.'

'But you've helped me. It's the least I can do.'

'Don't worry about it,' Johnny waved the thought away. 'Everyone knows I'm here… Anyway, just to mention, try not to look in living rooms when you go up the path to people's houses.'

Thwaite hardly needed Johnny to tell him how to deliver a leaflet.

'And it will stand you in good stead if you remember the position their gate was in when you went through it.

12

Was it closed – latched? Could you *just* squeeze through the amount it was open? Number six East Road never shuts; it's always banging in the wind. And *do* go back through the gates. You've heard the expression, "Quick as a mailman"?'

'Yes.'

'Well, don't be. Don't just do a quick hop over to the next house like the mailman sometimes does. People don't like it. He tramples things sometimes.'

'I won't.'

'I'm sure… So, where are you staying?'

'I don't have a place yet.'

'Check out Sky Cottage. It's been empty for a while, furnished. In Jones Place.'

'Joan's Place?'

'Yep. Named after Mr. Jones.'

'OK… Is he still around?'

'Popped his clogs long ago.'

Sam cocked his head.

'Sorry,' Johnny rasped. 'Just one of those English expressions we use. I'm sure if you stick around you'll hear them. Anyway. It was Mr. Jones's parlour pew in the church?'

Sam nodded, but he couldn't remember if the programme had mentioned Mr. Jones. 'Is there a map to Jones?'

Johnny shook his head. 'Jones *Place* – there's also a Jones Lane and a Jones Walk. The cottage is just round the corner,' he gestured. 'You can't miss it – small bungalow all by itself, if you like that. It's on at a fair rate.'

'How much?'

'I think I can get it for you for a hundred.'

'You know the person.'

'Everyone knows everyone.'

Sam's impulse was to just get it done, but what did he have to lose; there'd always be somewhere.

'Is that a month?'

'Yeah.'

'Including utilities?'

'Yep.'

'Would he do it for 90?'

'It's a she. Mrs. Cantrell.'

Johnny gave him a slightly questioning look, but Sam didn't flinch. 'That should be alright,' he said.

Johnny held out his hand and Sam shook it. 'I'll check with her; back in 15 minutes if anyone comes in. Can I get you a cup of coffee.'

'Sure. Thank you.'

FIVE

As the train began to slow, Tris looked out at the sun-dappled trees, still apple-green. *It's the yellow that dapples,* he thought, *the yellows to the light have it this year; the yellows have it.*

The programme had intrigued him enough to go out and buy *South Dakota: A Guide to Remote Towns*, and he opened it to the bookmarked Goodmews section. To read the *Guide* again now, nearly in situ, was to him the most pleasurable way to read a book about any place, as pleasurable as the feeling he got from wearing socks that still fluffed with life, or when flopping down on a bed with the current issue of a magazine.

He skimmed through the potted history of the town, with its still-unfinished church, its celebrated cemetery, its special regard for its 'glacial sharp' moon.

'Tackle your belongs with you,' he thought he heard. 'I'll be making my wee through the train. Any questions, hesitate to ask.'

He saw a WELCOME sign with the moon above a scaffolded church.

The train pulled into the station, its wooden platform open to the sky. When he alighted, what struck him as a warm summary of raindrops fell for a moment.

By the time Tris reached Goodmews Way, the morning sun had emerged, enveloping and buttery. *Why is it the done thing,* he wondered, *to stick your face up to the sun on the beach, but not on the street?*

The pink pavement was spread out ahead of him like a Yellow Brick Road, but pink, and was as pretty as the *Guide* had described it. It was almost *pink*-orange, a colour he'd marvelled at in pictures of old timber-framed houses in English villages.

There were few cars or people out yet, and the air had a green-hedgey freshness. Tris could turn a blind nose to the smell of dope if that happened to be in the air, but not to the sweetness of plants. He got that triad of spring all at once – scent, breeze and sun. 'The birds and the be-ees,' he sang in a drawly voice, 'are sweeter than huh-ney…' – the wrong words, probably, but the tune was close.

A couple of shops looked like they had just opened. One was MOLLYCODDLE.

FOR CREATURE COMFORTS
SOFT FURNISHINGS SWEETS TRADITIONAL TOYS

Mollycoddle, he thought. *Mommycuddle.*

'A Hard Day's Night' was coming out of another shop – SORRY WE'RE OPEN, that looked like it sold antiques. Either next door or the same shop was BECAUSE WE'RE OPEN! He liked that; it was fun. He walked against a snake of uniformed schoolgirls tailing a teacher about three times their height but wearing the same horizontal stripes. A couple of the lither-looking girls were doing dancing moves and twirls.

He found himself outside the church.

To Tris, it was a famous place – a place read about suddenly made flesh, and he felt privileged to be in its presence.

Upstanding gravestones walled-in the churchyard, the 'final resting place', as the *Guide* put it, for some unusual inscriptions and artistic headstone carvings. But it felt like more than just a busman's holiday for him.

Many of the stones were sharp, dark, sleek slate, which he'd been told by carvers was their favoured material to work in, as it behaved as they expected, giving them almost complete control over the material. The carving, though, was the hard part, often having to be done quickly if the work was outside in the rain or cold. The proofreading was easier.

He began to walk amongst the graves, looking at the dedications and decorations and always to see if there were any misspellings or anyone had died on today's date or his birthday. Many of the stones were weathered and old, their chiselled messages hard to read, like writing reflected in water might be.

He saw a memorial to an Inspector Honeymoon, with a magnifying glass etched on his tombstone, and saw one to an assistant auto mechanic, Mrs. Decent, her stern face embossed in relief above her name and a sculpted car. SHE URNED HER REST was on a vase next to her grave. Another quote was on John Dainty's headstone: 'WE LOVED HIM TO DEATH', with quotation marks for some reason. An engraved trail ran up the side of the headstone to a few rough-hewn trees. The quote marks had made him think about air quotes. *Do people draw them in single or* double *quotes? Does it depend on where they live? Do some people even take the trouble to do sharp-cornered ones if they're written that way in their country?*

One stone, lying flat on the ground, had a Jewish star on it. The epitaph read:

'The moon is falling down on the ground — God's big tear.'
— From a poem by Jan Maria Gisges-Gawronski,
an inmate of Birkenau.

Below that was the person's name.

The cemetery seemed remarkably devoid of Hallmark-like messages. Maybe they'd been banned, or people just knew they wouldn't belong there. The oddest dispatch he saw, as he called them, was to an administrator, the 'aforementioned' Mr. Adams. It was written in bullet points on what looked like a scroll and used management-speak acronyms, some of which he knew. One was 'BSR' – Blue Skies Research, a term that had come into use as a result of Sputnik a decade before. But would other people know these? And how funny would they find it? Management-speak was killing English. Dead-speak. But the dead don't speak.

Tris went up the church's concrete steps and pushed through the heavy, unlocked doors. Nobody had been about, and it did feel like a place that had lain undisturbed for years. It was peaceful; the outside world was blocked out, and there was that church quiet, unlike any other quiet –

contemplative, trusting. It was cold – 'cold in the isles', he played with, as he walked down the aisle, between stone pillars and the box-pews the programme had shown, pews enclosed in orange wooden panels. He could pick out the large 'parlour pew' that had apparently once been as lavishly furnished as a living room and used for the town grandees to entertain guests and observe sermons. Now its fireplace was bricked-up, and dust covered the table in the corner.

He walked back on to Goodmews Way, smack into the slipstream of someone's unmistakable English Leather. It was the first bum note he'd come across. He would have liked Brut or Ambush; English Leather smelled like furniture polish. It wasn't as bad as exhaust fumes, but he'd always found it overwhelming, like incense that sucks the fresh air out of formerly scent-free places. He wondered why someone would want to emanate such a scent. It would only attract the few who liked the smell; otherwise it was like a force repelling everyone else. He held his breath until he was pretty sure he'd walked for long enough to escape any trace of the cologne's smelly wake.

He turned up Fred Cougarman Balconies, another side-road named after a local, he supposed, the street sign marked with their birth and death dates. He wondered who these people were and what they'd done to deserve to be remembered.

Close to the station, Tris passed by a corner shop with its name on a bright pink hoarding above it: SORRY FOR ANY INCONVENIENCE. In the shop window it said YOUR LOCAL CONVENIENCE STORE. *No need to apologize*, he thought. *Thank you for spelling it right.*

Outside JOHNNY'S he read the sign in the window: YOUR ONLY DIETARY REQUIREMENT – TO FEEL HUNGRY. He tossed that around in his mind. *Yes, the hungrier you are, the tastier the food – at least until you let yourself get so hungry that you lose that edge and your stomach starts to hurt.* He recalled coming across a similar quip: 'The best analgesic is distraction.'

He could see 'Johnny', he assumed it was, an older man who was standing just inside, looking out. It occurred to Tris that it would be a great place to linger if you were the sort of person who was addicted to engaging passers-by in conversation. You could smile and wave at people you knew, with the hope of enticing them in to chat. He wondered if Johnny – if that was him – was like that.

He was smiling at Tris. Tris half-smiled back and walked in, though he probably would have avoided such a person back home.

'Welcome.' The man had a rough friendly-sounding voice, but his protruding nose-hairs made his face a bit difficult to look at. FEEL HUNGRY was on his T-shirt.

'Thank you. Are you Johnny?'

'Yes, sir, that's me. Can I get you something?' He pushed the words out in a slightly strangled way. It didn't sound like he didn't want to talk, but that it was just how his voice was.

'No. Thank you. Is it OK if I have a quick look around? I've only got a few minutes.'

'Sure thing.'

The café seemed to sport a ubiquity of ketchup bottles, and the walls were festooned with garish paintings. There was also one of those 'sun' clocks, with pointed brassy 'rays' coming out of it.

'Can I ask… Are these *moon* pictures?'

'They are.' Johnny pointed to a large black and white drawing. 'Jules Verne. Right over there. Just a copy of course. Did you know that in one of his books about a rocket to the moon three astronauts were launched from Florida – and landed back in the ocean? And that was *200* years ago.'

'I didn't know that.'

'And over there – that's a photograph.'

'Of the moon?' It was a blotchy-looking round image.

'Yes.'

'How *old* is that?'

'Hundred years?'

'They took photographs of it back then?'

'Yes…'

Tris heard 'Ramblin' Rose' in the background, a relaxed, loping-along song, no airs and graces, like Johnny's felt. Nat King Cole, Tris knew it was, and was pretty sure he'd heard recently that he was ill.

'Can I have a look at the menu? I might be back.'

Johnny picked one up and handed it to him. Just about every menu Tris had ever seen had something wrong with it – a spelling mistake, or something only a proofreader would notice or care about, like a letter that was higher or bigger than the others. Scanning Johnny's, though, he didn't see anything wrong. At the top it said, 'One Size Fits All'. Johnny was near enough. Tris pointed at the title. 'What does that mean?'

'Well, we're all different sizes, aren't we. But everyone everywhere gets the same size portion of food as everyone else when they order. And pretty much everyone finishes what's on their plate, don't they.'

Tris realized that when he walked into restaurants and made his way to a table, he usually looked first at what people were eating, not at the person eating it. He'd never thought about the size of a helping in relation to the size of an eater.

'I guess that's right,' he said. He could see that JOHNNY'S wasn't the sort of place that would have a children's menu, in any case. He decided not to ask about the odd-sounding items like Vulgur wheat salad and Million-raisin pastries. He said thanks and left, to strains of 'I'm a Believer'. *Who would want a pastry overwhelmed by raisins?* he thought. *Nobody likes raisins that much. Though sultanas are worse. You can spend a morning picking them out of a Belgian bun.*

At the clock tower, he looked up at the .GO.OD.ME.WS clock face.

What a great idea. And a beautiful clock.

The long hand was at the S, the short hand just before the dot at the top. 11.55.

The train was moving. Seated in an empty coach, Tris saw a THANK YOU FOR VISITING GOODMEWS sign out the window. Thank *you*, he thought. Though he'd only spoken at the café, he'd come away with the feeling that Johnny was probably a typical Mewsician, as they called themselves, with his unprepossessing nature – so unlike those faux-nice types in expensive shops, where they call you sir just because you're somewhere where things cost more.

And he liked the music in Johnny's and around town.

Goodmews had an innocence, like children playing in a paddling pool, or someone raking leaves. Tris found himself quietly singing 'Oh the shark's tooth…', the way he remembered Mack the Knife's opening words and as far as he ever got.

Goodmews was within striking distance. Maybe he *would* be back. Maybe he'd be able to add something of his own to the town.

SIX

Goodmews, the briefness of her visit notwithstanding, had carved out what felt like a permanent place in Francine's heart, and during a break at university it had dawned on her that she could have her cake and eat it. For 'older' students like her, the university offered her course, Astro-Geology, by correspondence. It was an opportunity she couldn't pass up, and there was nothing keeping her in Arizona. She could spend her final year in Goodmews, using her savings to experience life there. It would seem to be the apt place to study, especially since she'd chosen the moon as her field of interest.

*

Francine's move felt right. The time went quickly for her. The people were friendly, she explored the area, she got what she needed to furnish her flat.

One afternoon she treated herself to the horse-and-carriage tour which, she had read, was once conducted

24

in sedan chairs, though now by coachwomen in yellow waistcoats and wide-brimmed Ladies' Day hats.

The woman shouted out sights to the group as she giddyapped the reins, in that accent Francine no longer found coarse, but neither was it plain.

They rode past the ingenious clock face then stopped by the church, where the woman pointed out the dilapidated message board high up on the side. The white paint was peeling like a birch tree's bark but without the wispy beauty. The woman said that, years before, a new saying was put on the board each week, and recited one.

' "Faith, hope and charity, the virtues..." '

Francine jotted it down, and the rest:

health, safety & comfort: the necessities.

Back on Goodmews Way, the woman said, 'If it's OK I'll just take five more minutes,' which Francine knew meant she was going to. She stopped the carriage and pointed. 'That yellow door is Daff's, like in "daffodils", that it becomes every spring. In September you'll see it change back to Heather's, with a pink door. And that bench in front. Has anyone seen the dedication on it? It's that famous line, written by a poet named Ernest Dowson: "They are not long, the days of wine and roses". And the bench in the park? It has what one of our own once wrote: "If you're tired of reading benches, you're tired of Goodmews"... You laugh, but messages on benches are much loved here, and in fact until recently, "dedication defacement" was a fineable offence... Goodmews has retained some of its own community regulations, though, which you may have read about. One is the prohibition on picking daffodils anywhere in town.'

Good, Francine thought. *It's unthoughtful to pick daffodils, uncommunity, if that's a word.*

'Well, this is the end of the tour. Are there any questions.'

There were a surprising number, most of which Francine recalled as having been debunked as rumour in *Remote Towns*. She had the sense that her fellow riders, probably tourists, didn't have any real interest in Goodmews but since they were here they would ask questions to demonstrate their keenness to learn about it. If they'd read the *Guide*, though, they would have had to come up with questions other than those they were now asking: 'Was there ever a muezzin in Goodmews?' 'Was there once a coat of arms?' 'Was a plague pit ever found here?' 'Was there a time when money wasn't exchanged for certain services, such as the sewing on of a button?' 'Have there ever been moon murals, or walls where people wrote the date they viewed the moon and how they reacted?' 'Wasn't there a shop where you had to tell a joke to enter?' 'Was there really a Mr. Bedroom?'

The woman had answered everyone with a polite no. 'Anyone else?'

'May I?' said a man at the back. The woman nodded.

'Can you tell me where "Goodmews" comes from?'

'As you may have read, no one knows for sure. The most widely accepted explanation is that the founders and some of the earliest residents were English, or at least Anglophiles: you may know about celebrating Bank Holiday here and you've probably seen the English-looking houses and the church. And it's probably why we have a so-called Wet Fish shop. Mews are English too – cute backstreets that used to

26

be rows of stables with living quarters above them.'

'Are there any here? Or even in America?'

'Not here. Only in New York I think.'

*

Sometimes, just for the fun of it, Francine would walk around town wearing her tinted sunglasses – imbuing everything, including the wettened green grass, with red. There was a path that carried on west, out to the countryside, and if it was close to sunset she'd take her shades off and gaze down the path, through the shadowing arch of leaf-full boughs that joined the trees on either side, trees whose leaves in the breeze sounded soothingly crackly-windy, like raindrops spattering. At the end of the path she sometimes saw a semicircle of softly coloured light, shaped like the moon's top half, lit in a pale pink – a Van Gogh-washed pink, a Giacometti rock-pink. It lowly glowed salmon, like the Goodmews pavement or the deeply streaked piece of polished celestobarite she'd seen for sale in the Happy Goblet.

*

With some trepidation, once she felt ready she took herself on the long walk up to the orangewood grove to locate the bamboo cup. It was still there, fixed to the gamboge tree. It appeared to be undisturbed and was nearly half-full with a substance that looked like shiny lemon curd. Pleased with the colour and how much she'd collected, she had a walk through the more open areas of the grove and found what seemed to her to be a geologist's dream. Mineral-rich rocks

– their crystalline molecules giving them their colour – lay all around, and she collected some she knew and some she didn't. She was always on the lookout for meteorites in places like this, having learned how to recognize them from her course. The prize for her would be to find one from the moon, or Mars, but she knew the likelihood was low; almost all meteorites were simply fragments of asteroids.

*

Francine picked up the day's post, on the floor in the common hallway inside the main door. Four copies of a typewritten sheet were amongst everything else and she put what wasn't hers – everything today – onto the side table and took one of the sheets back into her flat.

<u>The Goodmews Occasional. Issue 1.</u>
Tuesday, August 3, 1965

To the residents of Goodmews,

I would like to introduce myself. My name is Samuel Thwaite. I first visited your town in the spring, attracted by the 'Decade of the Moon' episode that some of you contributed to and I would guess many of you saw.

So, she wasn't the only one who'd come here because of the programme.

I decided to return, because it's beautiful here and – for want of a better expression – it feels comfortable here.

She'd have to meet this person; maybe she'd seen him around.

> I can't know at the moment how long I'll be here for, but I'm here for now, and I would like to contribute something to your town as a thank you for your warm hospitality. Hence this newsletter, which you have received a copy of as one of the households in Goodmews. I hope it hasn't come as too much of a shock. I know I am new here and some of you may feel that an 'incomer' starting a newsletter so soon doesn't seem quite right. I understand that, and ask that you let me know if you feel this way. In the meantime, here are my thoughts about it.
>
> As long as people are happy with the idea of a newsletter, I propose to call it <u>The Occasional</u>, and, with your approval, would put it out around every two weeks.
>
> My plan is to keep it small and at this stage do it myself, typing it up at Sky Cottage, where I'm staying.

She'd seen Sky Cottage on her walks around town. It had looked neglected, by itself at the edge of a field. But she could see that someone had just moved in.

> I would like the newsletter to be a two-way organ of communication, and as my first order of business I am asking that you let me know, by August 15, your thoughts on not only whether you approve of having a newsletter, but how it might function as a forum for community news and discussion.
>
> If I may suggest one other thing. Everyone is aware of Goodmews's beautiful moon; as much as anything else, that has helped to put your town on the map. I feel it could give the newsletter a special 'flavour' if it included some

of your own thoughts about the moon here. They might be thoughts similar to – or beyond – those expressed in the TV programme. Please let me know what you think about this idea too.

I look forward to your responses, which will help shape the newsletter's direction.

Thank you.

Samuel Thwaite,
Sky Cottage

A newsletter sounded like a good idea, but it seemed best that she leave it to the true Mewsicians to Yea or Nay it. Maybe she too should give something back to the town. She felt lucky to be here.

*

<u>The Goodmews Occasional. Issue 2.</u>
Wednesday, August 18, 1965

I appreciate all the notes of welcome and support I have received over the past two weeks. There has been no opposition to the idea of a newsletter, and your comments in favour of it have been greatly encouraging.

Over and above that, the enthusiasm with which some of you have expressed your thoughts about the moon here has given me another idea. (This newsletter is already becoming the two-way organ I hoped it would be!):

The town has an identity inseparable, it seems, from the moon. That is partly what drew me here in the first place, and perhaps drew some of you as well. And I can see that The Occasional, in addition to its news function, will be a great way for Goodmews to 'compare notes' on its moon.

However, from what you've taught me in my short time here about yourselves and your town, I believe that Goodmews can become something more, and I would like to run the following idea by you.

The world has entered the Space Age, and Goodmews's relation to its beautiful moon could fit in with this, from Goodmews's unique perspective.

I assume we all respect the feelings of those who wear their 'alternative' look 'on their sleeve', openly declaring their beliefs in what the moon represents for them. My proposal, however, would entail a much more straightforward view of the moon.

In the light of President Kennedy's promise to get a man to the moon this decade, I think the timing of this couldn't be more right. And it would mean, for Goodmews, a step into the future.

What I would like to now propose is, of course, dependent on what you, the residents, want for your town.

I would like to establish what I would call the Goodmews Moon Centre, if that's not too grand a title. It would be housed in my living room at Sky Cottage.

It wouldn't contain anything fancy, not even a telescope at this stage, but it could include your thoughts about the Goodmews moon and also exhibit moon facts. I've done some research in Goodmews Library and, as far as I am aware, this would be the world's first Moon Centre! That would be a feather in Goodmews's cap.

I await your responses to this proposal. And if anyone at this stage so desires, I would also like to hear your personal thoughts about the moon here and even receive drawings of it if you have any. Perhaps you've now decided to start doing some.

I would appreciate your contributions by the end of this month.

Sam Thwaite

The world's first Moon Centre, Francine said to herself. *What an idea.* Who was this Mr. Thwaite? He sounded like a man with a mission – a vision – but someone who was clearly putting the wishes of the town first. A Moon Centre. That could make sense for it to be in Goodmews. And it could dovetail perfectly with her own interests.

She had to stop herself, though, from thinking about how she might contribute to such a centre and how it could be a way for her to get involved with the town. It hadn't even happened yet; that was up to Goodmews. But it seemed to her that she had landed in the right place at the right time.

SEVEN

Francine had seen notices bordered in red before, tacked to the hackberry trees in Goodmews's streets, and had stopped looking at them as they were almost always about someone's lost cat. But when she finally read one of the ones that had recently appeared, with a double red border, she saw that it was different. It was an announcement of an upcoming town meeting.

THE INAUGURATION OF THE
GOODMEWS MOON CENTRE
SKY COTTAGE
7:30 P.M.
SEPTEMBER 4, 1965

So it was happening!

*

She was curious about who went to these things. Other

people she could see, seemed also to be walking towards Sky Cottage. Was that where everyone was going? Probably. Where else could they be going at this hour? She had a sense of the disconnected world connected, that something big was happening. Everyone had left their house to come together at the same place, to get a sense of this Mr. Thwaite whom they'd only met through *The Occasional.*

Fleetingly, the pavement smelled of cat. Twilight was approaching, nearly the time of the joggers, but it still felt like day. A bird swooped, suggesting a guillemot pirouette to her, but seabirds with that plumage, that featherage, wouldn't be anywhere in the neighbourhood of Goodmews. The usual here was magpie, crow, but mainly pigeons, plapping their weight around.

She passed a garden with an unusually late – months late – crop of crocuses in the corner. Had she seen the same crocuses in the spring? They couldn't last this long. She recalled seeing spring's first, distant, glowing fields of rapeseed beyond Goodmews, that were now completely gone. And it was a week now, since she'd stood watching an oak tree pummelling the ground with its first hailstorm of acorns. 'The unremitting, unavoidable changing of the seasons,' she thought, 'but every time it's different in some way. And every autumn seems the most beautiful.'

Another random thought crossed her mind as she walked by a shop that had been something else recently, though she couldn't remember its name. 'What if we, like deciduous trees, shed our leaves and renewed ourselves each year, instead of just growing old.'

Some of these shops did just that – their lives seeming as short as some isotopes' half-lives, though of course those were measured in – infinitesimally small – zeptoseconds.

As she headed towards Jones Street, Francine noticed the beginnings of a building she didn't remember seeing before, and stopped for a moment to look at it. It may have been envisioned as an office block at one point, harbouring hopes of growth, but two rusted blue cranes – at least they looked blue in the darkness – still towered over it. A patch of weeds surrounded a lift shaft, waiting forlornly to be made the centre of the structure.

The front door to Sky Cottage was slightly open, and she walked in to the living room. Soft piano music – Moonlight Sonata, familiar to Francine – was mixed in with the chatter. Even as background, it was melancholy. But it was soothing – the slow, simple notes rising and falling predictably, sounding like the graceful fingerings of some long-fingered primate.

A couple of the forty or so people who were standing around looked familiar: that woman with the hard, unhappy poverty face Francine often saw on the bus, and the one with the glasses and long brown hair who reminded her of her sister. The chatter grew louder, rising steadily to that too-loud sound of wall-enclosed din, with single voices and laughter still pushing through. Francine picked up a glass of wine from the table and sipped at it. No one appeared to recognize her.

A tall man in a green suit walked into the room. The noise sank to a murmur, then died. He gestured to the rows of metal chairs where some people were already sitting. It had to be Mr. Thwaite. He stopped next to a bookshelf. Francine and the rest of the crowd sat down.

'If you would move up, please,' he said, motioning. It was interesting to hear him speak, after just seeing his newsletters and notes.

The chairs in front were dutifully filled.

'Thank you, thank you very much... As some of you know, my name is Samuel Thwaite. Please call me Sam. I want to extend a warm welcome indeed, to everyone who has come out tonight to inaugurate the Goodmews Moon Centre.'

He had one of those voices, flat and fast, that tended to make Francine feel sleepy. She hadn't been sitting for long, and maybe that was the reason she suddenly felt tired – or maybe the chairs were too comfortable. She doubted, though, that others were falling asleep.

'I thank you for your enthusiasm and your – overwhelming – support for the idea. I assume that most of you will have read the two newsletters I've put out. This showing tonight indicates to me that you have been happy to receive them.' There was a purr of approval.

'Tonight is also a wonderful opportunity for me to meet all of *you*. Most of all, I'm grateful that you have given me the go-ahead to begin this Moon Centre – for all of us, here in Goodmews. You have been very generous.'

To Francine, this Mr. Thwaite seemed confident that those who'd come to hear him were on his side. Judging by numbers alone – unless this many people always turned up at Goodmews meetings – the town was giving him its imprimatur.

'This new Centre, thanks to you, already has a growing body of your descriptions of the moon, some as seen from your wonderful orange grove.'

'Orange*woods*,' a man in the front row interjected, without raising his hand.

'Of course. Sorry. I haven't been up there yet.'

'That's OK, Sam.'

Thwaite swiped a finger across his forehead in a mock 'phew' gesture, and the man continued speaking to him, but in such a quiet voice that Francine doubted anyone could hear, though no one said anything. *Why does there always seem to be someone, in every group, who feels entitled to have their own conversation with the speaker while everyone has to wait.*

Mr. Thwaite looked up and began addressing the room again.

'One description was brought in by a young girl, after she saw the crescent moon near Venus. She wrote, "Venus was sitting in the moon's lap, like I do with my dad." That was Cynthia, 11. Are you here, Cynthia?' Francine and others nearby looked around, but there were no children.

Francine was relieved that Mr. Thwaite had slowed down to a reasonable, intelligent pace, and was allowing people to comfortably settle in. He wasn't trying to say a million things at once, as it had seemed at first, when he'd been speaking like a politician might who needed to quickly stamp his views upon a new group of potential supporters. Perhaps he'd been taken aback with his 'orange grove' mistake and realized he needed to slow down, and connect better with his audience.

'And "Jack" – are you here, Jack?'

A man with thinning, scraggly hair raised his hand about halfway and put it down.

'I imagine you all know Jack.'

Francine could see some wry-faced nodding amongst the sea of mostly greyheads.

'Jack has donated his charcoal sketch of the moon. It's on a foggy night, he says, and the river is filled with frogs. The caption reads: "The moon, a disc of light in the cool fog muffling the trickling creek, the creaking, the croaking, muffling the rustling". Thank you, Jack.'

Jack stood up slowly. Still stooped, he cleared his throat, a long, drawn-out clearing that sounded like a horse whinnying.

'Would you like to say something, Jack.' It didn't sound like Mr. Thwaite really wanted to hear from him.

'I would, sir.' Jack gave a quiet laugh that kept plunking along for a few seconds, like a car knocking after the ignition is turned off. He cleared his throat again, indicating he was ready to speak.

'Some say people who come to these sorts of meetings are an ailing, illing dench of bundicated individuals, fruity as nutcakes. I know we aren't the wellest heeled, our sweaters aren't the best pilled – some say they're Beyond the Pill. And maybe *you* think all Goodmews is niberts, sad as battered bananas, I don't rightly know.

'But, sir, if I may say so: I betch'I've had more birthdays than you've had anniversaries... Anymoons, I've been around long enough to know an honest man when I see one – someone who's not here to hornswoggle us. You've got that special thing – that thim and thigour. The world is rich with impossibilities – it's just a pithy that no one had the noggin to 'bark on somethin' like this before.'

'Hear, hear' came from somewhere.

'Thank you, Jack; I appreciate that.'

Francine wasn't sure what Jack had said, but it was clear he had given Mr. Thwaite his blessing.

Jack cleared his throat again.

'What you're doing,' he said, his voice gurgling up like a large black bubble from a tar pit, 'is bringing our old moon, our old town, into the future – in the reasonably near. I say you're the guv'nor, and in my book we should all be giving you long shrift... I'll sit down now. I've had my fill of German wine – maybe too much of that sweet leave-for-me – but if there's anything we can do you for, I'm your man.' He cleared his throat again, and in a low voice began singing in a Dean Martin imitation:

> 'When the moon hits your eye
> like a big pizza pie,
> that'sa Goodmews...'

He sat down to a ripple of applause, which Francine joined in motion, though not in sound. It had been embarrassing, she thought, and a bit much, but brave.

'Thank you Jack. I don't think any of us expected that.' Mr. Thwaite smiled. 'Jack's sketch is over there on the wall, which I'm sure most of you have seen, along with some of Johnny's pictures that he's lent us for this opening. It's also Johnny's copy of Beethoven's Moonlight Sonata you've been hearing.

'Some of you will have seen that I've also posted a few facts you've brought in about the moon – like it takes 1½ seconds for moonlight to reach the earth; that the next February without a full moon will be 1999... Someone brought in two interesting ones the other day. I think we all know that the moon is mainly responsible for the tides here on earth, but I, at least, hadn't known that the sun also exerts force on them – about half the moon's force. And also, that it's been calculated that when man finally lands on the moon, the simple action of opening the lander door will double the moon's tiny amount of atmosphere.'

Francine pictured the moon. Because of the lack of atmosphere, sunset there was abrupt – the moment after was as dark as midnight, with no lingering colour like on earth. And a fact that had always intrigued *her* was that from the moon, the sky would always look black, the sun and stars shining even during the day.

'And as some of you mentioned to me, I've also posted the lyrics to "Moon River" and "In the Misty Moonlight", with pictures of the songwriters. And "Shine on Harvest Moon". The pictures aren't perfect, I know, but they'll do for now. I was able to make copies of them at your great library. Thank you to those who made that suggestion and of course all of you who are teaching me about the moon.'

Francine heard a heavy breather, or a sleeper, behind her.

'And over there is Emily Dickinson's poem "I watched the Moon around the House". That's that picture of her, of course, above it.' Francine had seen it before, as probably many had – that old-fashioned black and white photograph, maybe the only one of Emily, in her long, dark dress staring at the camera, her hair pulled severely back.

'And a moray,' someone shouted, to general chuckling. '*Amore*', Francine realized; the Dean Martin song.

Mr. Thwaite nodded.

'If I may close with this… I thought I might be putting the cart before the horse with the Moon Centre idea, but

40

I know now that that's certainly not the case. My hope is that the Centre will prove to be worthy of inclusion in your community.'

Francine had spotted a few people glancing at their watches. They had made her feel like checking hers too, as there was no clock in sight. But it hadn't been a long meeting. Besides, she'd adopted subtler ways of coping with boredom when she needed to – by doodling, or repeating the speaker's words to herself as he said them, so she would fall behind and lose his train of thought. But she hadn't been bored at all. And it sounded like the meeting was almost over anyway.

Mr. Thwaite must have noticed the watch-glancers too, but Francine had learned – from the few times she'd spoken in front of her class back in Arizona – that unless a speaker, without comment, allows audience members to covertly employ small release-valves like checking the time, the door might be open to their walking out.

'Are there any questions – or comments?' The audience was still, as if they were now all sitting at the feet of their guru, there only to absorb his plans for their future.

'So, tonight feels to me like an exciting new direction for Goodmews. I hope it feels the same for you. Have a look round if you haven't done so already, have another glass of wine – though the *Liebfraumilch* is finished – and please leave a comment in the Visitors Book on the table.'

After some polite applause, people got up to mill about. Francine wondered for a moment why speeches never had encores, with some of the bits that had been left out for time.

From the back, one of the taller men in the room had that distinct straight-cut hair that the mailman had, but when he turned his head to the right she saw that it wasn't him. She sat in her chair, slowly finishing her glass of wine. She didn't have to engage – it wasn't as if she was in a tour group, where everyone was expected to be friendly with everyone else. What she wanted to do was go home and write Mr. Thwaite a note.

By the time Francine was back at her flat, that feeling she'd had at the end of the meeting had faded. Why had it felt so vital that she write the note the minute she got home?

She could give herself some time to think about it.

But she already had. It was a great opportunity.

Would 'Dear *Sam*' be OK? It's what he said to call him.

The first scent of autumn was in the air, not yet mulchy but leaves had begun to fall. Francine could hear the russet dry rustle of someone raking, which sounded to her like waves breaking.

She took the street parallel to Goodmews Way – South Street. The Orlons song went through her head – 'Where do all the hippest meet? South Street, South Street.' She was pretty sure it would get her to Jones Place; and off the main road it seemed more sheltered, less windy in the cool night air.

Some men were in winter scarves – *as colourful as most men get*, she thought. A woman had stopped at the corner – Brown Facades, Francine saw, a street she didn't recall. *You don't see people who are on their own just standing around much here, unless they're waiting for their dog.* And there was the dog. She'd seen it before with the woman, who she usually recognized by her dog – 'Matt', she'd heard her call him.

Why do people give dogs human names? Why not just a number, or something like that.

Sky Cottage was dark and quiet, as Francine had hoped. She put her note through the letterbox.

*

Sam picked up an envelope with Samuel Thwaite, Moon Centre on it that was lying on the entranceway floor and tore it open.

September 5, 1965

Dear Sam,

Hello. My name is Francine Robb. I moved to Goodmews recently, as I believe you also did. I am from Phoenix and have continued, as a 'distance learner', in my last year as an older student (I'm 35) at Arizona State, at the Tempe campus. I'm studying for a second time. My first time round I studied Colour Science; now I am studying Astro-Geology, a new course in the Department of Planetary Science.

My particular field of interest is the moon.

I was at the inauguration last night, and I hope it's not too soon to let you know that I would very much like to be involved with the Moon Centre. What a fascinating concept!

Of course I have no idea, beyond what you outlined last night, what your plans are for the Centre, or if others have also already become involved, but – if I may be so

43

bold – I would like to offer two ideas on how I might be able to contribute.

The displays of lyrics and moon facts that you spoke about and have already mounted are wonderful. My main thought is that a Moon Geology section, which I would be happy to set up and run, could be a logical addition to the Centre. It would depend of course on whether you were interested in the idea – and indeed if you feel there is room for it in your living room.

A related thought is the following.

I believe you mentioned that you haven't yet had the opportunity to get up to the orangewoods, but when you do, you will see beautiful rocks lying on the ground. The area is rich in minerals, and as a geologist I've collected a number of them already. If you were interested (and again had room for it in the Centre), I'd also be happy to set up a small 'rock shop', which I think could bring in some revenue, if that is important.

Please let me know if any of this is of interest and if you would like to discuss it with me.

Yours sincerely,
Francine

19 Red Rock Road
GOodmews 23071 (GO2-3071)

Why not, he thought.

*

She scanned the note. He'd signed it 'Sam'.

44

September 5, 1965

Dear Francine,

Thank you for your note and your encouraging words. I'm glad the idea of a Centre has excited you. I like your ideas. It may have felt too soon to you to suggest them, but they come at the right time. There is room for a small Geology section. It would be a worthy addition to the Centre. (I like your rock shop idea too!)

I will be at Johnny's tomorrow around noon. Coffee's not great, but it would be good to meet you, if that suits your schedule.

I'm sure it's going to work out, and I would like you to be known as the Centre Geologist.

And just so you're aware, you would need to work as a volunteer, at least for now, and at this stage I'm only planning to be open a couple of days a week.

Yours, Sam

EIGHT

Tris saw Sky Cottage up ahead. Back home the week before, he'd seen the headline 'The World's First Moon Centre'. That had sounded interesting enough, but what had surprised him more was that the article was datelined Goodmews. He had mixed memories of the place – had it been a bit too cutesy? – but he had a soft spot for it, mostly for its out-of-the-way feeling and slow pace, and it seemed odd that something so Space Age–sounding would be here.

He came to a wooden sign, like an estate agent's, stuck in the lawn. MOON CENTRE. He walked up the path. The door was unlocked – it 'swang open' he thought to himself, and went inside, to the living room. The tall woman standing at the far wall must have heard him, and turned round. She had dark hair cut in what he thought was called a pageboy or maybe a bob and had glasses on and an orange and yellow striped muumuu. It was an odd-looking 'dress', Tris had always thought, if you even called it that.

'Hello,' she said, and took a few steps towards him. In the background was some Latin-like jazz that was soft and saxy, but not foot tapping. 'Please come in. Your first visit?' Tris could see a crumb, he thought, on her lip.

'I was here a few months ago,' he said, 'before there was a Moon Centre. Thought I'd have a look, if that's OK... Are you Francine?'

'That's right!' She looked surprised.

'My name's Tris... You were mentioned in an article about the Centre?'

'OK,' she said, with a sour-y but not unsmiley look.

'You're the colour person and the... geologist?' He'd forgotten her title.

'*Astro*-geologist,' she nodded quickly, with an understanding smile that said, 'I don't expect everyone to remember.'

'Astro-geologist?'

'It's the study of rocks on other planets. My speciality is the moon.'

'There aren't any moon rocks anyone's got yet, are there?'

'No. Soon we hope. When they get there.'

He liked her straightforward tone and wondered if this was how scientists – 'astro-geologists?' – talked, crisply, enunciating their consonants. And he liked the catch in her voice; it sounded natural, not like the kind that some pop singers seemed to put on.

'Is astro-geology a course?'

'Hasn't been for long. It's only taught at a school in Arizona, where I took it, before I moved here.'

'Is that hard to get into?' He wasn't sure if he should be asking that, but she smiled and looked him in the eye.

'I thought it was when I applied, and it wasn't cheap, but the others didn't seem to know much about geology, or planets.'

'Money speaks louder than words.'

He could see a Was-that-worth-saying wince on her face. 'Anyhow. It was a great course. It's taught pretty close to a crater where the Apollo astronauts train.'

'For the moon?'

'Yep. Since it's in the desert it's hardly eroded.'

'For millions of years, like the moon?'

'50,000. Just as far as the course, since you asked… Have you heard of Gene Shoemaker?'

'I've heard of Bill Shoemaker. The jockey?'

She grimaced with a downturned-mouth. 'He's known as the father of astro-geology. Should I give you one fact about him?'

'Sure.'

'He was supposed to be the first geologist to walk on the moon, but it doesn't sound like that's going to happen now. He's been diagnosed with Addison's disease.'

'Is that cancer?'

'No. But as far as I know, it weakens the muscles and you get very tired.'

Tris nodded. He felt they could get back to Goodmews.

'This didn't feel like a place that would have a "moon centre" when I visited, but I can see it's not a gigantic building.'

'It's just an idea this man—'

'Samuel Thwaite—'

'Yeah. So, where are you from?' she asked.

'Des Moines.'

'Do you work there?'

'Yeah. I'm a proofreader.'

'You check spelling.'

'And punctuation, capitals, that sort of thing. But mainly letters carved into solid objects.'

Francine's large eyes looked up at the ceiling. It wasn't a questioning look, but more one of anticipation, as if she was seeing her next thought. Tris wanted to look behind him at where she'd been looking, but she brought her eyes back to him first. 'Do you think anybody ever checked the Rosetta Stone?'

He gave a short, appreciative snort. 'Good question. I check things *like* that – plaques on walls, dedications on benches, gravestones... You've got some good ones on benches.'

She nodded. 'Someone here came up with the saying, "A bench without a dedication is like a church without pews".'

'I like the benches here. That oval one, without a back? At the water fountain? I haven't seen one like that before.'

'I think they're unique to Goodmews. There's one outside the library too.'

'Where's that?'

'Blue Gable Way.'

'I saw *one* bench that looked big enough for only one, too. Outside the Post Office.'

'People call it a bench chair. Though – and I think you'd like this – it's spelled as one word, with only one "c-h".'

'But you don't say "benchair"?'

'No.'

'And I saw another odd one – two benches linked together. If you look length-wise, one slopes to the left and the other to the right?'

'The one in the park.'

'Yeah.'

'I still don't understand, Tris. Why would they need someone to specialize in reading stones or benches? A spelling mistake is a spelling mistake whatever it's on, *isn't it?*'

'It's slightly different when it's going to be "set in stone", as it were. You have to be perfect.'

'But isn't it too late to proofread them by the time they're carved, or however they do them?'

'You check them before.'

'Oh. Of course.'

He could see that she was slightly embarrassed. 'And then it gets carved exactly as you've proofed it, and then you check it again. I've only found one mistake, spelling anyway, on anything commemorative I've ever seen that I haven't proofread.'

Francine tilted her head into about half a question mark.

'It was a plaque on a pier that said "beachuts" – one word, with one "h", like your bench chair.' It didn't look to Tris like she cared much about that.

'So you have to be extremely good to do it.'

'I dunno. There's usually so few words, especially on things like gravestones, and often they're the same words. So you concentrate even harder if there *are* some new words.'

'And they *are* permanent.'

'Yeah. You don't want there to be a mistake for everyone to see forever.'

She nodded. 'Do you proofread things like signs and placards, like the ones explaining paintings in art galleries? I know they're not "literally" – if that's the word – carved, but sometimes it's almost like they are.'

'I'd rather not. Can't bear them. So much waffle in them, so much hype. I don't even want to *read* them, let alone proof them.'

She sniffed an almost-laugh. 'But someone's got to do it. It would be *work*, wouldn't it?'

'I'm not trying to get rich from proofreading. I can usually say no to jobs I don't want… Does Goodmews *have* a gallery?'

'No. But we could probably do with a proofreader. Are you a professional? Is there such a thing for proofreaders?'

'Yeah. I belong to a guild – of Letter Carver Proofers. The GLCP. It's the only professional society for letter-carver proofers in the country.'

She nodded, but he doubted she'd ever heard of it. Probably no one who wasn't a proofreader or didn't chisel gravestones or have solid objects proofread ever had. He scanned the walls and saw a photo of a rainbow. He nodded towards it.

'Does that picture have something to do with the moon?'

'Yes. It's a moonbow.'

He tried to see what she meant.

'They're like night-time rainbows,' she said.

'They exist?'

'Yes.'

'Have you seen them?'

She nodded. 'The thing is, in real life they usually look white. But if you take a photograph it's in colour.'

'How's that possible?'

'The reflected colour is usually too faint to see, but a long-exposure photograph will pick it up.' It sounded like she was probably tired of explaining this, but Tris found it interesting, something he'd never heard of.

'Hmm. Is that a real map of the moon?'

'It's the one, the Geological Survey map.' Tris looked at the bright yellows and browns. 'It's as much as we know… It's the only wall it would fit on.'

It sounded like something *he* would say. 'I better go soon. I'm getting the train back. But I like Goodmews, Francine; it's different, and now it's got a moon centre.'

'First in the world, we think.'

Tris nodded. 'Good luck with it.'

'Thanks. Maybe you'll come back and see more of the place one day, go up to the orangewoods. Have you heard of them?'

'Yeah. They're in the *Guide*.'

'*Remote Towns*.'

'Yeah.'

'Say hi if you drop by. And if you ever felt like giving Goodmews a go, I'm sure there'd be plenty of work. Besides all the "letter carvers" around, we're beginning to print information here at the Centre.'

He felt a gentle yank at his comfort zone and a small lashing at an eyebrow. *Is my comfort zone so narrow? Or maybe so wide that my whole life fits into it.*

'Could happen one day I suppose.'

'Have a good trip home. You know about Johnny's?'

'Yes, I dropped in last time.'

'Grab a copy of *The Occasional* there – it's the local paper, something Mr. Thwaite also started. It'll give you an idea of what goes on here. I'm not a professional like you, but I check it over for mistakes.'

'He's bad at spelling?'

'I think he just doesn't have the patience.'

We spoke very easily for a first time, Tris thought to himself. *That's rare. And we could have spoken for longer. She listened, and asked questions. The fact that she was female didn't seem to matter; our exchanges were innocent – just ideas and opinions.*

Johnny stood looking out of his window like the time before. Tris could see that the glass was wavy.

Is that how he spends his life?

He seemed to recognize Tris.

He walked inside, still no one there.

'Hello young man. I remember you.'

'Thanks. It's been about six months.'

'I'm sorry I don't recall your name.'

'I don't think I said. Tris.'

'Then, good to see you again, Tris.'

'Thanks. I just wanted to pick up a copy of *The Occasional.* Francine – from the Moon Centre? – said you kept some here.'

'Right there. Compliments of the house.'

Tris knew he always found it hard to resist anything free, even a local newspaper, though he did draw the line at Jehovah Witness magazines.

'I'll just take one.'

'Sure.'

He walked over to a stack of folded newspapers in a wire holder on the floor. *You never know which day's a free paper is.* But this one was current, he was happy to see. He took the one under the top one.

He found a seat on the train with no one next to him.

With a jerk, they were on the move. He unfolded the paper.

... Everyone will be aware that visitor numbers to Goodmews have been going up – one indication being that Crescent Bakery runs out of cakes at the weekend. The Moon Centre itself, now open the whole weekend, has had a threefold increase – in the past month! – in people coming through its doors.

Our resident population is also growing. New houses can be seen going up.

The train hurtled along.

Also, no one can have failed to notice the enterprising ways in which some of our new residents have entered into the community spirit, for instance the young lady who has set up her desk near the station, selling envelopes and writing pads and helping people write letters.

Stationery! She wouldn't have as much as a shop and it would probably be basic, like down a supermarket aisle, but she might have something different.

Near the clock tower you will now find The Barkery. This is not to be confused with the bakery, nor is it a meeting place for dogs! It's a collection of sculpted figures using the papery bark found on the ground in the orangewoods.

There are new restaurants, shops and offices, with their domino addresses now in the teens, along Commercial Row on the Way. The Post Office has hired another part-time mailman, and Goodmews Printers are producing a new and larger phone book which will be available at the beginning of next week.

Oh! he realized. Those small blocks of wood above doors, with orderly dots on them, were addresses. They had looked like dominoes, or dice. It would have been a squeeze to put his address back home – 17836 Catalina Street – on dominoes.

But the name Commercial Row will be left in place, as the Goodmews Historical Society has requested. In short, Goodmews is keeping alive its connections to its past, as it grows. It is a town that respects its history, while its eye is to the future.

He could live there, he thought. He could probably even get work there.

NINE

December went quickly for Francine. She would sometimes see people lugging carry-bags of wrapping paper as she walked the residential roads. There was the welcome of winter woodsmoke, which pepperminted the air, and sometimes snow's silent ice would fall, or simply a random snowflake would whizz by like a daytime shooting-star. She began to feel that all of Goodmews was like one big neighbourly neighbourhood, the sort of place you need to leave your house five minutes early because there's a good chance you'll see someone you might want to have a chat with.

Her first New Year's in Goodmews passed, and soon it was February, always a stutter of a month: spring seemed imminent, then not. Was there a lessening of the nip in the air, or the slightly sweet hit of a hint of the year's first daffodils? In Goodmews, there was an unmistakable sign – the new season's moonflowers in crescent-shaped beds that were obvious in their municipal pride. One of the beds sat before Francine in the bright sun.

Since coming to Goodmews, she had read about moonflowers and that they blossomed at dusk, softly glowing and exuding their sweet scent. She'd guessed it was the fragrance she'd breathed in on her first evening. She wanted to watch them open, and breathe in that fragrance again.

She returned at sunset. She waited, and recalled watching a cup of flowering tea until its flower fully opened.

Then it began. The flowers' pregnant stirrings grew stronger, and their outer petals unfolded into sunray-like spikes. The centre exploded into a starburst of liquid-white colour, and the perfume came, a honey unlike any Francine could remember.

*

She continued to compile moon facts, from the library and her course, perhaps for a booklet, and spent time adding to Geology Corner. In the small glass case left for the taking, that she'd picked up on the pavement in front of someone's house, she displayed the rocks she'd brought back from her orangewood walks. She'd even taken it upon herself to make Sam's living room – the Centre – feel less musty, look more welcoming, by doing some cleaning and dusting when she had time. Someone had once said to her that she had 'dust vision' – that she could see dust no one else could, or couldn't be bothered about. If that's what they called it, then she also had broken-glass-on-the-floor vision, lost-keys vision, litter-in-the-bushes vision, missed-belt-loop vision, sleep-stuff-in-eyes vision, and the knack of being able to spot a spray bottle's transparent dust cap, as small as it might be, and dropped black tyre-valve caps, that others couldn't see.

One of the library books Francine had brought home about Goodmews's past particularly intrigued her, and she decided to put together a leaflet based on the book. It was a way she could add to people's knowledge of the town, something she'd wanted to do ever since she'd been on the tour the previous summer.

<u>Once Upon a Time in Goodmews</u>

In 1949, the widely respected Goodmews historian, B. Lawon (1876–1960), published her only book, <u>Myth or Fact?: Once Upon a Time in Goodmews</u>. The book was the result of Lawon's research into widely held beliefs about the town. Here are some of her more interesting findings.

1. <u>Goodmews's beginnings</u>

There has been a settlement here since at least the late 1700's. Beyond that, nothing can be proven. However, there are many accounts that have been passed down concerning the village's founding by a local Indian tribe, said to have been drawn to the area by the brightness of its moon. Although no records have ever been found, it is also believed that moon-viewing evenings were an important feature of these early days and were held on the night of the full moon, both to bring people together and for 'a night of oaths', to be sworn by the holding of a stick with feathers to the moon. It is also believed that 'moon calls' were developed to announce the rising of the full moon, and that moonflower petals, from the fragrant, white, night-blooming flower that we still see around town, were scattered on the ground to sleep on.

2. <u>Our moondial</u>

Early this century, also on full-moon nights, there was moondial viewing. Some will have seen the concrete moondial, now mossy with green, in the cemetery.

Moondials tell time using the light of the moon, in the same way sundials work by the light of the sun. Sundials, however, are far more precise.

Moondials are only accurate once a month. It's hard to picture, but this is explained by the fact that the moon rises about 50 minutes later each night, making the moondial read an additional 50 minutes slower each night following the accurate reading on the full moon. This would also mean that a dial will be 50 minutes fast on the night <u>before</u> a full moon. Thus our moondial served little purpose beyond being a gathering point; one week either side of a full moon it read close to six hours before or after the correct time.

The idea for our domino addresses is said to have come from our moondial, which used domino-like dots, instead of numbers, to indicate the time. These 'dominoes' have worn away over time, as has the fragment of Shelley's poem <u>To the Moon</u> inscribed at the base.

Art thou pale for weariness
Of climbing heaven and gazing on the earth

3. The Goodmews Committee

Popularly known as the Bestmewsicians, the Goodmews Committee existed from around 1870 to 1935. It was a self-appointed, changing group of ten locals who volunteered their time for the betterment of Goodmews. Their records indicate that the local populace in general approved of their activities. Besides ensuring that the town street maps posted on notice boards faced the same way as the person viewing them, the Committee is probably best remembered for the following.

1. Encouraging the building of the church.
2. Approving, or not, all inscriptions submitted for cemetery headstones.
3. Supervising the building of some early houses in an Edwardian style.

4. Pareidolia

Contrary to widespread belief, there is no evidence that Goodmews was ever known as Pareidolia. The word has to do with the human perception of faces and images where they don't exist, such as the Man in the Moon.

5. Ankle rips

Although still questioned, it does appear that for a time early this century, there was a local fashion for 'ankle rips' in trousers and in long dresses called Aunt and Uncle dresses.

6. 'They've gone to Goodmews'

This phrase was said to refer to any resident who had been temporarily blinded by the brightness of the moon. There is no record of this expression having ever been in common use, nor indeed of anyone being blinded in this way, but other terms were said to have arisen from it, such as 'He was treated for moonstroke' and 'He should have been wearing moonglasses.'

7. The moon stick

In the library's glass case, there is one of the few surviving 'moon sticks' used by the local Sioux to measure time. According to (Miss or Mrs.) B. Lawon, with the rising of each new moon the Sioux would make a notch in their sticks. They would note the changing of the seasons, and learned they would come again.

Francine recalled her thoughts about the ankle rips; they wouldn't have fit in the leaflet. They sounded far from fashionable, and had brought to mind the Jews' yellow star under the Nazis, and the 'A' Hester Prynne was forced to wear in *The Scarlett Letter*. And they had also brought to mind the Beothuk of Newfoundland, whose use of red ochre was so central to their culture that forbidding someone from wearing it was their way of punishing them. And when Francine had read about red ochre, after learning that it was the world's first coloured paint, there was a historical footnote about the Beothuk. Europeans were led to refer to them as Red Indians due to their practice of decorating everything with red ochre – their houses, canoes, weapons, and even their newborn children to welcome them into the tribe.

But she couldn't wait to make copies of the leaflet. She smiled at the thought that the street maps, always with Goodmews's landmark, the church, were still dotted around town on the orangewood notice boards stuck into patches of grass. And the central street names, like Fred Bartleby Buildings and Dr Francis Windows, that had their namesakes' lifetimes added, gave her the sense that Goodmews had a continuity, a settled identity that was happy with itself. Neither the church, nor Goodmews, was built in a day.

And then she thought about blind people, and how they wouldn't even be able to read her leaflet. *Were* there blind people in Goodmews? She'd never seen anyone walking with a seeing-eye dog or a white cane, though statistically shouldn't there be? Should she have an occasional reading of it at the Moon Centre? It meant nothing in the scheme of things, but at least it was about Goodmews, people's home. But beyond the leaflet, could she, or anyone, ever adequately describe the beauty of the orangewoods to someone who couldn't see, or the moon here?

*

Except for weekends, she hardly saw Sam. She wasn't sure where he was or what he was doing, but she was happy to be trusted to organize things the way she wanted. And when a visitor dropped in and asked her about the moon, especially its mountains and craters, being Centre Geologist felt to Francine like pure indulgence: she was talking about what she loved.

She could tell people that most of the craters were named by the Italian astronomer Riccioli in 1651, naming many of the dark, smooth ones after weather, like Mare Frigoris, the Sea of Cold, or states of mind, like the Sea of Tranquility. Sometimes, if people were still showing interest, she added that the largest craters were technically 'basins', in a similar way that, in some places, sardines that are longer than six inches are technically 'pilchards'.

She'd also taped some poems to the wall, next to where Sam had put up song lyrics and the songwriter pictures, and labelled the section Moon Songs and Poetry. She made copies people could take of the first poem she'd posted, which included an introduction.

HILAIRE BELLOC
The Early Morning

TAKE THIS POEM OUTSIDE AT THE END OF
A FULL-MOON NIGHT, WHEN THE MOON IS
SETTING IN THE WEST AND THE SUN IS RISING IN
THE EAST. BEFORE YOU READ THE POEM, FACE
THIS WAY: THE SETTING MOON ON YOUR LEFT AND
THE RISING SUN ON YOUR RIGHT.

The moon on the one hand, the dawn on the other:
The moon is my sister, the dawn is my brother.

The moon on my left and the dawn on my right.
My brother, good morning: my sister, good night.

TEN

At Goodmews Post Office, Sam scanned the envelope he'd slid out of his private box. In the left corner was a recognizable logo – a blue sphere, with a futuristic red wing slicing through it, and NASA in white letters across the middle. In the other corner was a red, white and blue CAMP FIRE GIRLS postage stamp. The letter was postmarked CAPE KENNEDY. Sam opened it carefully and read it where he stood.

April 16, 1966

Samuel Thwaite
Sky Cottage
Goodmews

Dear Mr. Thwaite,

If I may introduce myself, my name is Ray Block. I am Deputy Communications Director for NASA.

Word of the Goodmews Moon Centre reached us some time ago. Last month I visited your Centre anonymously, and reported back to my superiors. You have not only created what we believe to be the first Moon Centre anywhere in the world, but the wide-ranging displays and the Geology and the Songs and Poetry sections were impressive and educational.

As you may be aware, NASA's founding principle states that we are to be 'For the Benefit of All' and, from the beginning, we have endeavoured to bring community Space programmes under our 'wing', so to speak, so that we can provide support for them as well as exchange information with them.

We would like your Centre to be another such venture for us: we would like to invite you to become a NASA Affiliate – or 'satellite', as we refer to our partners. This would mean that NASA will fully fund your Moon Centre, initially for two years. We will also pay you a salary, commensurate with your position as director of the Centre. We will also fund the position of an associate director.

The small print, if you agree to the above:

As your Centre would have our backing, we would procure ownership of it and the property immediately surrounding it. Crucially, however, we would maintain a 'hands off' relationship: you will continue to be in charge of day-to-day operations. We would request that you inform us as to improvements you intend to make, but we would only need to approve projects that require substantial investment. For your consideration, included is our Infrastructure Allowance Limits document, our Terms and Conditions and our proposed contract.

All the above is details. What underlies everything is

our belief that local enthusiasts like yourself will not only stimulate wider interest in our efforts, but will give NASA a more human face.

Please let me know by return mail if you feel you may be interested in our proposal. Please send it Special D, as we consider this a matter of priority.

<u>We invite you to join us in the Space Race.</u>

Sincerely,
Ray

Raymond Block
NASA Deputy Communications Director
Ext. 442

He'd done it.

He clutched the letter as he walked. He hadn't even thought about them. But something always came along. And who better could they have chosen, to expand their… galaxy.

And he had free rein. *Sky Cottage – the new Moon Centre.*

Pay *Francine. A geology* room; *Songs and Poetry if she wants. Bigger exhibits. Hire a guard.*

The future was suddenly secure. What more could Goodmews have wanted? How could they ever thank him?

*

April 30, 1966

Dear Sam,

We are pleased that you have decided to become

66

a NASA Affiliate and have returned the signed contract. We are as enthusiastic as you are to have you on board. We will now proceed to procure ownership of Sky Cottage and the adjoining land.

Sincerely,
Ray

cc: Patrick Sanford, NASA Affiliates Secretary

*

May 7, 1966

Dear Ray,

Please confirm NASA's approval of my Centre extension and improvement plans, the details of which are enclosed. As you will see, the current 'corners' and sections will become rooms; and, to help generate revenue, there will be a Moon Café. To stimulate Goodmews's economy, I plan to hire local builders to do the work, if that gets your thumbs-up. We will close for these refurbishments, which I'm told should take about six weeks.

I'm unclear about one aspect of these changes – whether I need your permission to put into place the following (which I would like to run by you in any case):

To more clearly distinguish the Centre, now that it is a NASA 'satellite', I feel it should be renamed. I would suggest: Thwaite Moon Centre. I believe this would be appreciated by the people of Goodmews, as it will give the Centre more of an identity. Townsfolk, in time, may even come to refer to it fondly as 'Thwaite M.C.' – which almost sounds like it could be the name of their local soccer club – if Goodmews was big enough to host one!

Thanking you in advance for your agreement on all this,

Sam

*

May 20, 1966

Dear Sam,

We are in agreement with your expansion plans.

At this point, our normal procedure is to restate two subsections from our Terms and Conditions, which you have had sight of:

(a) All documents produced by a NASA Affiliate must include the NASA logo. It must be rendered in black and white. (I have included in this package a set of inkpads and engraved ink blocks for this purpose. I have also included coloured NASA decals for you to use wherever you see fit – though please don't go overboard with these.)

(b) All persons having any connection whatsoever to a NASA Affiliate are required to sign a non-disclosure agreement – the Oath – regarding any material they are working on or have knowledge of. I enclose the Oath, which you may copy freely. Please sign one copy yourself and return it to me; keep all other signed Oaths at the Centre.

Two final points:

1. We are happy for the Centre to be renamed; in fact we were about to instruct you to do so. However, we require that 'NASA' be part of the title. Accordingly, we would suggest that, incorporating your idea, the Centre be renamed NASA Thwaite Moon Centre. We trust you will be in agreement with this.

2. As you may be aware, the U.N. Outer Space Treaty is due to be ratified next year. Weapons of mass destruction will be banned in outer space, and measures will be taken to prevent the exploitation and accidental contamination of the moon.

   The essence of the treaty is that all celestial bodies are humanity's common heritage, and can only be used for peaceful and scientific purposes. To indicate our agreement with this tenet, we will require that our motto, 'For the Benefit of All', be posted in your Centre and identified as NASA's. As befits all our Affiliates' individuality, you have the freedom to render this motto in any appropriate way you choose.

   Sincerely,
   Ray

*

Sam would have preferred that 'NASA' didn't precede 'Thwaite' in the new Moon Centre name – why couldn't they have shown their arm's-length acceptance, their belief in his Centre's future, by running with his suggestion to use just *his* name?

At least they had left it in. That was their seal of approval, for all to see – their acknowledgement of what he, alone, had brought to Goodmews.

*

Francine read the latest *Occasional*.

<u>The Goodmews Occasional</u>
August 9, 1966

Just before the start of summer, the Moon Centre received news that will secure its presence in Goodmews. To my surprise, and great joy, NASA took it under their umbrella, thus conferring upon the Moon Centre an honour, a responsibility and a bright future. We will be known as the NASA Thwaite Moon Centre. I remain Director. Francine Robb, now Associate Director, also continues as Centre Geologist.

Tomorrow the Centre will close for refurbishing. It will reopen towards the end of this month, with new rooms and a café. I myself will be moving out of Sky Cottage, which will become the new Moon Centre.

We will be using the vacant lot adjacent to Sky Cottage to lay the 'groundwork' – literally – for the new Centre. That land and Sky Cottage have been sold to NASA.

I trust that we have everyone's backing for this new venture. The greatest beneficiary of the new Moon Centre will be Goodmews.

Francine and I thank you for the support you have shown the Centre over its first year. We are sure that you will be proud of your <u>new</u> Moon Centre. We hope to see as many of you as possible at our reopening.

A final note. To accompany Goodmews's growing identity as a 'Moon town', I have decided to begin printing <u>Space Bulletins</u>. These will be brief announcements of worldwide Space events, for local consumption. I will be drawing on information supplied by NASA to the Moon Centre.

I've included 'Bulletin 1' in this <u>Occasional</u>:

Two months ago, on June 2nd, NASA's Surveyor 1 achieved a 'soft' landing on the moon, the first successful landing in American history. Four months earlier, in February, the Soviet Union's Luna 9 accomplished the same feat.

Surveyor is NASA's programme to send unmanned missions to the moon to prove that soft landings are possible, and that men can touch-down safely on the moon.

Samuel Thwaite
Director
NASA Thwaite Moon Centre

It would have been interesting, she thought, for Sam to have also mentioned Luna 10, launched shortly after Luna 9. When Luna 10 had entered lunar orbit, it became the moon's first artificial satellite. And for Francine, as a geologist, Luna 10 also meant something else. It had found the first evidence of mascons – 'mass concentrations' – on the moon. She had been thinking about mascons lately, perhaps because the new Beatles song, 'Yellow Submarine', had been on the radio

71

all the time. It was about living beneath the waves in a yellow submarine, and Francine knew, that like coral reefs beneath the ocean waves, mascons lurked below the surface of the moon's largest craters, making them highly gravitational compared to the rest of the moon. As NASA put it, these large craters were 'anomalous gravitational regions', making the moon the most gravitationally 'lumpy' body known in the solar system. What that meant for the space programme was that mascons posed an invisible and possibly devastating hazard. They exerted enough extra gravity to pull a spacecraft in low orbit into a crash trajectory.

ELEVEN

August 29, 1966

Dear Ray,

The Centre's reopening today was attended by over 100 people, including a good many from outside Goodmews. Your idea of a Suggested Donation box in the foyer worked well, as did the visitor surveys you suggested, which told us two main things:

1) The news of Surveyor 1's soft landing in June (which we put in our local Bulletin), increased (or initiated) people's interest in the Centre and the Moon Race.

2) People are appreciative of NASA's involvement with the Moon Centre, which they continue to see as a boon for Goodmews.

NASA's motto (now on the wall) has given us the idea to create our own – To Know the Moon – which will be put on the doors to the Centre's rooms.

I believe you are off on your summer vacation soon.
Have a good break.

Sincerely,
Sam

*

Francine popped her head round his office door. 'Sam? I just wanted to let you know something.'

'Come in.' It sounded brusque.

He might have been picking his nose, crossed her mind, but she didn't really want to know. 'Thanks.'

He motioned her to take a seat, on the wooden chair, and turned some papers over.

'What's on your mind?'

'Sam, I've been thinking about all the descriptions of the moon that people brought in in the early days.'

'They're still here.' He motioned to his file cabinet, one of those metal ones about chest high.

'Now that we've got more room, don't you think it would be a good idea to display them? Wasn't that the original idea? Maybe even use one of the small rooms, call it something like "The Goodmews Moon"?'

'There's no great demand to see them.' Thwaite's eyes looked down as his mouth kept moving. 'I don't hear people talking about them.' *His face doesn't match his eyes,* Francine felt. *Though maybe that's just me.*

'They do to me, sometimes.'

'Really. And what do they say.'

'That they're glad they're being preserved, but maybe more could be done with them, maybe acknowledging how they inspired the Centre.'

'And what do *you* say?'

'I've agreed with them. I think they *should* be available for people to see.'

'That's not what the Centre is for.'

'Why not?'

'It's about facts, *real* things. Things move on, Francine... I'm concerned with the Centre's future, not its past. I'm thinking about adding a NASA room – maybe call it The Race for the Moon. I'll let you know about it soon.'

Even as Francine was leaving Sam's office, she was making up her mind.

By the next day, she had decided, and when Sam checked in with her in the morning she told him.

'Sam, I've been thinking about the conversation we had yesterday. I've decided to move in to the church.'

'What? It's not even fit for habitation.'

'I'll get it cleaned up... I'm going to call it the Moon Church.'

'I'm *sorry*?' Sam's pitch had gone up a notch.

'That fits in with the Moon *Centre*, don't you think?'

'Why do you need a *church* for that?'

'I don't *need* a church, but it's a beautiful building under all that scaffolding and it's been neglected. I might even give some talks about the moon.'

His look was more mocking than baffled. 'And start a new religion?'

'It's nothing to do with religion. I'm not religious. But no one else seems to want to "resurrect" it.' She knew he wouldn't like the word.

' "Resurrect"? So the church can be a place where the hippies can come down to perform their rituals to praise the moon?'

Sam had never mentioned them before, though everyone knew that a group of shabby young people had set up camp in the orangewoods.

'What rituals?'

'I don't know. I've heard. They're not good for Goodmews. Why would you want to make them feel welcome.'

She hadn't realized he was so opposed to them, but she stood her ground. 'That's not why I'd be opening the church, but they'd be welcome to come along if they wanted. They're not *harm*ing anyone. In fact I think it says something for the beauty of the area, that they've chosen to come here. "Let and let live".'

'I think you're out of your mind, Francine. We don't want them here.'

She wasn't sure who this 'we' was, but she didn't pursue it. 'Sam, I'm excited about this, about bringing the church back to life. Don't you think it looks bad for the town that its most historical building is rotting away?'

'If you change it' – he chuckled at himself – 'you'll have to change the sign outside the town.'

Francine never knew what to make of Sam's chuckle. Was it a smugness? It made her think of strolling couples who had that self-satisfied look, like they had no worries, that everything was 'sorted'. Sometimes after watching him laugh at another of his own jokes, she felt like saying, 'You can be comfy, Sam, but don't be so comfy in my face.' He was like the leader of a reading group she'd been in where everyone was always asked what the next book should be, but no one was ever asked if there should be a next book.

'It's an old sign anyway,' she said.

He shook his head. 'Is that what you want to use your money and time for? Maybe I'm paying you too much.'

She let that pass. 'I'm going to have it repainted too. The scaffolding's already there, isn't it.'

'It's a symbol, like you say. Let it be. There must be plenty of other things you can spend your money on.'

'I've taken out a lease on it, for five years.'

'No...'

'Yes... Have you ever looked at it, seen the cupolas and gargoyles?'

'No.'

'Have you ever been inside?'

'A moon church. Is that what you want Goodmews to be known for? Your *ser*mons?'

'No sermons, Sam. It's just a church in name. The Moon Centre will still be the most important thing. There's no reason, though, not to use the church. And making it moony, at least in name, relates to what this town is about now.'

'I don't want it to be connected to the Centre in any *way*. You do with it what you want, but it's *not* part of the Centre. It's a "spaced out" idea, as those hippies are supposed to say. The Moon Centre is about *real* Space, not inner space.'

'Sam, I think, in a way, it could balance the Moon Centre. We have all these facts and science here. The church could be a place where people could *muse* on the moon, *celebrate* it if they want. I'm thinking of reinstituting Moon Viewing Evenings.'

'If they ever existed… You're making me concerned about your work *here*. You need to make sure you do your hours.'

'You don't need to say that. That's not going to change. You *know* how much extra time I've put into the Centre.'

He had no response to that.

'Sam. I want to give something back to Goodmews.'

'You don't *owe* it anything. You're doing plenty.'

'The Centre's great. It's been great for the town, and for me too. But I need something more. On those days we're not open, I feel I should be doing something of my own. I want to.'

He shrugged. 'Well, good luck to you.'

He had no reason to doubt her commitment to the Centre, she thought. There was nothing disloyal about her idea for the church or, for that matter, her disagreement about the hippies. The truth was, she felt, she and Sam were perhaps more alike than not. Neither was a joiner, neither 'went with the flow'.

She felt lucky to be able to be an individual. The horror of horrors for her would be to speak for a group – like people do for a political party, cocooned by the group's support.

But had he been right? Was her redoing the church just – in today's parlance – an 'ego trip' on her part? It wasn't how she saw it. In hippie-speak, couldn't the church be a sort of 'yin' to the Centre's 'yang'?

Bringing back its beauty had to be good for Goodmews.

She let herself again feel excitement for it. She'd use the parlour pew for her room and refurbish the other wooden pews, maybe add some – moon-themed? – cushions. And after the weathered signboard outside got cleaned up, she could revive that tradition of posting sayings – of *hers*? Was that being too vain? Though who looked at church billboards anymore anyway. Why should they. They were almost always about God's love or something like that.

She recalled a few proverbs, or whatever they were, and noted them down.

The extent to which a song has entered the mainstream of popular culture can be measured by the frequency it is heard around campfires.

A learning experience:
a label we apply
to an unsuccessful try,
to convince ourselves the attempt was worthwhile.

Though would either of those fit on a signboard?

TWELVE

As he gazed out of the train window, Banno heard that song intro in his transistor-radio earpiece. It was just the right train-serenade, and added that extra dimension to the journey, making the outside world seem ten times as interesting as it was. He tried to picture the passing countryside in the same way he liked looking through a viewfinder, screening out in his mind any unwanted foreground, like the window smudges, so he could focus on what was beyond.

He saw the ticket inspector, in her blue uniform a long way down the gangway, through the open door between the coaches. He turned off his music and put the transistor and earpiece into his backpack. He'd known an inspector would appear – they had the right to swoop from anywhere, anytime – but still, the moment of arrival was always a sudden signal to Banno to be wary, to stop what he was doing and do the right thing. They had the power.

He patted his shirt pocket to be sure he had his ticket, where he knew it was. What would he do if it had disappeared? He wondered how some people had the guts to try for a freebie, pretending they'd lost their ticket. Some people would even try to say they'd shown it earlier; but they didn't stand a chance of outwitting a ticket inspector, a person who possessed incomparable seat-memory, like a barber who always remembered the length he cut a customer's hair the last time.

She entered Banno's coach, pausing at each row of seats, looking left and right, relaxed enough, bending down a bit, having a glance and chat, her bandolier-strap slung sash-style over her shoulder. She got closer, but would pay Banno no heed until she got to him.

'Ticket, please.' Her smile was unforced but it wasn't large and free like a happy person.

He proudly presented it, and received that day-brightening 'Thank you' that comes from the sort of person who does their job without ceremony – ticket inspectors, librarians – their main task being to make sure everyone understands what's expected.

'Thank you,' he responded. What a pleasant thing to be able to say – a confident response-in-kind for the service and courtesy shown.

Mainly, he'd passed. He was in.

The train crept along. Banno could see a WELCOME sign out of the window with an image of a church and a moon on it, though the church was scaffolded, which seemed odd for a tourist sign.

At the station, Banno grabbed his bags and guitar and went out into the wan light of the morning. As he walked along the pavement, the window display in the Lost Property Office caught his eye, its seemingly random arrangement of suitcases, dog collars and other left-behind belongings making him smile.

He read the directions again he'd been sent.

> Cross Old Road. Turn left. Turn right onto Goodmews Way. Pass The Tipping Point restaurant. The Moon Centre is on the right, just past Johnny's cafe.

As he crossed the road, a car suddenly braked to his left, making him jump. He hadn't heard or seen the car. It must have been going slowly and quietly. The driver smiled, and Banno waved a thank you back. *That's important. If you smile and the other party doesn't return it – or like if you move aside on the pavement for someone who's nudged into the centre and the other party doesn't thank you – the event is incomplete. Incompletions build up.* He continued across the road, happy to be walking in Goodmews, even as he lugged his luggage. *People here are more polite than back home. They fulfil their civil – civic – traffic-duty.* He recalled stopping his car once, as someone was manoeuvring through an endless three-point turn in front of him. He could have zoomed around them, but waited patiently. But the person, finally finishing their manoeuvre, just roared off, without even a thumbs-up or flashed rear-lights.

A warm breeze barely brushed his cheeks and a flowery smell from somewhere reminded him of grape-flavoured Lik·m·aid and licking its powder right out of its package.

He stopped outside JOHNNY'S. Here too was a window display worth looking at. Maybe someone in Goodmews was known for creating them.

In this one, on an easel, there was a small painting of a mountain. The colours of the rocks and trees were muted;

everything was in blocky browns, yellows and greens. Banno had seen similar paintings – it looked like an Impressionist – though they were often confusing to look at. He could relate to this one, like a sport he grew up with as opposed to a foreign one he didn't understand. But there was also something about this painting, something he couldn't put his finger on, that made him think that when the world first saw it they must have seen it in a way they'd never seen a painting before.

Next to it was a typed caption: PAUL CEZANNE: 'HILLSIDE IN PROVENCE'. Were these blocks of colour how Cezanne saw it, or was it just for fun? It didn't matter. No one had ever done it, and it was pleasing. The work of a master.

He arrived at the building. It said NASA THWAITE MOON CENTRE above the glass doors. He heard church bells, three steady ones that sounded like door chimes. 11.45. Fifteen minutes until his appointment. He went up the road, careful not to get lost, then doubled back and walked up the Centre steps and through the revolving glass doors.

The receptionist looked up as he arrived at her desk.

'I'm Banno Culdrun?' The job was his, *but you can't take anything for granted*. 'I'm here to see Mr. Thwaite?'

'Yes. Just a moment. Take a seat please.' The woman was the gatekeeper here but, from her smile, not one to make things difficult. She pressed a button on her phone. Banno could see its little indicator light go amber and heard a faint buzz in another room. She had a short exchange with someone.

'Mr. Thwaite will be about 20 minutes,' she said. 'I'm afraid he's running slightly late this morning. If you'd like to get a cup of coffee and come back—'

'That's OK. I'll wait.'

It felt like a dentist's or optometrist's waiting room. Banno took out the job description, in case Mr. Thwaite asked him about it.

> The Moon Centre is a repository of knowledge. Our collection, much of it on long and short term loan, includes information on the science and history, and the music and poetry, of the moon. We offer this knowledge to the public, in our various themed rooms. All persons hired as Visitor—

Outside, without introductory flourish, the church bells began to toll, one by one, the same note. Banno counted twelve. Who needed anything more?

> —Assistants (VAs) in any of our rooms will be subject to the following regulations (as per NASA Code Section 31).

1. <u>Definition of VA</u>

> Carries out incidental janitorial work in connection with the upkeep and care of the assigned room, including: sweeping floors, dusting furniture, polishing glass exhibit cases and straightening frames, posters, etc. on the walls; follows established rules and procedures relating to security activities; performs related responsibilities as requested; and has a proven ability, or be able to demonstrate the ability, to work effectively as part of a team and to stay cool and calm under pressure.

It seemed important enough to be rereading this stuff; but, Banno thought, *how much does it matter?*

I don't want it to be torture, but I want it to be over.

2. Duties of VA

In assigned room, protects exhibits from theft, damage or accident, and enforces rules and regulations governing conduct of the public. During emergencies, assists in the removal of exhibits.

3. Behaviour of VA

Demonstrates a neat appearance to visitors; provides information to visitors; walks inconspicuously towards visitors; does not pace up and down; is friendly, outgoing, and professional; is comfortable enforcing rules; and, overall, leaves a lasting and positive impression.

Interview Date: September 1, 1966

A door opened and a tall, thin man appeared. He walked over to Banno, smiling and holding out his hand.

'Nice to finally meet you, Banno,' he said. Mr. Thwaite's voice was as clipped as his crewcut. 'I was most impressed by your application and letter of recommendation.' Banno felt a surge of relief. Mr. Thwaite did sound like someone who knew what they were going to say before they said it, like a caller to a radio phone-in show; but it didn't matter. He seemed a nice enough person. And he hadn't asked about the short gap in Banno's CV.

Banno stood up and shook hands. 'Thank you. Nice to meet you too, Mr. Thwaite.'

85

'You can leave your bags – and guitar – with Reception.'

He must have looked unsure to Mr. Thwaite. 'They'll be safe... Let me take you to your room, and we can talk there.'

He led Banno down a hallway, to a door with the words SONGS AND POETRY written on it, above the smaller TO KNOW THE MOON. He let Banno in. The room smelled smoke-soaked and woody musty, but he could see framed exhibits all over the walls – the photographs, vinyl records and sheets of paper, probably with lyrics on them, that he'd read about.

Thwaite motioned him to follow as he crossed the carpet, past a small desk to a window. He opened it, letting in some fresh air and muffled car noise. 'We've had to close the room for a while,' he said, 'until we got the right person... There's your cottage.'

Banno walked over and peered out, towards the back.

'A classic old Fireman's Cottage – second from the left. Number 2.'

A white, wooden bungalow.

Banno followed Thwaite over to two stools, just inside the entrance to the room. 'We'll sit here for a minute,' Thwaite said. 'The one against the wall is yours; the other's just for today. Hold on.'

Banno sat down on his stool and watched Thwaite go over to a record player and lift the needle on to the beginning of a record. It played at a low volume.

It was *Moonlight Sonata,* one of the few classical pieces Banno recognized besides *Für Elise.* The rest was wallpaper to him and found no entry point into his soul; he could never tell if a piece was going anywhere or was supposed to mean something. But *Moonlight Sonata*. It was tuneful, and calming, at least until Thwaite spoke over it. 'It's what you play during the day. It draws people in. Then you can turn it down.' He rattled all this off, in dry, rat-a-tat words, like he was reading the legal small print at the end of a radio commercial. He took the needle off and came back over and sat next to Banno.

'Am I supposed to keep playing it?'

'As much as you can. But don't drive yourself insane. The first six minutes is what everyone knows, but you can let it play for the full fifteen if you want, especially if someone's in the room already. See how it goes on your half-day tomorrow.'

The job was confirmed.

Thwaite gestured to the room. 'As you may have read, we've procured, with NASA's assistance, original, handwritten lyrics to some famous moon songs.'

This was the introduction. 'Yes. I do know about that. It's very good.'

'They're kept here so the public can see them, but they're also entrusted to the Centre to protect. Your job. Those signed photos are those of the songwriters – Johnny Mercer, Henry Mancini, and so on. They're especially precious. There's more about them in the notes you'll get. Over there are early pressings of the original records. Poetry Corner,' he pointed, 'has moon poems, including Emily Dickinson's, and that's her picture above them of course.'

Banno liked the idea of saluting the songwriters; they were so often overlooked, while the singer got the fame. But *poetry?* Mr. Thwaite didn't strike him as a literary person.

'Happy?'

Banno wasn't sure what he meant.

'Do you think Songs and Poetry will suit you?'

'It's great,' Banno said normally. 'I like music and' – he had to be honest – '*some* poems.'

'You're sure it's the room for you.'

Banno's heart raced a little; *I don't say what I don't mean. I don't really need to answer that, don't need to be asked the same thing twice.*

'Yes.'

'You'll have the chance to change rooms if you want.'

'It's fine.' Was Mr. Thwaite not listening to him?

'Just so you're clear about what we expect from our Visitor Assistants…' Banno could tell he was about to race through more information. 'Most importantly you must always be neat and always courteous to our guests. Some will want to get out as quickly as possible but you must treat everyone with respect. Often it's just standing at attention and keeping people behind those yellow lines. Most often you'll find yourself waiting on your stool for any questions unless someone wants you to show them around the room.'

'It would keep me awake,' Banno said, feeling brave enough to half-joke with Mr. Thwaite – 'getting up to explain things.'

'As long as you get up with a smile,' Thwaite said tonelessly.

Banno felt heat around his heart. He wanted to say he didn't play that game, that he hated the idea of false smiling, and he'd done what was needed in all his jobs without being dishonest like that. He could never tell Mr. Thwaite that his honesty had cost him the job at Harold Grandy's. But to have lied to customers – that their dry cleaning had taken 'longer than expected' and they had to pay more – was something he hadn't been prepared to do.

'Remaining polite can be difficult,' Thwaite continued a bit more slowly. Had he sensed Banno's discomfort? 'It doesn't happen often, but the odd visitor in other places I've managed has become verbally abusive. I don't know why, but some of them, after asking a question of an Assistant – or someone else they see as subordinate – and not getting the answer they want, say things like "You should know more than you do" or "Never mind. You're only hired help. You're not supposed to know anything." Someone once told an attendant at another museum that she was wrong in her *opinion* of something. She argued with them, and they complained to me about her, and I had to let her go for the sake of our reputation. So it's best to keep your opinions to yourself. Just get on with what you're supposed to do: give accurate information; never argue; keep that smile; and treat everyone in a professional manner. In short, make sure they have a good experience.

'Let me introduce you to your colleague, and then I have to shoot off.'

They walked quickly to the open door of the Geology room. 'Francine?' She appeared at the doorway. 'This is Banno Culdrun, our new Songs and Poetry man.'

She smiled what looked like a real, warm smile to Banno. 'Welcome to the Moon Centre,' she said, 'and Goodmews, "Banno?"'

'Yes.'

'I've never heard that name.'

Banno shrugged. 'It's short for "Bancroft".'

'Francine works here mornings. She's been with us

almost from the start, knows everything about the Centre. She even made up a colour – Floor Yellow – for the bright lines in your room. She also' – Thwaite rolled his eyes – 'runs the *Moon* Church. Maybe you saw that old tourist sign on your way into Goodmews. Maybe you've seen the church.'

'I did see the sign. I haven't seen the church yet.'

'She's planning to save everyone, hey Francine?' Then Thwaite smiled and winked at Banno.

Banno smiled back, like he was on Mr. Thwaite's 'team', but he only managed a twitch, like David Janssen in *The Fugitive*. Out of the corner of his eye he could see that Francine wasn't smiling, and he felt bad that it looked like he was in cahoots with Mr. Thwaite.

'We'll let you get back to your work, Francine,' Thwaite said.

He led Banno to his office, in a roundabout way it seemed, and had him sit across from him at his desk.

'The final thing for today… Since we're a NASA outpost, you're required to affirm this loyalty oath.' Banno felt himself freeze. He was being given the official 'We trust you'; that felt good. But Mr. Thwaite couldn't have known how important signing an oath was to him. It was more than just a piece of paper, it was more than a guarantee to an organization. Signing it was Banno's solemn pledge that he would keep his word. Like all the other promises he made, to himself and others, it was iron-clad, inviolate, a straitjacket that suited him. A lifejacket.

'It's not a problem, is it?'

Banno could hear a hint of concern in Thwaite's voice, like he thought Banno might be hiding something.

'No.' An oath was serious, but it was not a problem.

Oaths had no grey areas. They were the black and white of honesty.

Thwaite pushed the piece of paper across the desk.

Banno scanned the half page; he'd read words like these before – I will not disclose any confidential information. He signed and dated the form and slid the piece of paper back across the desk.

Thwaite glanced at it. 'Welcome aboard' he held out his hand. Banno complied.

'See you at 1 tomorrow. Jan – the receptionist – should be back from lunch soon. She'll give you your uniform and the key to your cottage—'

'Great.'

'—and your m.o. for setting up the room every day and tips on what to tell people.'

Banno sat down to wait. He spotted a buzzing fly hovering with intent, then landing, watched it take off, and saw it land somewhere else, a sitting target. He watched it out of the far corner of his eye until it hurt.

So boring. Though boredom is better than pain. And he had the job, and free rent.

A copy of *The Occasional* was on the table in front of him. It looked like a local paper by the way it was printed. He turned it over and saw the 'Mooncross' on the back page and began to work through it.

He knew the answer to 5 across: 'Who was the goddess of the moon?' – Diana; and 'Galileo' fit – though was that right? – for 'Who coined the word "crater?"'. Others he had no idea about and were going to take time, if he ever got them, like 3 down: 'Six letter astronomical term for conjunction of earth,

91

moon and sun.' It started with an 's' if 9 down – 'eclipse' – was right, which it probably was, and had 'g' as its next to last letter if 'Gagarin' was right, which must be. But it was a word he didn't know.

Jan saw him as she came through the revolving doors.

'Sorry to keep you waiting, Mr. Culdrun.'

She crossed the foyer. 'Let me get you what you need.'

She reached behind the counter, then came back over to Banno and handed him a bag. 'Your uniform and key and a few sheets of paper are in there. Let me know if you need anything else.'

'Thanks.'

'See you tomorrow.'

He went out the front and round the side and walked the yellow paving stones that led to the cottages at the back. The door was unlocked. He removed his shoes just inside and went in, putting everything down. The cottage had a distinctive smell. It wasn't a bad one; just a smell, the smell of the cottage.

He took his slippers out and put them on, then walked over to the bedroom and, from habit – shoes off at front door, slippers at bedroom – took his slippers off and had a pad over the givingly soft carpet. It smelled new.

The bathroom was bright. The tap was dripping. Perhaps someone had given the cottage a cleaning. He turned it off. There was no clunk. That was a relief – the pipes were alright. He tried out the toilet seat; it didn't 'sit' as well as the one in his apartment back in Iowa. *Always new things to get used to.*

In the small living room, Banno straightened the two just-off-level, nondescript paintings on the wall. The only sound he could hear was a ticking clock somewhere – or was it a steady-dripping tap? He went back to the bathroom to check. The tap wasn't dripping. He waited. He needed to be as sure as he could that he wouldn't be bushwhacked by it starting again. It would be like the time he'd woken to fresh mouse droppings after he thought he'd got rid of it. No drip. 'Showertime,' he sang, 'and the livin' is easy. Tap ain't drippin', and the water ain't high.'

He went over to the TV and turned it on, changing channels until he came upon *Tidiness*. How lucky was *he*? Should he have been surprised that it was on on the same day and at the same time as back home?

He stood there, letting the programme draw him in. He'd got to know the names of the four panellists, who competed against each other, and the three 'Domestic Judges' who sat in a separate room and decided which panellist was tidiest each week.

For some reason that he could never understand, the show often involved new electrical devices, which afterwards were awarded to audience members as prizes. In a recent episode – 'The Electric Lawn Mower Trial' was how Banno remembered it – the show had taken place in a large garden close to the studio. The winning panellist had been the one who, after an acceptable mow, rewrapped the electric cord around the lawn-mower the neatest and fastest. Another episode had been 'The Cutlery Trial', or something like that, that took place in the *Tidiness* kitchen. Clean cutlery from the dishwasher had to be transferred to the cutlery drawer. The judges' decision had been based on speed, least cutlery dropped, and accuracy and quietness of transfer.

Today it was 'The Holiday Trial'.

Each panellist described, in one minute, what they would need for a two-week cruising holiday and what they would need to do to leave their house more clean and tidy than the others. 'One lucky audience member,' said the deep-voiced presenter, 'will win a cruise for two to the new state of Alaska, where the Anchorage earthquake three years ago was the second most powerful in recorded history, reaching a magnitude of 9.2. But,' the man continued, 'it's all over now, and you can be part of the first group of tourists that Alaska is welcoming back.' The Stones' twangy song 'It's All Over Now' flicked through Banno's brain.

As always at the end, 'all that remained', as the presenter said, was for each panellist to offer their own four-line definition of domestic tidiness. Their lines were about to be flashed on the screen while they read them out, and there might be laughs, or sometimes just murmuring.

'BELONGINGS ARRANGED
BED MADE
DISHES WASHED
ROOM SWEPT.'

Then:

'DOG HEALTHY
DEBTS PAID
NECESSARY FOOD PURCHASED
NECESSARY ITEMS PURCHASED.'

The next one sounded partially spontaneous, but Banno never knew whether these TV things were.

> 'DESIRED FOOD PURCHASED
> DESIRED ITEMS PURCHASED
> LETTERS ANSWERED
> CAUGHT UP ON READING.'

And the last one:

> 'DESIRED PLACES VISITED
> THINGS EITHER FIXED,
> IMPROVED
> OR THROWN OUT.'

As the applause died down, the presenter intoned, 'And we leave you with this. Tidiness for some means...

> NOT IN A ROMANTIC TIZZY:
> EITHER SETTLED ALONE OR SETTLED TOGETHER,
> AND FEELING NO GUILT
> TOWARDS ANYONE.

'Before we say goodbye, we offer you today's tidy hint. On your towels and washcloths, tuck those little labels out of sight. "Better neat than not".'

Banno turned off the TV. *No guilt towards anyone,* he thought. It was good not to have to feel it anymore.

It had gone with the days of Debbie. So many times, after saying something hurtful to her in the heat of the moment, when they'd flip-flopped from lockstep to loggerheads, he'd apologized. It had assuaged his guilt and made him feel like it wasn't the end of the world, but it only made things better until the next heated moment.

Suddenly he felt lost. Was worse than feeling guilt, not feeling it? He recalled a friend who'd had a vasectomy before he got married, and every day, out walking, his heart sank in guilt when he saw children.

What am I doing here, in this strange cottage, Banno thought. *I'm so lonely. It's the last place I want to be. Should I go back home, forget this job? Go back to my old one? – they'd take me. And at least I know people there.*

Who? He pictured them. There was no one he could call to ask what they thought.

But he'd done it. He'd discovered a sense of adventure he didn't know he had, and he'd got the job.

THIRTEEN

September 16, 1966

Dear Ray,

Thank you for your note of congratulations on the recent reopening of the Moon Centre.

I congratulate you on Lunar Orbiter 1. Whether the world will remember that it was America's first spacecraft to orbit the moon, I can't say, but I am sure that millions will never forget that photo. It may be grainy and show just the southern half of our planet at night, but for NASA to be the first to have snapped the earth from the moon is a great triumph.

I would like to bring up one issue at this point, if I may.

As you know, even before the Centre's reopening, our numbers had been growing steadily for some months. Goodmews is situated in a beautiful canyon and, with the Moon Centre as an additional draw, many people have been finding this to be an area they not only want to see

– and some to return to – but additionally, an increasing number have chosen to stay. The town is growing into a city.

Most incomers have settled in comfortably and are contributing to Goodmews's prosperity. However, there is a problem with some who've chosen to stay: we've had a large influx of drifters – 'hippies', as they call themselves. As I understand it, they have set up tents and shelters in the hills near our beautiful orangewoods.

They are not appreciated here. They come down into the town looking for thrown-away food and cigarettes, swearing and shouting, and they smell. I have become increasingly concerned about their being here. I'm sure their presence will begin to have a detrimental effect on the number of visitors to both the town and the Moon Centre.

The Centre was a world first, and NASA's brave plunge in taking it under its wing has proved to be very beneficial, both for Goodmews and, I would venture, NASA's reputation as a community-spirited government agency.

So, regarding our 'hippie' invasion, I have a solution to propose: NASA designates Goodmews as the world's first 'Moontown'. Besides being another NASA world first, I believe it would benefit everyone else, for many years (please see below).

As a popular NASA satellite, who of course wants the best for NASA, ourselves and all other satellites, I believe we 'speak the same language', and I would like to present the following idea.

NASA could stipulate, in its articles of incorporation for any so-designated Moontown, that for any town to be granted Moontown status, it would have to ensure that all of its inhabitants accept certain responsibilities in exchange for having this honour bestowed upon it. The key agreement would be that all able-bodied residents would be required to work.

This would attract the right type of incomer, as the town would be known to neither harbour nor accept 'ne'er-do-wells', such as Goodmews's hippie chaff. As a result, a Moontown would become a proud place with a reputation for hard work. It would attain, besides renewed pride in itself, self-supporting status in the public eye.

I know this proposal, being out of the blue as it is, will require thought on NASA's part. Far be it from me to suggest to NASA how it should frame its proposals, if indeed this one is of interest, but I do believe this would be good for all concerned.

For Goodmews, as an example, this would accomplish the crucial goal of ridding us of the hippies.

I await your considered response.

Sincerely,
Sam

*

October 10, 1966

Dear Ray,

I know I wrote three weeks ago.

Firstly, let me say that I'm sure that the crash-landing of Surveyor 2 on the moon two weeks ago must have been a great let-down for NASA, and for you personally. From the reports I've read, it sounds like it was a very unfortunate accident.

Thus, I hope you don't find this short letter impertinent. I had prepared it before the crash.

I understand that there may well be more pressing issues there now, but as I hadn't heard back from you regarding my letter about the possibility of a 'Moontown', I had one further thought about it, which I have held off sending to you.

There are towns in the U.S., and probably beyond, that have 'moon' or 'luna' in their name, like Moonbeam in Ontario, but as far as I am aware, there are no 'official' – or even self-styled – 'Moontowns'. I believe that bestowing such an authorized designation, firstly upon Goodmews, would not only emphasize Goodmews's uniqueness – to its benefit, and the Moon Centre's – but would accord NASA a good deal of publicity and an even more 'futuristic' feel in the public imagination.

Thank you again for your consideration of this idea.

Sam

*

October 19, 1966

Dear Sam,

Please excuse my delay in responding. Yes, Surveyor 2's crash has been a blow. You may have learned some things from the news reports, but to put you in the fuller picture as you are part of NASA's structure (this is not public information): Surveyor 2, as you know, was expected to be NASA's second unmanned lunar lander. Our investigation indicates that a mid-course correction failed: Surveyor 2 lost control, then contact with it was lost. It is assumed to have crashed.

All we can do is pick ourselves up again. Surveyor 3 is scheduled for next April (also confidential). Not only will it be the first mission to carry a surface-soil sampling-scoop, but the soil samples – and the mechanical surface digger at work – will be photographed by Surveyor's camera, along with the moon and Surveyor itself. These images will be the first ones from the surface of the moon to be transmitted back to earth.

This letter, however, is in response to your 'Moontown' suggestion, and I think you will be pleased with it.

Prior to Surveyor 2's crash, and though I myself was highly sceptical of your idea, I conveyed it to my superiors. Surprisingly to me, they reacted positively. Then the crash intervened and nothing further was mentioned. However, I have gone back to them and they are still positive about your idea. They want to look to the future in as many ways as possible and have instructed me to communicate to you the following.

'The NASA Thwaite Moon Centre in Goodmews is an important outpost in NASA's campaign to stimulate public interest in Space. We hereby designate Goodmews as the world's first NASA Moontown. This is further evidence of NASA's support for the Goodmews Moon Centre and the principles it subscribes to, as we continue our joint role in taking the citizens of Goodmews into the future.'

As stated in the three-page enclosed documentation, Sam, please especially note that Goodmews's Moontown status will be 'official'. NASA will determine how this designation is to be promulgated and retains the right to withdraw it at any time.

Congratulations are in order.

Yours faithfully,
Ray Block, NASA

*

Thwaite finished reading the official information and dialled. 'Ray? This is Sam, from the Goodmews Moon Centre.'

'Hello, Sam. Good to hear your voice. I don't believe we've spoken before.'

'I don't believe so… I want to thank you for your help in getting NASA's agreement to my Moontown idea.'

'I only presented it. I had nothing to do with its approval. But you're welcome.'

'I know it will work out well, Ray. And the proviso that able-bodied residents must work, will help our hippie situation immensely, immediately.'

'That helped sway NASA. They're sympathetic to your problem and they feel that that proviso will set a good precedent for future Moontowns. Between you and me, NASA has its problems, too, with some people who don't seem to fit, who aren't completely "with the programme".'

'Yeah. I do see articles about that sometimes.'

'Did you see the one recently, quoting Kennington Varnen?'

'I did, yes. Wasn't it about some chemical NASA's involved with?'

'Close. It was about a chemical element – actually an isotope: helium-3. With a hyphen before the 3. It's something that was discovered in 1939. Kennington is a chemical engineer and a rocket specialist. He's been our helium-3 advisor for a number of years.'

'You have an advisor for one chemical?'

Sam could sense a pause on the line.

'If you don't mind this reminder, it's something your oath of secrecy covers.'

'Of course, Ray.'

'Of course. I know I didn't need to ask.'

'Thank you.'

'Helium-3 is important. It could be a clean source of fuel for nuclear fusion in the future. You don't need to understand how that would work; but why it's a major concern of NASA's is that although helium-3 is rare on earth, it's plentiful on the moon.

'Kennington went further in public than NASA would have liked. As you may remember, he feels that its extraction from the regolith – the soil on the moon – would be too involved and expensive, not to mention the problems of bringing it back to earth, and it shouldn't be part of future human lunar landings.'

'But he can't be the only voice at NASA.'

'Of course not. But his view carries a lot of weight, even though *we* – perhaps half of senior management – feel it's vital to at least attempt the extraction.

'We've tolerated what he's said in the past about why NASA's lagging behind the Soviets – we're wasteful and bureaucratic – and "risk-averse", as he puts it. And there are *some* truths in what he says. But this article felt to many at NASA like a bridge too far, especially coming so soon after the crash.'

'It must have been a blow for him too, wasn't it?'

'I'm sure it was. For everyone, and he's one of Surveyor's chief engineers. Maybe the crash tipped him into openly airing his thoughts on helium-3. We don't know. But it hasn't been good for morale. It's not the image we want to project. Like everyone, he has to be part of the team. He can't just go off in his own direction.'

'Can't you fire him? There must be other excellent chemical engineers.'

'There are. Like your hippies, many here would be glad to see the back of him. But he's a great engineer. We need him… You did well to convince NASA about how to "legally" expel *your* problem. It's good for NASA, of course, to have a "clean" Moontown, but it also chimed with NASA because of our "Kennington" problem. In fact we're revisiting our guidelines regarding what our employees can say in public. You deserve thanks for that, which NASA can not give you publicly.'

'I understand. Thank you… Ray, what I would appreciate is if NASA could issue an official "Moontown" statement regarding Goodmews, which I'll put in our local paper. I don't want anyone in any doubt about what will now be required of everyone living here. Do you think you can get that from your bosses for me?'

'I'm sure they'll be happy to do that.'

'A final thing, Ray, that I wanted to run by you. I would like to rename some of our streets so they sound more associated with the moon. It would fit well with our new designation. Should I have NASA's agreement for that?'

'No. NASA does not want to be seen to be involved with local issues. It sounds good, though, very appropriate. It will make Goodmews even more of a Moontown.'

*

The Goodmews Occasional
November 10, 1966

NASA DESIGNATES GOODMEWS AS WORLD'S FIRST 'MOONTOWN'

NASA has asked me to release the following statement to Goodmews. It is great news:

'In recognition of the NASA Thwaite Moon Centre's promotion of public interest in the moon and in Space exploration, and in expectation of our long-term future partnership with the Moon Centre, NASA hereby designates Goodmews as the world's first Moontown. This is a unique honour, and we expect Goodmews to be the first of many NASA Moontowns.

This Moontown designation will be for selected local NASA centres of moon interest that are part of hard-working, thriving communities. NASA will now require all residents of Goodmews, as a Moontown – and all residents of any future Moontown – who are not natives and are over the age of 21, to be employed or self-employed. In other words, those not in work will be deported by town officials, with NASA assistance if necessary.

These regulations will be distributed to Goodmews Station and to relevant travel agencies. NASA also expects there to be extensive press coverage of this Moontown designation.'

In England, 750 years ago, Magna Carta was issued. It has been a symbol of justice and freedom all over the Western world ever since. And, as everyone will be aware, the Declaration of Independence, nearly 200 years ago, led to the recognition of this country as a sovereign nation.

NASA's designation of our town as the world's first Moontown may not yet be seen in the same light as these two documents, but I believe that this pronouncement is of great moment for Goodmews and will pave the way for other Moontowns to come.

Goodmews will be, as never before, 'on the map'. Our visitor numbers will no doubt increase, as will investment in our town and the number of (appropriate) people choosing to settle here. I have been assured by NASA that they will provide any additional officers we need, to enforce the new regulation that requires incomers to be employed. As everyone will know by now, our temporary 'residents', who were camped out near the orangewoods for months, have already been cleared from their sites.

Finally, to befit our new Moontown status, it has been proposed that some of our central roads be renamed so that they bear a connection to the moon rather than simply to past Mewsicians, who I've been told many have never heard of.

I would ask that residents bring any suggestions for these street names to the Moon Centre in the next two weeks. Barring objection, ten new names will be decided upon by myself and Francine and put in place, and an updated town map will be published. Please keep your suggestions anonymous so there can be no hint of favouritism.

Francine, hands strong-swinging, passed slower walkers on her way to work. 'I'm not a dog walker,' she thought, 'or one of those people who look like they're racewalking, or a radio-listener walker, or a child-in-pram walker. I'm just a walker. But I know what it's like to move fast. I did athletics.' She pictured herself striding out like the walking man on the green traffic-light. The fewer-people morning's fresh-air always invigorated her more than afternoon's noisier heavier-air walk.

She checked her watch. 8.45. On time as always. 'Francine?' It came from his office as she crossed the foyer, and she went over to it.

'Good morning, Sam.'

'Church looks good, I have to admit.'

'Thanks.' That was great to get his approval. She hadn't even known he'd seen it.

'Good riddance to the scaffolding,' he said.

'It's going back up for a while, I'm afraid. They've discovered the roof needs doing.'

He nodded, almost to himself. 'At least we won't have to change the sign coming in yet.'

'Yeah.'

'It looks nice; grey and white if I recall. They looked different somehow. Did you get the colours in Goodmews?'

'I made them.'

'You *made* them?'

'Yes, in the church.'

'In the church?'

'Yes.' Francine tried to ignore the grating feeling she got when Sam repeated what she said. Was he hard of hearing? She didn't think so. He was too young for that. Was it just a bad habit? Or something they did out where he used to live? It seemed like a way to stall for time, to think.

'From paints?'

'I mixed different shades. I did study Colour Science before switching to Astro-Geology.'

'Sorry. I forgot.'

'I wanted to create some colours that look like the moon to me.'

'Can you trademark them?'

'I don't know. Why?'

'You could give them names. Make them special; "Goodmews" colours.'

'Hmm. I did give them names in my head when I was making them. Crater Grey, Sunlit White.'

'I see. The grey craters…'

'Lava seas probably.'

'Of course. And the white we see.'

'The mountain peaks lit by the sun.'

'This is sounding good, Francine. What struck me, when I saw the roof, fresh and bright like you've made it, is that the rest of Goodmews has always looked pretty shabby, "barny". Do you think you could create some colours for some of the other buildings, cheer up the place a bit?'

'I suppose so.' She felt slightly embarrassed, like a child who's done some finger-painting that someone was saying was great. 'That would be fun. I *have* made two other ones, now that you've asked, that I've called Sun Yellow and Wet Brick Red.'

'How about using the yellow for the Centre?'

'OK.'

'Who'd you use for the church?'

'The decorators who did the G-Mall.'

'Perfect. I'll get them. Is there a formula you've got, so I can get more made?'

'Yes. I wrote it down.'

'Great. And I'll pay you a bonus for that colour and the red one and any new ones you come up with that we use in the town. I mean, we're a Moontown. Why not also have our own "Moontown" look?'

'I don't want to be paid, Sam.' She felt a certain dignity in saying this. 'I enjoy creating colours; it's like science experiments. And to be able to use them to beautify the town will be enough. I *could* do with some measuring beakers and a microscope, though; I've been using bowls and a bucket. And I'll need to get some more paint.'

'Get what you need and give me the invoice.'

It was another of her ideas that he'd accepted. She felt she was now nearly a full partner, remaking – bettering – Goodmews in ways no one could have expected, even a few months before. It was the perfect place for her to use her talents. Colour could be beautiful anywhere – an azalea-flowered golf course, a blue-surfaced tennis court, the blue water of a swimming pool, the smooth black of a newly tarred road.

FOURTEEN

Sam's new idea was clever and, he knew, an easy way for NASA to officially salute the central role the Moon Centre had played in Goodmews's development.

December 9, 1966
Dear Ray,

I hope Surveyor 2's failure in September has not continued to put too much of a brake on life at NASA, and that plans for Surveyor 3, and all you hope it will accomplish, are still in hand for next April's launch.

I want to reiterate my gratitude to NASA for having taken seriously – and taken on board – a number of my suggestions, including – crucially – Goodmews becoming a Moontown, which has contributed to NASA's reputation as much as to Goodmews's.

I would like to run another idea by you, which I think will neatly 'bookend' the Moontown idea.

Goodmews's main street – the old Goodmews Way, soon to be Copernicus Broadway – is playing host to an increasing number of shops. I plan – with the town's consent – to request the government (perhaps with NASA's assistance?) to demarcate the area as a Central Business District or, in Census Bureau terms, an 'unincorporated place', which has 500 or more people. This future, for various reasons that you will understand, will include parking enforcement and the levying of rent and business rates; as you will appreciate, this is an inevitable by-product of growth but will also be a basic source of municipal income. As importantly, it will help to define the key areas in our expanding town.

A secondary business area would be marked out on the edge of town, where the Moon Centre is situated, and in line with the above, I feel that it would be a good time to rename the zone immediately surrounding the Centre. As this land is owned by NASA, my suggestion is that it be called something like Moon Centre Park – or even Thwaiteville (if that's not too rich a suggestion!).

This would give the Moon Centre new significance and, at the same time, raise its, and NASA's, profile. I'm sure the idea would be welcomed by Goodmews, as it would be further recognition of its unique identity. As importantly, it would be another clear signal of NASA's intention to cement its 'long-term partnership' with the town.

I believe the case could also be made to assign this special sector its own postcode, as distinct from the new central district and Goodmews as a whole. We could perhaps discuss this at some point.

For now, I await your – hopefully positive – response to this idea.

Faithfully,
Sam

This issue of <u>The Occasional</u> is expressly to thank everyone for their suggestions for new street-names, which will further enrich our identity as the world's first – and still <u>only</u> – Moontown.

All entries were appreciated. The ten renamed streets in the centre of town will be:

Copernicus Broadway
Crescent Crescent
Galileo Court
Impact Street
Meteor Avenue (leading to Meteorite Close)
Moon Parade
New Moon Road
Tidal Lane
Waning Gardens
Waxy Way

*

Abed in the middle of the Goodmews night, Tris woke and woke from his 'pitch-black catty-naps', triple-checking the silence, hearing it as a total deletion of noise – motorised and otherwise – that no human can guarantee. When dawn broke, he woke for good, to a punctuation of caws, then chirps, then the cooed paragraphs of the doves' Morse code, all finally overwritten by the bold bells of the Moon Church.

He was surprised he hadn't recalled a dream, as he'd woken up so many times. *Most soon go up in a puff of effervescent irrelevance – as is their nature,* he thought. And the ones that did stick around? Not the nightmares, but the ones where something he wanted to happen did? Was he glad when he'd had them, or not? Because when he woke to the sudden reminder of the real world, he would realize they had only been dreams.

Work from Francine waited downstairs, in his pocket-size office on the ground floor of his flat. Double-checking her weekly sayings, as little as the work was, still gave him a veneer of respectability, and he'd put his sign up outside. It was his salute to Goodmews's quirky spirit, and to himself for finding the *h* missing on the plaque on the pier: T E S OP WIT OUT AN – 'The Shop Without an H'.

He was glad Francine had planted the idea in him to return, and when he'd read she'd started a 'moon church' with sayings posted regularly, he was pretty sure that was what had finally convinced him to come back. In settling in Goodmews, he felt a bit like the giraffe he'd seen at a drinking hole in Africa: it approached, checked for wild animals; moved away, approached, checked again; then – feeling safe enough to drink – stayed for a little while.

Even though he'd been here twice before, Goodmews still felt as fresh and unique as a great first album. This time, before he'd even popped in to the Moon Centre to say hello to Francine, he'd been an eager tourist. If he'd run into her, that would have been OK, but he hadn't.

He gave himself a week, wandering around, and he still hadn't been inside the refurbished church or been up to the orangewoods. He should have treated himself to more meandering time. Unlike the harried hurried urban horridness of back home, Goodmews had a relaxed rhythm.

He'd strolled slowly across roads, taking advantage of the town's extended pedestrian-crossing times, just enjoying the colour of the crossings, which reminded him of a friend's Competition Orange Mustang.

He'd also spoiled himself with daily 'stand outs' – standing outside his flat and doing nothing. He should have done this more before 'doing the right thing' and settling in to a new proofreading routine. As he knew, one only gets one chance at a first week in a new town.

Life now was fine inside his flat too, at 15, Crescent Crescent; and the way his address was shown, in the 'dotty' Goodmews fashion – on two wooden blocks, with one dot on the first, and five on the second – had given him the idea for a dice game. He knew he probably played it too much. In the past, real-world problems, or even just niggles, would sometimes render him unable to immerse himself in whatever game he'd invented. But here his flat was childhood cosy and his time was his own. The phone never rang. And he wasn't offending anyone; no one even knew what he was doing.

My first morning-decision, he said to himself – *how to slice my orange.* He cut through it, halving it, revealing the glisten inside, then chewed the sweet juice of the sections he'd sliced and raised his plate for the sip. The few seeds were all that had lessened the perfection. *People argue about which are the best novels,* he thought. *I'd like to know where to get the best navels.*

He had a quick cup of instant coffee to jump-start the day. *It's a lousy, lazy way to do it; I should make the effort to brew it – so I could 'wake up and smell the coffee' and be fully awake for proofreadery concentration; but it's such a hassle. Instant's got no packaging, just need to open a jar.*

The world's divided into those who can open a package correctly – or know whether to push or pull a door open – and people like me. Asking me to tie on a hospital gown properly would be like asking me to help a classical musician find their place in a score.

Blessed are the bedmakers, for they know how to fold the sheets.

The bread, with its weave, flavour and freshness, was almost good enough to eat without jam, though he only had strawberry today – *the anodyne of jams*, he thought. He picked at his final bits of breakfast – clumped in their own islands of colour in a semicircle round his plate.

'Light my Fire' was on the radio again; it was on every day. Not a great song to him, the lyrics – like most rock songs – rhymey-stupid; but it had that catchy build-up to the chorus and it was the first long song he could remember ever being played on the radio.

He did his morning shave, always worth the wait until after his shower, for bristle-ready efficiency. Like always, he tried to get his sideburns even, but it was like trying to get trouser cuffs turned up equally, or a car's tyres inflated to the same pressure. Not even barbers got his sideburns to match.

He gave his clothes their brush-off and went downstairs. He settled in at his desk, his dictionary to hand, thinking, *Where would I be without it?*

Gavelling to a start his proofreading day, he rapped the rubbish-bin rim with his pencil sharpener, emptying yesterday's remaining blue shavings. Then, with poised blue pencil, and ruler under the words, he whisperedly, expertly, read Francine's message of the week:

Good listeners are rare. They are an endangered species.

Like good interviewers, he thought, *who should just let the interviewee talk.* He checked the words for mistakes; as with any proofing job, no matter how small, he used all his concentration. As he'd taught others, errors are often overlooked in short lines because one assumes the words are correct. These were. He looked over the proofed words again; it gave him the same type of satisfaction he got when looking out over a lawn he'd just mown, or raked.

He went upstairs, trying to pay attention to how he moved, knowing from experience how easy it is to twist an ankle and ruin the day.

He stood looking out of his rain-spotted window, chomping at a crispibly edible apple, almost as crunchly juicy as a pomegranate but without its impenetrably pulpy pips. It was pouring outside, but life streamed by below: the couple – the husband walking, as always, ahead of his waddling wife; the flame-haired woman from across the road, pulling her old-lady-type shopping trolley behind her like she was dragging the weight of the world; that man with the best posture; the three-doors-down-man going off to the shops with leashed dog and lipped cig.

A parallel parker was manoeuvring his bonnet to just the right distance from the bum of the car ahead, trying to match the distance of his own car's bum from the nose of the car behind. Was the man being so overly concerned in case anyone happened to be watching? – in the same way that someone writing a letter to a proofreader might watch their spelling? *He's going for the perfect front, back and sides,* Tris thought. *But I'm not my neighbour's peepers. A 'nosy parker'? An English expression I can look up at some point.*

The passenger got out, fingernail-clicked the bonnet to say goodbye, then rushed indoors from the heavy wet with child and child equipment.

Tris watched as the light-grey clouds began to evaporate the rain into overcast, and two ladies emerged to brazenly chat. Someone cycling smilingly past gave them a slow-motion wave, as unreal as Miss Gulch flying by Dorothy's window, cackling at her from her broomstick-bike.

A couple of weeks earlier, when he'd read about the renamed streets, he wondered if some of them would be replacing the ones named after people. What an honour, he'd thought. To have a street named after you. Or a town named after you. Or... a dessert. What about a month!

The renaming had also given him the idea of inventing a Goodmews board game – To the Moon Centre. Players would move using little coloured models of local buildings, like the clock tower or the G-Mall. On certain squares you'd pick up a card, and if it described something beautiful, like the Goodmews moon, or the pink pavement, you'd skip a square. If it was something negative, like getting lost in the orangewoods, you'd lose a turn. The winner would be the one who got to the Moon Centre first, in the middle of the board. But Tris hadn't taken the idea further. He had his dice game. He went back down to his desk.

His chair, covered with some sort of material, was comfortable. He drew a vertical line down the middle of a sheet of paper, making two columns, then picked up his favourite pair of dice – small, brown, Bakelite-feeling ones

117

– and shook them in one hand, then shook them cupped in both, slightly muffling their soft sound of almost like teeth. He opened his hands and let the dice drop to the desk. A six and a five.

He grabbed his blue pen and recorded the total in the left column. He let fly again, picked up his black pen and recorded the total on the right. He shook the dice and recorded the score in blue, on the left, then shook again, for black's score. Equal. He shook again. And again.

He could stop. But again. And again. It was the same sort of pleasure he got from a warm, steady shower without any intermittent cold bits. He luxuriated in the indulgence, as he did with soft toilet paper or the sweet suds of scented soap. There was nothing he had to think about, nothing he had to do.

After each round – ten throws for blue, ten for black – he totalled the scores, which he liked doing. Then he drew an x in a small box at the bottom of each colour's column, like recording a strike on a ten-pin-bowling scoresheet.

The dice dots began to blear, but he wanted to have the icing on his cake before he stopped. He added up all the scores for each round, to get the day's totals for both colours, and drew a zigzagging line – as it usually turned out – across another sheet of paper, graphing the results. Today, black had beaten blue. He'd update his other charts – his record charts – later, and see if there were any new bests for things like the longest winning streak for either side or the most double-1's rolled in a row.

He realized he'd been sitting there for two hours. His game had spellbound him as much as if he'd pitted famous boxers or racehorses against each other. And all was still

OK. The world hadn't fallen apart just because he'd been playing his game.

*

The church phone rang.

'Francine.'

'Hi Sam!' She was surprised he was phoning.

'I wanted to ask you something.'

'Okey-doke.'

'You know we have various files of moon facts that we keep adding to.' His voice sounded scratchy and tired.

'Yes. They must be building up.'

'I'd like to get a number of them proofread.'

'Should I do it?'

'I'd like to get a professional to do it.'

She'd thought he'd been happy with her checking over *The Occasionals*. 'You want someone from *outside*?'

'I haven't decided yet. But the files are an official part of the Centre and I intend to publish some of them in the future. Isn't there someone you've been using for your "messages"?'

She could sense Thwaite's slight sarcasm.

'Yes.'

'Is he trustworthy?'

'Yes. He's a good guy.'

'Do you have his name?'

'It's Tris Palman.'

'Can you give me his number?'

'Yes.'

'Is he good?'

'Very good.'

From his desk, Tris could see that the grey had given way to pillow-white billows and some nearly spring sun. A gossamer of spider web – his wind gauge – bobbed around on the outside of his window.

He could hear chirping singing thingies cheering the blue – sweet peppering the air with their squawks. A police car appeared, prowling. Suddenly its blue lights flashed on – a proper prowl car, he said to himself. Its siren began howling as it raced away in its real-world sound.

He hadn't realized at first that the siren had disappeared, like not noticing that a burn mark on the skin has disappeared. He was back in *his* world, his warm, wordy, bookshelved encampment, as quiet as the inside of an elevator when there's one other person, but without any of that tension.

A few Mewsicians moseyed by. They never looked in at him.

The ringing phone shocked him into full attention.

'Hello?'

'Hello. Is this Tris Palman?' It was a new voice; was it male?

'Speaking.'

'This is Sam Thwaite. Director of the Moon Centre?'

'Yes,' he responded, showing that he knew of it. 'Hello…'

'Do you have a minute?'

'Yes.'

'You've been recommended as a proofreader by Francine?'

'OK.'

'Would you be available to do some proofreading for us at some point? Here at the Centre?'

He'd grown used to working at home – snug, with the right amount of light and his bed available for an afternoon nap. That was where he'd rather work. Would it be letting Francine down to say no? It was nice of her to mention him as a proofreader – he hadn't done *that* much work for her. And maybe the work would be interesting, to do with the moon.

He should. 'Sure.'

'We need you to sit our test first. I'm sure you understand.'

Tris bristled at the idea of having to prove himself. He was a long-standing member of the carvers guild; Francine would have told Mr. Thwaite that.

'Would this be soon?'

'Could you come in on Monday, the 19th, at noon? It's the last day we're open before Christmas.'

He was asking for help, and Tris didn't like saying no to someone he'd been recommended to. To be recommended was a professional's highest accolade.

'That would be fine.'

'When you arrive, if you could go to Reception and ask for me. The test should only take about ten minutes. I'm sure it will just be a formality in your case, but it's one of those things that NASA requires for any "outside" contractors. It's *their* test.'

'Of course. See you then. Thanks.'

Tris phoned Francine.

'… Thanks for telling Mr. Thwaite about me.'

'Good – he called you. Did you get some work?'

'I have to take a test first.'

'That's alright. Won't be difficult for *you*. Let me know how it goes.'

He wanted to go downstairs and play. But he didn't move. He knew that, in some sense, he was addicted to his game – to the roll and clatter of the dice; to the recording of the totals. He'd wondered if it was like other addictions, that were within arm's reach and so predictably pleasurable that they were almost impossible to resist, like alcohol or heroin, and he'd once tried to find out if there might be an organization – Dice Aware? Game Aware? – that he could phone for counselling. Mainly, he knew what would happen after a game, and that was what gave him most pause, wanting to dive in but knowing he shouldn't.

Often, sitting at his desk he would bring the desire for a game upon himself. At other times, it brought itself on. If he happened to be out somewhere and heard the roll of dice – or its cousin, as he called it, the shuffling of cards – his soul would be bated; and when he got home he would need a game, which would turn into an afternoon of rolling the dice, over and over, and he'd get lost in all the battles and scores. After certain crucial rolls, he'd find himself announcing, like a play-by-play commentator who made a game exciting, 'the balance has suddenly altered' – or 'the game has been put on ice' – or, most noteworthy, 'a new record has been set!' Pushed into the background would be what he had already felt approaching: the headaches. And the more he thought about them, the more he felt them being dragged back on to the stage, by the concentration he'd forced upon himself to make this dice world of his as all-encompassing as he could.

The headaches were bad, and would last for a day or a week; and when he left his flat, still suffering from them, and saw someone who looked as if they wanted to talk, he'd find it difficult to smile, let alone speak, inwardly cursing himself for succumbing to this compulsion once again and, as always, paying for it. He'd think, '*Why couldn't I have abstained, remained alert and pain-free, primed to engage?* He'd find his headached-self mumbling, and people would wonder why he seemed like this basket-case; and, as dispiriting as his headaches already were, they'd be compounded by the fact that he needed to keep this embarrassing, useless urge a secret.

A nap beckoned. He turned on his bedside lamp and lay down with the day's *Occasional* and a pen. His clock and radiator were in tick-tocking rad-knocking interplay, as if the rattling rad was nodding off as time marched on. His mind genuflections, though, were to the sounds of heat when it was cold: the softer clatter of the rad reigniting; the trusty boiler humming away. He knew he was lucky to have central heating. Not many people in Goodmews had it, though he'd heard the number was increasing. If he'd believed in God, Tris would have thanked him at these times. Instead, he'd find himself promising that if the heat came on and saved him, he would do penitence, like dusting shelves.

He read the newsletter like he usually read them, starting at the back and tearing out articles he wanted to save, and enjoyed a spot of 'nail-letting', as he called it – like 'blood-letting', but pleasurable.

His eyes were beginning to tire. He read 'good news' as 'Goodmews', 'Moontown' as 'Motown' and found himself proofreaderly puzzling over the look of 'oomph' on the page. He wanted to get through as much as he could, but he knew he was losing his train of thought. 'Train of thought, ship of fools' went through his mind before he dropped the paper onto the carpet and closed his eyes.

He didn't know if he needed to, but he put on a tie. He wouldn't be the best-dressed test taker ever, but he'd be presentable, acceptable. He collected the mechanical pencil and red pen he liked to use, along with his plastic ruler. He still hadn't found the perfect mechanical pencil, where the lead always came out the right amount and didn't break, but this one was as good as any he'd tried.

He pinned his carvers badge to his shirt. *Quarter to 12. Have to get to the Centre on time, but no rush.* He walked up Waxing Gardens, and down Waning Lane. Even at his easy pace, he moved more quickly than the drivers coming towards him, stuck in traffic. He stopped and looked back at the cars inching their way away, then sat down on a bench to guiltily, gratifyingly, take in the full view for a minute, observing the cars in the same way rubbernecking crash moths might when they've flocked to an accident. He got up, as quick off the mark as a bus suddenly pulling out; and so he could continue to watch the backed-up cars, the drivers no doubt fuming, he decided against taking a side road. He walked smoothly against the slow flow of traffic, the tyres quiet on the road.

Francine's billboard with the week's 'churchinition', as he called them, came into view:

IF YOU DON'T FEEL LIKE
RUNNING FOR THE BUS, DON'T

He turned into Copernicus Broadway and reached the Moon Centre.

He pushed through the glass doors, and as he was walking towards Reception, Mr. Thwaite emerged and held out his hand. 'Hello, I'm Mr. Thwaite. Thanks for coming in, Tris.' He zipped the words along, slurring them together like they didn't seem to matter, getting them over with.

'Nice to meet you, Mr. Thwaite.'

Tris followed him down a corridor. Why did he say yes? He wasn't a beginner, like ten years before. Why should he have to 'perform' for Mr. Thwaite? Could he say he wasn't feeling well, and split? This world of work. He didn't need it. They weren't his people.

He wanted to go home, read, hide like on Halloween when children came round.

But it was only for half a day.

He was led through an open door with TO KNOW THE MOON on it; inside, in a nearly bare room, Mr. Thwaite indicated the small pile of papers on the table in the middle.

'Please take a seat.'

He handed Tris the non-disclosure form. 'If you could sign this please, so we'll have it on record. It's just a matter of procedure, as you'll technically be a NASA contractor for any job you do here.'

Tris took it and read…

... Its an offence for anyone to disclose information regarding any Moon Centre document they have knowledge of or have had sight of...

'That's fine,' he said, not mentioning that 'Its' should have an apostrophe. He'd been through many such forms before, and how much did they matter anyway. He signed and dated it and gave it back to Mr. Thwaite.

'Thank you.' He handed Tris a sheet of paper, headed Language Usage Knowledge; Tris would have hyphenated Language-Usage for clarity. He flipped it over; there were questions on both sides.

'Quick explanation,' Thwaite said. 'NASA provides two different proofreading tests. This is not the one where you pick out mistakes and mark them with proofreading symbols.' He was speaking like someone speed-reeling-off terms and conditions, an insult to the English language. 'To be honest, I don't really understand them, even though NASA has supplied a guide. This test is just a quick check of – as it says – your "Language Usage Knowledge".'

Tris could feel that he'd cocked his head while Mr. Thwaite was talking, something he did when he was thinking about what someone was saying.

Thwaite glanced at the clock. 'It's very short, Tris. In the first section, if you could just circle "a" or "b", whichever's correct. I'll be back around 12.30. I'm sure you'll have no trouble with this, but do, please, give me a shout if there's a problem. Good luck, uh, Tris.'

It was annoying that Mr. Thwaite repeated Tris's name so often. It didn't feel like it was for courtesy; it was more like Mr. Thwaite was putting the conversation into a knowable box, to remind himself who he was talking to.

Tris took off his watch, laid it on its side, and let his ears adjust to the steady rhythm of the clock. He moved his lips: 'The time at the tone is… *Le temps est…*'

Whether or not he should have to take a test, he was taking it, and he would give it his full attention. He could at

126

least pretend to himself that he was hungry for the work, to make him try his hardest. No matter how much experience he had, he still wanted to be star pupil, like being the best patient, or the best son – though the way Mr. Thwaite had spoken to him made him feel more like a mailman than a proofreader, expected to know the quickest way around his patch, to stick to the route, and get it done in good time.

1 Spelling

| (She got her) | a. just deserts | b. just desserts |
| | a. minuscule | b. miniscule |

Tris circled the correct letter, and continued down the page, his pen ready for each number.

2 Apostrophes

| 1 | a. the people's candidate | b. the peoples' candidate |
| 2 | a. Jack Daniel's (whiskey) | b. Jack Daniels |

3 Plurals

| (keeping up with the) | a. Joneses | b. Jones's |
| (two wet) | a. Februarys | b. Februaries |

4 Hyphens

1	(it was...)		
	(excessive)	a. too-too	b. too too
2	(he was...)	a. colour-blind	b. colour blind
3	(all was turned...)	a. upside down	b. upside-down

He scanned his answers. They were all 'a's; he was pretty sure they were all correct. There was another question:

PLEASE USE THE SPACE BELOW TO MAKE ONE OR
TWO BRIEF POINTS/SUGGESTIONS ABOUT ONE
OR TWO PUNCTUATION MARKS. THIS SHOULD BE
FROM YOUR PROFESSIONAL PERSPECTIVE.

He wasn't sure what the purpose was, but punctuation
was his meat and potatoes, and nobody had ever asked him
about it.

He decided he'd leave out the full stops after his numbers
to match the test.

I The question mark

1   There could be a half–question mark – perhaps a
    question mark with an x below it – for a question that
    doesn't sound like a question.
2   There could be an upside-down question mark at the
    start of a sentence as well as at the end, as in Spanish, to
    alert the reader that a question is coming.

II The exclamation mark

Exclamation marks are integral to printed advertising
come-ons like 'Free coupon!' or 'Win bonus points!' In
addition, expressions such as 'Oh Wow!' seem to include
an exclamation mark.

There was still room. Tris decided to add one of his
pet ideas; after all, this was a test of his 'language-usage
knowledge' – though he wasn't sure if Mr. Thwaite would
appreciate it.

I also feel that the English language needs another punctuation mark — an upside-down exclamation mark, that would look something like ¡. My reasoning is this: let's say one wants to use a punctuation mark to emphasize the negativity of a phrase — for example, numbers indicating someone's dangerously high blood pressure, such as 180/120. If you use the normal exclamation mark after that measurement, it looks like you're saying it's exciting information, which is the opposite of what you're trying to convey — that the numbers are alarming and a cause for concern.

He looked over what he'd written, twice. 12.30. He heard the doorknob, and Mr. Thwaite appeared. 'Have you finished?'

'Yessss,' he crisply but elongatedly answered.

'How was it.'

'Fine, I think.'

'I've got to run,' Thwaite said. 'We're closing this afternoon. We're open again in January. I'll be back to you on the test then. Have a good Christmas.'

'Thank you. You too.'

*

Just before popping down the road, Sam wrote down a few ideas.

Ask NASA?

Centre charity? for investment in the Centre and Goodmews. Plaque on wall — 'The Moon Fund'.

<u>Tourism</u>:

      Centre gift shop. Mugs. Erasers. Orangewood crafts (not little wooden ships).

      Postcards – moon over orangewoods.

      Skywrite – or skytype! – ads outside GM? 'Visit GM'. 'When a man is tired of the moon, he's tired of GM'.

      See world's only Moon Centre, Moontown.

      Moongaze in dark 'moon nooks' in GM.

      Walk down Copernicus Broadway, Galileo Court. Fun shops.

      <u>Property</u> cheap, growing in value.

At the post office, there was one letter for him, postmarked 12/17/66, with the red, white and blue NASA insignia on it. He counted: the letter had taken only three days to get there. He tore it open, and read as he walked.

... and while we appreciate your latest idea, I am afraid that it is a non-starter.

What?

Our modest profile, on the outskirts of Goodmews, suits us: our intention has always been to be part of the town, not separate from it, and certainly not to be seen as in any way 'lording' over it.

Additionally, you will be well aware that we have contributed far more to the Moon Centre than was originally envisioned.

And my *contribution? What are you talking about? You think without me there'd* be *a Moon Centre?*

We thank you for all your ideas, many of which we have incorporated. We were happy to accept the granting of 'Moontown' status to Goodmews – even if there are yet to be any further Moontowns. And, as you requested, we have included 'Thwaite' in the Centre's name.

Well, la-di-da.

But – I trust you will understand – NASA's current position (in light of monetary constraints that you will be fully aware of) is that we have contributed more than enough to the Centre and have spent more than the allotted time considering your ideas for its improvement, which we have taken seriously.

We have concluded that the Centre should now be functioning as a stand-alone institution. If you desire to remain a NASA Affiliate, please inform me immediately and that will be discussed at the next Development meeting. Whichever option you choose, you are entitled to continue to use our name for the duration of the contract you originally signed, which was for 18 months and will not expire until October 1967. Additionally, we will pay you 50% of your salary until then (please see subsection (t) of our Terms and Conditions, a copy of which I have enclosed, in case your copy is not to hand).

You will be aware that a side benefit for you has been the enhancement of your reputation – far beyond Goodmews.

'My' reputation? What about yours? Who are you *to tell me how much you've done for* me?

To be honest, Sam, we are surprised that at this stage you would still want to enhance it further. Specifically, while it may have been tongue-in-cheek on your part, we find it alarming that you entertained the notion – even for a moment – that we might be interested in your suggestion of renaming some of NASA's land 'Thwaiteville'. Our relationship with you and the Centre has always been a formal, serious one, and we feel that you should have been well aware of the absurdity of this latest idea before proposing it.

It has taken much of my time over the past year to respond to your many ideas. I am sure that you agree that I have always been courteous and have responded in a timely way. I am afraid that I – and NASA – no longer have time for that.

Thwaite's heart was pounding. *Well, you think I need you, Ray? You think I'm your* boy? *you two-faced pen pusher. What are you saying: 'Run along now, Thwaitey, we're done'?*

I don't think so.

What about a new motto: maybe 'Ask not what Thwaite can do for NASA, but what NASA can do for Thwaite'?

The Space Race, hey? Watch this *space.*

*

December 21, 1966

Dear Kennington Varnen,

I'm sorry to be interrupting your Christmas holiday. If I may introduce myself, my name is Samuel Thwaite.

I am the founder and director of the NASA Thwaite Moon Centre in Goodmews, South Dakota. Perhaps you are familiar with the Centre. (I enclose a Goodmews history leaflet put together by Francine Robb, the Centre Geologist.)

I obtained your address through Information, here in Goodmews; I hope you don't mind my writing to you. I trust you will respect the confidential nature of this correspondence.

I understand that you are one of the NASA Surveyor programme's chief engineers. I have read with interest your public comments in recent months concerning NASA's position vis-à-vis the Soviets in the Space Race. I agree especially with one of your criticisms of NASA, which echoes my feelings about them: individuals' ideas are listened to only when it suits NASA, and in my experience they don't take kindly to suggestions from people they consider to be on the 'outside', like me.

You may not be aware of the fact that it was my idea that NASA designate Goodmews as the world's first Moontown. Besides raising Goodmews's profile, it has also turned out to be a great boost for NASA's 'community' reputation, as has having their name – at their request – as part of the Centre.

However, two days ago, NASA severed our relationship. It was a shock, but I can live with that. The Centre can stand on its own two feet. But I am angry with NASA for this sudden decision, their stupidity. Their motto may be 'For The Benefit of All', but the moon for them is no more than a target.

So, putting my cards on the table: I have never collaborated with anyone on a project. I am someone who prefers to do things on my own – it is more efficient that way. However, I realize that I don't have the expertise to take my next idea any further by myself. It regards the moon, and I would very much like to discuss it with you. Perhaps NASA doesn't hold all the cards.

If you feel you may have the time or interest to hear more, please get in touch.

Sam Thwaite

*

January 13, 1967

Dear Sam,

Thank you for getting in touch, and Happy New Year to you. Thank you, too, for the history leaflet. I found Goodmews's connection to the moon – both actual and purported – most interesting.

I am familiar with your Moon Centre. It sounds most impressive. I didn't know that the Moontown idea was yours too, but I'm not surprised. NASA is keen to take credit wherever they can. The idea of a 'Moontown' sounded crazy when someone here first mentioned it, but you've proven that it was a good idea – not to mention convincing NASA to take it on – and I salute your vision, and your entrepreneurial spirit. The world needs more people like you.

Your letter intrigued me. It sounds like we may have a meeting of minds. NASA won't try anything different if something has worked before.

I would like to meet you and visit your Centre. It's always busy here, but I will contact you soon. Of course I concur with your concern to keep any correspondence we have confidential. Unless you hear from me to the contrary, any communication we have should only be by mail.

Ken

*

January 20, 1967

Dear Ken,

I appreciate your warm response, and hope you will soon find time to come out to Goodmews. I want to tell you now my main reason for writing to you, so you can decide if you want to continue our correspondence and also make the trip.

I have not shared this idea with anybody, as there is no one else I can think of who might be both sympathetic and knowledgeable enough to be worth approaching on this matter. I don't believe you mince words. I don't either:

In my year and a half at the Centre, I have read about many, often absurd, ideas and 'thought experiments' people have had in relation to the moon. But I have never come across the idea of putting colour on the moon – colour that would be bright enough and cover a large enough area to be visible with the naked eye from earth.

Do you think this could be done? Could a march be stolen on NASA – could the moon be 'painted' before Man lands on it?

If this was possible, would you have any interest in being involved?

If this could be done, it would be as spectacular in the night sky as Saturn's rings. The other day, Francine showed me a piece of blue moonstone, polished smooth and round. She says it looks like the blue of Neptune.

Could the moon be like that? And you wouldn't need a telescope to see it.

And it would be created by man. And it would show the world that individuals – outside NASA, outside the formality of government – have the imagination and knowledge to make extra-terrestrial advances on their own – like Robert Goddard with his homemade rockets 40 years ago. You will know from first-hand experience what that has led to. (I came across Goddard not so long ago when I did a bit of reading on the history of spaceflight.)

I believe you may share my frustration with NASA. You will have surmised, though, that I know nothing about the physics of Space or, of course, rocketry.

I would greatly value your honest and expert opinion as to whether my idea of putting colour on the moon is worth thinking about at all. Is it even in the 'orbit' of possibility?

Sam

*

Occasional Space Bulletin
February 2, 1967

As this is our local record of major Space events, this Bulletin is to report last week's tragedy, though it has been worldwide news.

On January 27, in the worst disaster ever to befall the Space programme, the three Apollo 1 astronauts were

136

killed in a cabin fire on the launch pad at Cape Kennedy. It was to be the first manned Apollo mission, Apollo being the programme destined to put a man on the moon by the end of the decade. The three astronauts would have been the first Apollo crew testing low-earth orbit. I'm sure Goodmews's sympathies are with the bereaved families.

*

February 6, 1967

Dear Sam,

I will respond to your letter below.

To put you in the picture, the Apollo 1 tragedy has put everything on hold here. The incident is being investigated in the hope that nothing like it can ever happen again. In my opinion, it was an accident waiting to happen. True to form, NASA didn't listen to senior engineers like myself, who had flagged up possible problems with Apollo 1 some time ago, including the lack of emergency preparedness in the event of something going wrong in the cabin before lift-off.

The Apollo programme will likely be suspended for at least a year, and I don't know what the future will hold for it or if we will still be on course to get a man to the moon in the next three years. The Surveyor program, however, carries on. As you may know, I am part of the hands-on team that prepares for launch the rockets that will transport the Surveyor landers to the moon.

In the wake of this tragedy, all telephonic communication in and out of NASA is to be monitored for the foreseeable future. NASA is very nervous about what anyone might reveal, or say, especially about what happened. As regards us in this respect, you will no doubt appreciate that being seen to even discuss an idea which, as off the wall as yours may be, could be viewed as an 'end run' round NASA at this stage, could be a career-risking move for me.

In any case, the main point of this letter is the following. It won't be a welcome response.

While I admire aspects of your vision of a future that doesn't rely on NASA, I'm sorry to have to tell you that the idea of putting colour on the moon is a scientific and technological impossibility. I'm afraid it is fantasy – as you feared – and a waste of time to think about anymore. Just by the way... if it was possible, it wouldn't be a 'bright' colour that you would want. It sounds counter-intuitive, but a dull colour would work best. I'd be happy to explain the physics of that someday, but for now I need to put the kibosh on your idea.

I may no longer be your choice of person to meet, but I would still like to come out and say hello when I get time.

Just to conclude, I am aware of course that many experiments throughout history have had unexpected consequences. Wartime research into high-vacuum technology, for instance, led indirectly to better production methods for penicillin and other antibiotics, but also to the invention of freeze-dried coffee and Minute Maid concentrated orange juice (made from powder).

Needless to say, there are also ideas that may have seemed cockamamy at the time but, likewise, turned out to have great significance. Which brings me to Robert Goddard, one of my heroes as you surmised. I keep a quote of his handy. 'It is difficult to say what is impossible, for the dream of yesterday is the hope of today and the reality of tomorrow.' All the work that goes on now in human spaceflight began with him. As you may know, when he tested the first liquid-fuelled rocket 40 years ago, the motor was about the size of a roll of paper towels and the rocket only got up to 60 miles an hour, landing in a cabbage patch a few seconds later. He got much further with the next one.

Ken

Thwaite felt like his foundations had crumbled. He'd failed. His idea was no good.

If at first you don't succeed is what he usually thought at these times. Something always came along. But this time?

*

February 15, 1967

Dear Ken,

Thank you for your letter, and your honest response. Frankly, in the light of your expertise – and now the Apollo tragedy – I would have been surprised if you had reacted otherwise. The idea of putting colour on the moon must sound ludicrous to you. You have much more pressing matters to attend to.

I still hope to one day welcome you to the Moon Centre.

Sincerely,
Sam

FIFTEEN

It seemed to Tris that these early spring days were getting cloudier but 'mild-ier'. He found himself walking by the Moon Centre, as he often did in the afternoons. Francine only worked mornings, so there'd never been a reason to go inside. But he was curious about how he'd done on the proofreading test. Had Mr. Thwaite forgotten about it? Should he ask him?

Tris went up the steps. Mr. Thwaite was coming out, in his tie. *People his age don't wear T-shirts.*

'Tris! I've been meaning to phone you. I have your test results. Will you be home in a couple of hours?'

He could be. 'Yes. After three?'

Thwaite nodded. 'Grade A,' Tris thought he said. Was it how he'd done on the test? But he realized it was 'grey day' when Thwaite said, 'Better get to the library A.S.A.P. Before it rains.' To Tris, that was the ugliest acronym in English, as ugly as small print on packages.

As long as he was here, he thought, why not have a look inside, at some of the rooms. He pushed his way through the doors, waved hello to the receptionist and went down the corridor. He could hear strains of Moonlight Sonata coming from Songs and Poetry, and walked in.

The guard flinched at his entry, and he flinched back. He hadn't seen the guard on his stool, who stood up quickly, looking surprised – which seemed odd to Tris, as he must get visitors all the time. Maybe he'd nodded off.

He was looking at Tris, though one eye seemed to be looking elsewhere. 'Welcome to the Songs and Poetry room!' he said, in a voice that was fronted by a smile but sounded forced.

'Is this your first visit to the NASA Thwaite Moon Centre?'

'I've been here once, but not to this room.' Tris glanced at the name tag – Banno Culdrun – below a dirty or wet blotch on his lapel.

'Do you like music?' Banno asked.

Tris looked back up to his eyes, which seemed to reflect the grey of his shirt and were shaded by ridges, sort of beetle-browed.

'Yes.' Tris could have added 'of course' – The Beach Boys, The Byrds, The Beatles, Herman's Hermits floating into his head. It was the sort of rhetorical question – like 'Are you hungry?' – that a person seating you in a restaurant might ask when you walk in; or like 'Do you enjoy reading?', that a charity worker might accost you with when they are asking for money.

But Tris always liked speaking to visitor guides, in the same way he liked asking street-sweepers for directions and supermarket shelf packers where something is. It had nothing to do with getting the measure of the person; if he were to dig below the surface, who knows what their opinions about the world might be. But it was human interaction with people who could help him, more than he might need them to. It was a pleasant situation – simply a useful, clean interchange of words.

Banno motioned – 'All around are the original lyrics of some famous moon songs. You'll see as you go round that some are written on napkins, some are typed properly. All have the writer's name underneath and their photo next to their words.' Tris nodded. Banno spoke with a minimal amount of expression; it sounded like he was reciting a script, which he probably was. And it was disconcerting that only one of his eyes was looking straight at Tris. But Tris liked it when the songwriters of well-known songs were acknowledged, which they rarely were.

'Are you familiar with "Moon River"?' Banno continued.
'Yes.'

'Beautiful song. Do you know who sang it?'
'Andy Williams?'

'That's right,' Banno said, with just enough interest that Tris felt he could bat this one back to him.

'Jerry Butler had a hit with it in '61 before everybody heard Andy Williams in '62.'

'And *Danny* Williams,' Banno took it up, 'also had a hit with it, in the UK, in '61.'

'Audrey's version in the movie, sitting on the windowsill strumming, is probably the best.'

'Yeah. Do you know who wrote it?'
'You mean the words?'
'Yeah.'
'Johnny Mercer?'

Banno's teeth flashed 90% due smile, spilling a second's brilliance. 'Not many people know that,' he said, looking at

Tris as directly as he could. 'People know singers, but unless the singer wrote the song, they don't know who did.'

Tris wasn't sure how much of this was the script. 'I agree,' he said. 'You hear a great song and think, "Who wrote that?" Songwriters don't get much public acknowledgement. The power behind the throne.'

Banno smiled.

'Though,' Tris said, 'without the singer, the lyrics wouldn't come alive. They would just be words on a page.'

'That's true. Like quiz shows. Without the right presenter, the questions would just be questions... Do you know "Misty Moonlight"?'

' "Mr. Moonlight"? Roy Lee Johnson.'

'No,' Banno said, ' "In the Misty Moonlight", the one Dean Martin sings... But isn't "Mr. Moonlight" by the Beatles?'

He's a guide in a public institution, Tris thought, *not someone I've just met in a bar; but he's opening the door to more than mere banter. He wants to know my opinions and expects me to add something.* 'It's one of their shouty early ones,' Tris said, ' "from your beam you made my dream" – but Roy Lee Johnson... "Misty Moonlight" is Cindy Walker.' Saying this, Tris felt – almost embarrassingly – an affinity with Banno. Very unusually for him with someone he hardly knew, he quarter-sang: 'In the misty moonlight, by the flickering candlelight...'

Banno's head bobbed up and down. ' "Firelight".'

'Oh.'

'But how'd you know her?' Banno sounded genuinely interested, though his voice was unprepossessing, even timid. 'I never knew she wrote it till I worked here.'

'That's one of the songs I start singing sometimes, when I'm walking by myself. I go to the library and look these things up if I'm curious who wrote them – if I can remember to do it.'

Banno nodded. 'I do wonder why they pop into our heads...'

Tris could sense a generosity in the way Banno spoke – he left space for Tris to respond. He asked questions, or just let his thoughts trail off unfinished, giving Tris the choice of whether or not to pick up on them. Maybe that was just laziness on Banno's part, letting the other do some of the work, but Tris didn't think so. Together, they were 'on', firing on all cylinders.

Tris felt they had gone off Moon Centre-piste with each other and he could further broach those pre-agreed boundaries of a first-time conversation.

'Do any songs pop into *your* head?' he asked.

'Anks,' it sounded like Banno said.

'Angst?'

'No; "thanks".'

'No thanks?'

'No!: Thanks – for asking the question. "You talk too much".'

'Sorry?'

'Pops in for no reason.' Banno half-sang in a not-great voice, ' "You talk too much, you worry me to death..." '

'Or my version.' Tris half-sang back: 'People talk too much, they bore me to death, they talk too much, about themselves...'

Banno's smile went from dour to real, softening his face. 'The Achilles heel of conversation,' Tris snuck in.

Banno looked confused. Then he said, 'Good one. Whose is that?' His face had relaxed again, and he looked happy to go with the tributary Tris had opened up.

'Don't know. Mine?' Tris said, thankful they were back on equal footing.

Banno snorted a half-laugh, which prodded Tris on. 'Somebody once said, "If you're talking, you're not thinking." '

'Or,' Banno said, ' "The same faces talk too much"…

'Are you here on holiday?' he asked. 'Haven't seen you around.'

The music grew fainter, then ended. Tris thought of another couple of songs he sometimes sang to himself while walking – 'It's Not Unusual', 'Are You Lonesome Tonight?' – but enough; he hadn't even seen the room yet. 'I've been here steadily for about a month,' he said, happy to continue the conversation. 'I came for a visit once.'

'So you just dropped in to the Centre today?'

'Yes. I took a proofreading test a couple of months ago for Mr. Thwaite, and I wanted to check how I'd done. He's letting me know later.'

Banno's hands opened out. 'Is that what that pin is?'

'Yeah. It's the proofreading guild I belong to.'

'Is that a good job?' Banno's hands went back towards himself.

'For *me*. I mainly proofread engraved words, like on gravestones or plaques. I guess in general I just like working with words. And I get paid for finding mistakes. It's sort of my way into the world, I think – picking out mistakes on signs I see; in brochures, whatever.'

'You mean maybe like an architect has their way into the world, or a historian has theirs.'

'Yeah, I guess so. There's so many notices and signs everywhere and I suppose it gives me a reason to look at them, see if there are mistakes. I try not to look at most of them these days, but it's like trying not to look at where a loud sound is coming from, like a helicopter. And it was more of a challenge to find mistakes before people stopped caring about spelling.'

'Or architects stopped caring about houses.'

'Yeah. Like where I live. A modern block, but not a modern*ist* block: *they* have character, and *those* architects seem like the design heroes of the century to me... Have you seen my "office"? Below my flat?'

'Not sure. Where is it?'

'Crescent Crescent. The sign says "Te sop wit out an "? White metal letters and a black background?'

'Oh, *that* one. Some letters have fallen off? I couldn't work out what it once said, but also, it looked like a new sign.'

'It's all on purpose. It's "The Shop Without an H", written without "h"s.'

'Why?'

'Just running it up the flagpole to see if anyone salutes. I wanted to get into the spirit of the place. Goodmews. Its oddness.'

' "Goodmoon", they could have called it.'

'Or "Good Mood".'

'Or "Gad Zooks".'

Tris smiled.

'But it's *not* a shop, is it?' Banno said.

'No. I'm sure it's more confusing than anything. But I needed to use "shop" so I could do it without the "h"s. I wanted to have something "engraved", but with raised letters, if that makes any sense.'

'Not really.' That was funny. 'But,' Banno said, 'isn't proofreading a sort of negative way to look at the world?' His voice seemed halting, like he wasn't sure he should have gone back to that topic.

'I think you're right. It is. I'm mainly saying "what's wrong here". Proofreaders read with suspicion. The main thing they do is find fault – "This isn't right", or in the right alphabetical order or something else.'

'So you might be working here.'

'First I have to see if I passed the test.'

'Then would you like more work here—'

'No,' Tris whined, before Banno had finished. 'I'd rather work from home, if I had my druthers. At least when I do normal proofreading, words on paper... And you? Do you like it here?'

'You mean in Goodmews?'

'Either.'

'I like Goodmews. I came for the job. Suits me. They cheeve me a chone.'

Tris somehow instinctively understood. He repeated it back to make sure: ' "They leave you alone".'

Banno nodded.

'And,' Tris added, risking another slice of truth, 'it looks like you don't have to pretend to be excited about your room. You *could* just paste a smile on your face.'

'Tssss... It's fine.'

'Are you interested in the moon? Is that why you got the job?'

'Not really. But I'm here now. I've liked learning about it.'

Tris could see someone waiting at the door, and saw that Banno had noticed her too. He needed to show her around. And had he and Banno been getting unrealistically, inappropriately chummy too soon? I'll have a quick look around the room.'

'The exhibition goes clockwise.' Banno sounded like he'd flipped back into script mode. 'Do you like poetry.'

'Great poetry is great. Bad poetry I hate,' Tris said.

Banno smiled wryly. 'If you want to have a look, they're all moon quotes or poems – or parts of them – in that corner, under the picture of Emily Dickinson.'

The woman at the door came in, and Tris began to tour the room.

He stopped at The sad face of infinity – Jack Kerouac and her motionless balance in space – M.C. Escher, then moved to the sheets of lyrics. It *was* 'firelight', as Banno had said, in 'Misty Moonlight'. Next to it was 'Moon River'. He'd never seen those words before either. As he'd thought, but hadn't been sure of until now, it was 'Two drifters', not 'Dew drifters', and 'huckleberry friend' – whatever that meant – not 'Huckleberry Finn'. Next to that was 'Shine on Harvest Moon'. It also wasn't ' *'s'no* time, to stay outdoors and spoon', but *snow* time…

He heard the music starting again and Banno launching into his welcome-patter. He tread as quietly as he could on the carpet, so as not to disturb the mood. He felt as cautious as when he picked up the tiny pieces of lead that dropped out of his mechanical pencil on to his desk, so they wouldn't leave a mark on its laminated surface. The woman was already walking round the room. Tris quickly completed the circuit and arrived back at Banno, on his stool again, and held out a last strand of self. 'Did you know that Beethoven didn't call it *Moonlight Sonata*.'

'Yes. I've heard that.'

'Can it get a bit repetitive to you?'

'Is the Pope Catholic. I do need some heavy rock afterwards sometimes, like Hendrix.'

'My name's Tris.'

'Thanks. Maybe see you again if you passed the test?'

'I'll pop by.'

'Good luck.'

*

Banno felt close to tears. It was the same sort of satisfying swell in his heart he felt when he heard a beautiful, sad song. Tris had been the first person he'd had any desire to speak to since he'd come to Goodmews. They had things in common, like music, and they'd had a couple of laughs. Had the chat simply been relief, a break from the boredom of the job? No. They'd listened to each other; Tris had even understood Cheeve me a chone.

Mainly, they'd been honest with each other; and if he couldn't be honest with someone he felt he could trust, like Tris – a friend!, or possible friend – what would be the point of the encounter?

But he'd trusted Debbie, hadn't he. She'd dance around and sing 'My Guy', about never being untrue to *my* guy.

Who had she been singing it for? Had she *meant* it before she lied, and didn't phone him back like she promised? That last kiss was a Judas kiss.

I would never want to do that to anyone, and put them

through what she put me through.

So, isn't it safer not to trust people, and to protect oneself, one's soul from being chipped away at?

But don't connections, humans matter?

Could Tris be a friend? Am I the sort of person who has them?

Banno got out the piece of paper Jan had given to him on his way in. On his stool he read it.

As a Visitor Assistant, if for any reason you would like to move rooms, please indicate your choice by printing your name next to the room.

NASA Apollo
Geology
Moon Myths
Songs and Poetry

Why would he want to move? He had just settled in to *his* room. Besides, only his room and Francine's had anyone working in them. Maybe this was for the future. So, maybe 'Apollo' could help him learn more about the moon at some point. But Geology certainly seemed like *Francine's* bailiwick. And *Myths?* Who could care about that anymore? It was as meaningless as God. You might as well learn about Superman... And why have to have such a formal tick-box form?

He left it blank.

*

Tris pushed through the glass doors of the Centre and looked up and got that now-familiar Goodmews aspect, over the shops and the jumble of coloured roofs, to the hills beyond. He went down the steps more quickly than he needed to. 'Idiot,' he cursed himself, nearly tripping on his shoelace, but he hadn't. 'An untied shoelace is more unsightly than dangerous,' he thought, but he stooped to tie it. 'I'm nuts; k.n.u.t.z.

'It's great that we had a real conversation,' he thought, 'one that steered far away from those safe topics like weather and food and jobs and, the worst, family, where people are as polite and controlled as those hosting an Open Garden Day, showing off their plants. And how often do you meet someone who seems to chime with your own thoughts.'

Banno was odd, and Tris liked that, but there was also something sad, something vulnerable about him – he was bullyable, like a younger sibling one could scare; and Tris felt weighted with the sort of feeling he got after a doctor's appointment and reprimanding himself for forgetting to say something. 'But we'd connected,' he said to himself, 'in that short time. Friendships begin with some sort of mutual fingertipping, don't they? to see if there are wavelengths both parties are on? We'd done that. There was a symbiosis between us that was soft, like the Sonata. A sympathetic symphony. So why hadn't I talked to him more about real things, things that mattered, rather than trying to impress him with what I knew about pop songs? Why had I pulled up the drawbridge towards the end, been so "see you later" casual, like it was just another chat? Had I glimpsed the threatened intimacy of a looming friendship out of the corner of my eye, and made sure I ducked the blindside sucker-punch just in time?'

Should he go back and continue the conversation? No. It was too late.

He walked into the Safeway near his flat. It was too bright, and felt soulless after his time with Banno. He shopped quickly.

As he reached Crescent Crescent he gazed up at the bell-buckle contrails, criss-crossing the sky like Pick-Up Sticks, or blue and white lines of abstract art. He saw the clock tower. Did it stand out like a sore thumb today, like a conifer in suburbia? He'd always liked the clock, and the way that 'Goodmews' was spelt out around it. The thought struck him: 'Moontown' had the same number of letters as 'Goodmews'. What if the clock face got redone, like the street names had? It would wipe out more of Goodmews's history, like that town he'd read about in the Deep South whose streets had been named after Confederate soldiers and were now things like Liberty Street and Freedom Street.

Just outside his door, he was relieved to hear no beeping from the machine inside; at least he didn't think he could hear it. He hadn't asked for one, but these state-of-the-art incoming-message recorders were one of the advanced technologies that NASA had supplied to all residents of Goodmews as a thanks for hosting the Moon Centre.

He'd had one message so far, a few weeks before. He'd stood outside his flat, thinking he could hear the ominously faint beeping but unable to be sure that it wasn't just distant, random street noise, until a few seconds went by and that insistent, soulless beep, like a heart monitor slightly stretched, reappeared. His mind had started racing – What might be so important to require leaving him a message when he was out and couldn't get it? – and he had burst through the door, rushed to the phone and pressed the button that killed the beep, waiting on tenterhooks for the message. It had been a wrong number.

He went inside and upstairs to his flat and sat down at the kitchen table. In a crumpled white napkin he saw Banno's face – his receding hairline, his longish nose. Was there sadness in the face? Tris closed his eyes, and when he opened them he could still see the face.

He sang, 'Two, drifters, off to see the world, my huckleberry friend…'

Did he want the work from Mr. Thwaite? It was good to say yes, for the future. Maybe he'd decided on someone else, or had got busy and wasn't going to phone him. Or he hadn't liked him trying to be clever about exclamation marks and he'd phone and tell him they didn't need him but would 'keep his name on file'. Maybe that would be best, and he would have time for other things.

The phone rang, beating Tris's heart. He jumped up but let it ring a few times; it would be Mr. Thwaite. He picked the phone up, still standing as he spoke.

'Tris *Pal*man.'

'Hello Tris. This is Sam Thwaite, from the Moon Centre?'

'Yes. Hello Mr. Thwaite.'

'I'm calling to let you know that your answers were perfect, and we'll be in touch soon for you to come in again.'

'Thank you.'

*

Walking down Galileo Court, Sam saw the plate-glass library frontage and went in.

The lady at the Reference desk smiled a greeting. 'How are you, Mr. Thwaite? All well at the Centre?'

He smiled back. 'Very well. What I'm interested in, is any articles there might be about bouncing a laser image off the moon.'

'Has that happened?

'Apparently so. I believe it was a few years ago, and I don't know if it's happened again since.'

'Let's have a look. If you could come with me?'

She led Sam to a microfilm reader. She leaned into it, underneath its hood, switched it on and then scrolled through what looked to Sam like pages of indexes.

'Here it is.' She stood up. 'All yours, Mr. Thwaite. Let me know if you need anything else.'

'Thank you.'

He settled himself in front of the image of the *New York Times*, dated May 10, 1962, and read what was on the screen.

MAN'S LASER MOONSHOT

Last night, for the first time, man illuminated another celestial body. Had someone been standing in the mountainous region of the moon that is southeast of the crater Albategnius, the stark and darkened lunar landscape about him would have been lit by a succession of dim red flashes.

This light would have come from engineers at the Massachusetts Institute of Technology, using a device that produces a light beam. This is known as a "laser", an acronym for Light Amplification by Stimulated Emission of Radiation.

On earth, the dull reflection of this light could only be seen through powerful telescopes, as the light that fell on the moon is thought to have been limited to an area the size of a tennis court. The experiment showed that even a tightly focused beam will spread out hugely by the time it gets to the moon, a quarter of a million miles away.

However, even though the weak illumination on the moon's surface was roughly comparable to that produced on the walls of a large room by a flashlight bulb, the debate about future 'laser wars' seems to have begun: who will dictate what might be projected on to the moon? A laser could be directed from anywhere, with political messages, racial slurs, even advertisements. The only thing stopping someone from plastering their message on the moon would be someone else with a more powerful laser.

We have been assured, though, by engineers at MIT, that this is not something we need to worry about. Scientists roundly acknowledge that it will be a long time, if ever, before a laser beam image on the moon could be produced that is concentrated enough to be visible to the naked eye on earth.

*

March 24, 1967

Dear Ken,

I know you are very busy. I hope you don't mind my confirming one thing with you.

I went to the library today and read about the attempt to shine a laser on to the moon several years ago. It certainly sounds to me that – even if one wanted to shine a laser to try to project a large swathe of colour on to the moon – it's not a viable option, and won't be for a long time to come.

Can you just tell me if you concur with this conclusion, and why? At the very least, I can include your information (uncredited, if you wish, to preserve your anonymity) in the Moon Centre files.

Thank you once again for your time.

Sam

*

Banno felt settled, even as far as having worked out the perfect door-taps, closing them with just enough push so they barely touched their jamb.

At his mirror, the one he looked better in, he pinned on his name badge above his right breast-pocket and viewed himself in his uniform. It looked like a park ranger's, with its collared short-sleeved grey shirt and its khaki trousers. He had some pride in being part of the Moon Centre. It was famous, and he was a trusted employee. Yes, Mr. Thwaite could be pushy, and he was speedy. He rarely stopped whatever he was doing except to make sure that everyone else was doing what they were supposed to do. But who could blame him? He was one of those people who made things happen, who got things done. Where would the world be without people like him.

But the job itself was probably the dullest Banno had ever had, as calcifying as an occasional whole-family meal.

It didn't call for him to do much; visitors rarely spoke to him. In general he didn't mind – 'The less I have to interact the better' seemed to have become his motto; though when he had to respond to a question or enforce the rules by telling someone to take their bag off or stay behind the yellow line, it did stave off a few seconds of boredom. And he got paid and it gave him a place to live; and it allowed him to stay in Goodmews. Were those who came in to Songs and Poetry just drawn out of curiosity by Moonlight Sonata? He hoped it wouldn't become wallpaper to him, like Muzak where ethereal strings are imposed upon a great piece of music, tranquillizing it into the sort of hospital-room soundtrack he'd once been subjected to when waiting to be transferred somewhere else.

Banno's evenings were mostly spent watching TV and, always, the news, despite the fact that the regional newscasts were as off-putting as the ones back home. He could hardly bear the way stories were dumbed down with punchlines relating to the scene, as if viewers wouldn't be able to understand how difficult the issue was without reference to the stormy weather in the background. And it was just so dispiriting to be told by these same faces yet again what he almost always had already heard. Once was enough, and even that was almost never interesting. Why did they repeat the news so much? And it was confusing, like a boy who cries wolf. Were they telling us these things over and over because we should be concerned about them, worried about them?

And so many other things about the way the news was presented made it difficult to watch. There were the reporters who, upon being questioned by the newsreader, would so often respond with 'Good question', even though they'd obviously supplied the newsreader with the question in the first place. Then there were the younger reporters, who delivered their reports in three-word clumps, presumably to make themselves easier to understand. Three-word – or even two-word – clumps could work well, Banno knew, when beautifully phrased in a song, like Herman's Hermits' 'Listen People' : 'listen, people, to what, I say.' *But,* he'd react in his head, *why can't you talk normally when you read the news? And why do you have to do things like tell us what time it is or that we should wrap up in the cold or have a good weekend? And why do you have to be so sickeningly smiley and on a first-name basis with the weather reporters – because who could be against the weather? And spare us the sports reporters – always with the biggest smiles and the most boring things to say that they're so excited about and expect the viewers to also be. And what is the point of these politicians. Does anyone still expect them to offer an independent view on anything? Haven't we learned by now that you can always tell what's going to come out of their mouths, whichever side they're on?*

Banno often felt soiled after watching the news. He should wean himself off it. He should try to not turn it on in the first place. But 6.30 would roll round and, like the London tourist he'd once read about who was unable to resist stopping at a Blue Plaque, he would feel compelled to watch.

He sat down to breakfast and turned his transistor radio on, rolling the dial through different stations and lingering at one whose Twilight Zone-type music was fading out. As it did, the announcement came, with a dramatic, drawn out 'It'sss The Moon Quiz! on Goodmews Radio, your Goodmews station at 267.5 on the dial.'

Whatever this was, he was just in time.

'Welcome to the quiz that tests your lunacy. A reminder for our listeners… Both three-person teams – our illustrious Rockets, versus this week's challengers, who call themselves the Cadets – write their answer in their *Moon Quiz* ring binder. The teams read their answers out; I give the correct answer; and the point is awarded to whichever team has the right answer.'

The challengers introduced themselves and what their jobs were, or used to be, as some were retired. Banno liked that they introduced themselves, rather than, like on some other quizzes, a voiceover introducing them. Everyone on the show, including the presenter, lived in Goodmews; Banno had probably seen some of them already. And it sounded like a civilized way of scoring – just one point for a right answer, no bonuses.

'Let's make a start. As always, teams: to start the game, eight questions, eight points on offer. The questions get progressively harder. Both teams can be right, and there can be a tie going into the break, indeed even at the end of the contest.'

Banno liked the presenter's voice; it seemed to have a friendly smile to it.

'Question 1. How does the moon's gravity compare to earth's?' A pause while everyone wrote. Banno knew this one.

Each team said their answer. 'One-sixth' confirmed that everyone was right. There was some banter in the studio between the Rockets and the presenter, who shot back some jokey, quick-witted replies. He asked the new team, the

Cadets, what they did in their spare time, and they said the normal things like play board games with their children and go for Sunday drives. The one female member said her family had liked watching *The Flintstones* together until it had gone off the air.

'Who was your favourite?'

'Wilma.'

Banno wondered how he would have answered that question. 'I like watching quiz shows and playing guitar.' Though come to think of it, he most liked having a small orgy of scratching, or feeling sorry for himself.

He laughed out loud a couple of times at the repartee – too loud, probably – but it gave the show an air of levity that he liked, combining fun with facts. *The perfect medium in the message*, he thought to himself, the phrase close to the title of a book he'd read a couple of years before.

'Question 2. How long does it take light from the moon to reach earth?'

'About one and a third seconds' came the answer. 'Exactly 1.26 seconds.' Banno had had a pretty good idea of that too.

'Question 3. Sometimes the moon is closer, sometimes further from the earth, but approximately how far is it, on average, from us?'

'Around 250,000 miles.'

Banno had somehow known that too. Three out of three.

'Question 4. At what rate, in centimetres per year, is the moon spinning away from the earth?' Banno hadn't known it was spinning away.

'The answer, as the Rockets have it, is just under four centimetres – or about an inch and a half – a year, about the same speed our fingernails grow, or Iceland's tectonic plates are drifting apart, the eastern half drifting east, the western half west.'

Banno was impressed by the Rockets' knowledge. He had the sense that they were rarely beaten. He wanted them to win, as he almost always wanted the 'home' team on a show to win. But mostly he was enjoying the spirit of friendly competition that pervaded the show. He fancied himself as a quiz show connoisseur, and this was a good one. It moved at a steady, calm pace, with questions distinctive to the programme. *Who thought it up? Creators of great quiz shows never get the credit they deserve. Nor do people who read to the blind.* He liked that everyone was polite, sometimes one team even congratulating the other on their answer. It was relaxing too, just silence until both teams gave their answer – no sudden bell going off, no tense time-running-out music accompanied by the sound of a clock ticking down or of a kettle being filled.

The presenter's comforting, modulated voice came again:

'Question 5. A blue moon is the second full moon in the same month. How often do blue moons occur?' The tune of 'Blue Moon' flitted through Banno's head. He'd read that Richard Rodgers, who wrote the music, hated the sped-up Marcels version. *Twice a year*, Banno would have guessed. 'Blue moons occur about once every 2.7 years.' *A bit of a ways off.*

'Question 6. How fast does the moon orbit the earth?' Banno had no idea. 'At about 2,300 miles an hour,' came the answer, 'which means it travels about 1.5 million miles around the earth each month.' The Rockets' point.

'Question 7. When was the moon first viewed by telescope?' 1609 was the answer. Banno would have guessed some time around then, around Galileo's time.

'Question 8. When did man first see an image of the far side of the moon?' Banno didn't know. '1959. The picture was snapped by the Soviet's Luna 3. As the Rockets and others will know, the far side of the moon is the only place in the solar system deaf to earth's radio noise. Earlier the same year, Luna 2 became the first spacecraft to reach the surface of the moon.

'With the score Rockets 8, Cadets 6, we end this half. Join us again in a few minutes, when each team chooses whether to take a question or pass it over.'

Banno turned off the radio. He realized he'd been sitting there eating, with a smile on his face, for fifteen minutes. All was neat, tidy. Here he was in a Moontown, working at the Moon Centre, and he'd done reasonably well in a quiz about the moon. He didn't like leaving in the middle of any quiz; whatever the outcome, getting to the end gave him a sense of completion, something like getting the last piece of dust out of a carpet sweeper even though it would need cleaning again the next time. But he had to get to work. That's why, how, he was here.

*

April 13, 1967

Sam,

I do salute your thirst for knowledge, and I think it's a great idea to include the laser information in your files. Please feel free to credit me, as Senior NASA Project Engineer, with supplying the below information.

Briefly, as regards bouncing a laser image off the moon, it's a challenge for the future because the moon's surface is dark and fairly non-reflective – in technical terms, the 'albedo' of the moon is .12, meaning that only about 12% of the light that strikes its surface reflects off it. In other words, you lose 7/8 of the light you send there to begin with.

An almost incalculable amount of energy would be required to produce a laser powerful enough to overcome this: it would have enough power to slice an incoming missile in half and would potentially startle pilots, not to mention birds.

It will still be decades, at the very least, before the advent of a laser that could produce concentrated colour over a large enough area of the moon to enable it to be seen with the naked eye from earth.

As I think you will be aware, the launch of Surveyor 3 is 'go' for Monday, and that is where all of our efforts are directed at the moment. It is due to land three days later.

Ken

*

April 16, 1967

Ken,

This letter won't reach you until after Surveyor's launch and perhaps not until after it has landed. I hope all went well and the landing was soft.

Thank you for your explanation as to how lasers work. Sorry to be asking you for your expert opinion on something else so soon: but just to wrap things up concerning what we spoke about in the beginning, could I prevail upon you to jot down for me, when you get time, maybe just three key reasons why getting colour on the moon is not possible, by any known means? It would be good to include this information in our files.

Thank you once again.

Sam

*

May 12, 1967

Sam,

As I'm sure you've seen and read about, Surveyor 3's mission passed with flying colours. It radioed over 6,000 images back to earth during its first lunar day (14 earth days). One of the photographs (on April 24) was of the darkened sun as the earth came between it and the moon. It was the first photograph in history of a total lunar eclipse as seen from the moon.

As for your idea of painting the moon, I'm glad you accept that it's not a goer, that it's too 'far out', as they say these days. Between the lines, I hear your disappointment.

When you first approached me with the idea, I realized that if it could be done, it would be an extraordinary event, something I'd want to be part of. But it was soon clear to me that it threw up too many conundrums – impossibilities, really, and that was that.

I applaud your drive and spirit, however, and I feel that you deserve a more complete answer, if only for your

164

files, as to why your idea cannot be taken forward. Without getting too technical, here are three of the reasons:

1. Even if there was a way to transport paint to the moon, the amount you would need would weigh too much. Any rocket can carry only a tiny amount of extra weight. And extra weight requires extra fuel, which is additionally heavy.
2. Even if this weight problem could somehow be overcome (though I cannot conceive of how), there would be no way to 'spread' the paint over the moon's surface – and over a large enough area to be visible from earth.
3. There is the (significant) problem of the paint itself. It would need to be able to withstand the moon's wild day–night temperature swings of about 300 degrees C.

These problems appear to be insurmountable, and that's why I have been unable to offer you any realistic hope.

In any case, I too still look forward to meeting one day,

Ken

*

Bank Holiday for 1967
Brought to you by the Goodmews Historical Society

Bank Holiday in Goodmews will be held this year on May 29, 'Monday next', as the English might put it. The Day, which probably goes back to the founding of

165

Goodmews, has been celebrated in conjunction with the public holiday in England each year, often towards the end of May. As some will know, England is in the middle of a five-year trial period set to continue until 1970 in order to decide what to call the holiday and what day it should be on.

In Goodmews, we've continued this day as a 'cheeky' way to celebrate some of our first residents, who earlier this century constructed various aspects of the town in an Edwardian style. These include the brick houses and the curving roads. The church is in an even older style, the classically plain style of Hawksmoor, a famous 18th century English architect.

We hope the Day, for those who are new to Goodmews or have never participated, will be 'up your street'. It will, as always, consist of all things English. At the Renaissance Fayre, from midday in the park, traditional English ballads will be sung by a troubadour, and there will be maypole and Morris dancing, with instructors leading both. Other highlights for the Day (see the schedule below) will include Johnny's Full English Breakfast, and then, for High Tea, his Pudding with Hundreds and Thousands.

As most Mewsicians will know, the Day is made more fun if people 'have a go' at speaking with an English accent or using words or phrases that might be heard in England. If you can't be our local Cary Grant or Julie Andrews, you can still be our local 'Gazza' (Gary) or 'Shazza' (Sharon).

If you are unable to get out of work on the Day, as it is not a holiday in Goodmews, we still hope you can find the time to 'pop round'.

SIXTEEN
May 29

Tris wasn't sure he felt like being in the thralls of Johnny and considered taking a back street, a safe route, but continued down the Broadway.

Johnny was standing outside his café, as if he owned that piece of pavement as much as he owned his café.

'Tris! Hi how're you doing you alright?'

Tris felt he understood; though he was surprised that Johnny had remembered his name.

'Fine, Johnny.'

'Come on in.'

Tris followed him inside. There were a few people there, but like always, the place had a hollow feel. Johnny's would never have that warm hubbub of a stylish café.

'Will you be wanting something?'

Was that the English way of talking? It didn't seem to suit Johnny. He belonged in his normal American habitat – Goodmews, not in this once-a-year English version of it. It was like he was a guard out of uniform or a builder in a tuxedo; unrecognizable.

'No thanks. How's it going.'

'You off to the pub quiz?'

'Not sure. What's that.'

'That's England versus America, that is. At Frank's Place, about five minutes.'

'I'll check it out.'

'Good stuff. Off you go.'

Tris passed the Moon Centre, doubting there would be anything English about it today. Why would there be?

Johnny recognizing him had made him feel like he belonged. He was still mostly a tourist but he was becoming a resident. It was a middle-ground where he had the best of both worlds – he could get explanations afforded a visitor if he needed them, but with his growing local knowledge he wasn't dependent on them. *Maybe it's how older people feel, being offered a seat on the bus but not needing it.*

He stopped in at Frank's. The walls were hung with paintings of the English flag. Some were realistic, almost photographic, but a few looked like they were rippling in the breeze and others were torn and tattered and not red, white and blue any more, as if they'd been shredded in battle. It all looked more artistic than patriotic.

There were twenty or so people sitting around. Maybe he'd seen one or two before. He stood at the back and read some of the signs on the wall. A large one, written in dripping brown paint, said 'The Blokeroom', and below it he could see two typewritten notices.

UMBRELLAS SHOULD ONLY BE
USED IN HEAVY DOWNPOURS

BRANCHES FROM TREES IN BACK GARDENS
MUST NOT EXTEND INTO A NEIGHBOUR'S GARDEN

He didn't know what these were – jokey rules? – but he noticed the English spelling of 'neighbors'. He thought of what a firm of lawyers might be called if it was somewhere out in the mid-atlantic, acting for both countries. Favor and Favour?

Frank came out through a side door, wearing a flowery shirt. Tris didn't recall having seen him or this shirt before and wasn't sure if that was what he always wore.

Frank unbuttoned the top button and looked around. 'We are, all of us, in England now.' He tapped his finger on the side of his nose: 'but don't tell anyone.

'Most of you know how this works. I say the American; you say the English, albeit just general knowledge, nothing scientific like jography or jollogy last year.'

Tris didn't quite know what 'albeit' meant.

'Does that twitch your curtains?

'Right. Just a word for the new faces… but take a pew, those of you at the back.'

A few people sat down, so Tris did the same. *Close enough to hear*, he thought, *but aisle enough to escape.*

'It's our *sicth* year doing this.' It sounded to Tris like Frank was saying the word like it had a "c" in it. Was that the way they said it in England? 'It's not a huge giant competition – it's a "friendly", if you will. Enjoy our tiny little bit of England today in Goodmews. And welcome, those newcomers.'

Was Frank one of those people that every town needs – someone who starts groups, who has people over to their house? Someone who brings people together. And like other movers and shakers Tris had met, like Mr. Thwaite, he'd bet that Frank was someone who tried to direct whatever he was involved in, even just a conversation.

'In British parlance, Goodmews has gone from "strength to strength" since the advent of the Moon Centre. And we like to think that, here in the Black Hills, we will always *be*, our own mini-A.O.N.B.'

Tris wondered if that was supposed to be a rhyme. His mind was suddenly awash with acronyms, and he leaned over to the man sitting next to him.

'What's an A.O.N.B.'

'Area of Outstanding Natural Beauty.'

'In England.'

'I think so.'

Something felt different to Tris, just having this short exchange. He was no longer invisible, and the crowd was no longer anonymous.

'Who's been to England again?'

Maybe two hands went up.

'Jolly good.'

'Alright for some,' a woman at the side shouted out.

'Right. Let's get on with it.' Frank nodded towards what looked like a discoloured picture on the wall. 'The moon's made of green cheese, right?' No one responded. Tris recalled John Heywood's poem, maybe from around 1500, and its spelling of those words – 'The moone is made of a greene cheese'.

' "Have your cake and eat it too"… The English?'

Tris had no idea.

'Have your cake and eat it,' Frank said. 'Don't ask me why. It's like "raze".'

'Raze to the ground.'

'Nice one, mate.' *Did that word mean "friend"?*

'At the moment.'

'At the minute.'

'Well done, that man. How do you know these things?'

The man shrugged. 'TV?'

'There you go. Anyway, free drink to you. Two right, on the trot... Now. What are some other differences you might notice between England and America?'

'They tend to walk on the left.'

'I agree. Others?'

'One thought,' said a man sitting with a group at a table. 'Lots of things that are private here are public there, like swimming pools.'

'Lidos,' Tris heard.

'Well spotted.'

'And at outside basketball courts,' the man continued, 'you often see hoops without nets. Maybe they're not so rich.'

'Right. So, how else can you tell an American from an Englishman?'

Was this a joke?

'By their girth?' the woman from before piped up, to some laughs. 'I'm not being funny,' she said, to some half-grunts, 'but the English I saw were slimmer. Americans can look like trunks of mature...' The end of her sentence was unintelligible, obscured by her laughing at how funny she thought she was.

Frank shook his head. 'Any phrases anyone's heard over there?'

'Me bag's heavy cuz I've got a bevvy!'

'Meaning...?'

'Beverage?'

'Got it in one. Where'd you hear that?'

'Professional soccer game there – football, as they call it. One thing I noticed was that the players often shouted at the ref, argued with him. It looked threatening, which seemed odd, as the country seemed so peaceful otherwise. Sport's very different in that way. If, say, a baseball player here as much as looks at an umpire funny, he's tossed out of the game.'

'Alright. And, in England, if a team "just about" won, what would that mean… They won, but it was close…

'I know I'm banging on a bit, but never mind. Let's try some more. Popsicle' – no answer – 'Ice lolly.'

Tris made his way to the door.

'Mind how you go,' Frank shouted.

'Cheers,' he said back. He didn't really know what that meant, but he'd heard people say it and he liked the feel of the word. What was 'mind how you go' though? He'd watch out for dangerous holes.

*

June 4, 1967

Ken,

I appreciate your full and considered response. Yes, I am disappointed. Some things work out and some don't, but the 'drive' hasn't left me. I may come up with another way to 'best' NASA, who knows? And perhaps it may be something I can do on my own.

If I may crave one bit more of your already overstretched time…

My geologist Francine, who I mentioned, is also a

colour scientist. She has created Goodmews's bright colours that you may have heard about and I hope you will see someday. (If you've ever seen photos of the rooftops of Reykjavik in Iceland, the colours look something like that.)

I had a 'casual' conversation with Francine after your last letter, and asked her about the weight of paint, and she explained how, if paint was heated and dried, it could be compressed into a light powder that could fit into a very small space (like concentrated orange juice?).

I realize I'm grabbing at straws now, and I'm not sure why I'm bothering you with this, but I was wondering if a much lighter paint would be theoretically easier to get to the moon and be somehow spread.

Please feel free to tell me to shut up about all this and let you get back to your work, but if you could first just assure me that the answer is still no – thanks.

Sam

After Sam had posted the letter, he felt that it would be the last one. Ken had no doubt appreciated the fact that Sam had chosen him as his confidante, and he'd appreciated Sam's tenacity. But Ken had made it clear that this idea of colour on the moon could come to nothing. Besides, he had much more important things to do, like payloads to check, trajectories to confirm, rockets to launch.

*

Before coming to Goodmews, Tris had never heard of Claite Ticking. It seemed to be the callisthenics of the moment there, and though he was always looking for an excuse not to go to the class, he wanted to fit in to the town, at least to some degree. But did he really need to go? It had always seemed odd to him that you have to be healthy in order to do exercise that's supposed to improve your health. And was it so important, that he had to organize his day around getting to the class on time? Couldn't he just walk up to the orangewoods for some exercise?

And he was paying for it. Shouldn't the state pay people to work out, which would benefit society as a whole?

He left his flat, appropriately and bravely attired in his white T-shirt and grey tracksuit bottoms, or sweaty-pants, as he called them. A man too far away to recognize came into view, walking towards him. Tris felt almost bigger than Goodmews, like a holstered cowboy strolling down Main Street, a middle-of-the road walker in a Wild West town, his arms draw-ready at his sides. He watched as the man turned into a front garden and out of sight, like a cloud appearing and disappearing without notice.

A young woman in a vivid-peach tracksuit jogged towards Tris – the peach colour, he thought, no doubt enhanced by the woman inside. She swept by, blond hair breezing, white teeth visible, her blue eyes as Aryan as they come. *It's not fair to the rest of the world. If someone's beautiful, young enough and is a graspable size, they get more attention than someone who isn't. If I'd been a caveman – like Joanie Summers sang she wanted, in 'Johnny Get Angry' – maybe I would have felt that I had to have this woman, had the right to have her and would have gone for it. The face makes such a difference.*

He'd once read about a paranoid Roman emperor whose daily walks were in a gallery lined with polished moonstone that reflected everything behind him. For himself, Tris wished he just had a rear-view mirror; the passing glance he'd had at the woman hadn't been enough. But – a squiz in time saves nine? – it was all he was going to get. He did like looking back, as if he'd just seen the Lone Ranger and was thinking 'Who was that masked man?' But looking back was declaring an interest – even if you just wanted to appreciate something about the person, or just wanted to confirm what you were pretty sure you'd just seen.

He'd always known that you didn't look back if you cared about what the looked-back-at person would think if they knew what you were doing. Most people would be annoyed, or concerned; besides, the looker-back was the lesser person, and unless there was something suspicious about someone – or they were a child or had a dog with them – society only grants you that one-to-one scanning-second – even here, he was sure. The only time look-backs worked was when they were side glances – half look-backs, like when the person has just passed behind you on a perpendicular road. And he never did even a quarter look-back at someone in religious garb or a person who had a problem, like a limp, or was begging, or talking to themselves. And he'd never look back at a group of people who hadn't moved aside coming towards him. They didn't deserve it, nor did he want to get into a fight. He doubted they ever looked back. But few looked back – certainly not joggers, like the woman; people everywhere always seemed so intent on what they were thinking, or getting somewhere.

What if he had looked back at the woman and she had looked back at the same time – a 'double' look-back; what would he have done then? He would have pretended to not be looking back. And if there'd been a double smile-back?

He entered the barren room filling up with women laying out the mats and chatting to one another. He always mixed up two of them – they seemed to be about 60, were smallish, had the same sort of face, the same length of uncoiffed, straw-coloured hair and the same black tracksuit. When they spoke, though, he could tell them apart.

He was the only male and, probably, he thought, the only newcomer to Goodmews. He reached into the large bag of melon-sized coloured rubber balls in the corner; squeezing them to find one that was the right softness was slightly easier than finding a needle in a haystack.

The teacher entered, making straight for her spot at the head of the room. Like bees to a queen the class turned towards her.

'How is everyone? Everyone limber?'

The group of 20 responded as usefully as an audience answering a speaker's 'Can everyone hear me?'

The background music began – from somewhere, he was never sure where. It was a soft wash of some sort of strings, punctuated with a tinkle here, a soft bell there, and what sounded like bird tweets mingling with the tinkling. He'd once done some bogus eye-exercises, accompanied by a sappy melody, and this offensively inoffensive Claite music reminded him of that. It was a distant waterfall of sound, the poorest of cousins to Phil Spector's Wall of Sound, and it made him move in slow motion, like a slippery soap dish sliding towards a sink.

But – though the teacher was a bit airy-fairy with her music and her sing-song instructions – he liked her and her helpful manner. He did need to concentrate, or she'd say, 'Tris! Are you here.' But she didn't shout at the group like a P.E. coach. 'Breathe,' she'd gently instruct, and the extroverts amongst the class, unlike Tris, would exhale like an elephant.

He always needed reminding of how to do the positions, even though they were the same ones each week. Whether they were straightforward, like 'tip of nose to ceiling' and 'chicken wings', or some pretzel-like contortion, he kept his eyes on the teacher. But even if he didn't, she – even bent over backwards – seemed to have the uncanny ability to watch everyone at the same time, like she had eyes in her feet.

The Claite class always lasted the full hour, and much of this involved exercising both sides of the body – for 'balance'. Tris could just about bear the boredom of this when it was an easier stretch. Most of the time, though, it was muscle-straining, at least for him, and on top of that the flip side was yet to come. It was like knowing that the dental hygienist, having finally finished scraping one's upper teeth, still needed to do the lowers.

He generally began yawning – airy yawny giants that sent tears down his face – about halfway through the class. If he wanted to confirm the time, he'd sneak a glance at the clock, but he tried his best never to look at it, in the same way that he tried not to look at supermarket items still coming along the conveyor belt and would still need to be bagged. When it felt like the class had about ten minutes left, he would allow himself a look at the time, and know he could make it to the end.

'Now, slowly lie down.'

The rough winds of the hour would subside; the outside noises would drift in.

'Ree-lax,' she'd say, as if she had the power to make the class do it.

'Relax your toes…

'Your feet…

'Reeelax your legs…'

And she would conduct everyone up their bodies, to the top of their heads.

*

'Sam? This is Ken Varnen.'

'Ken!' His voice was more solemn than Thwaite would have supposed.

He would have seen Thwaite's letter by now. Was he calling to make sure Thwaite knew he shouldn't write to him again?

'You're happy using the phone, Ken?'

'Just this time. It's not a NASA phone. Sam, when you wrote about compressing paint – it must be almost a month ago now—'

'Sorry, Ken. It was just another one of my—'

'No. That's not what I meant. Let me explain. A few hours ago I was informed that Surveyor 4, which has been on the drawing board for a long time and has been delayed and delayed, has now been scheduled for launch on July 14.'

Kennington's voice sounded measured, like a newscaster with all the facts at his fingertips, and Thwaite listened intently.

'Target moon-landing date July 16. I don't know what's going to be happening with future Surveyors, or any other missions; I'm not even sure if I'm on them. But I'm on Surveyor 4.'

'Under three weeks.'

'That's right. It's all hands on deck. But I'm also calling about the paint.'

'The paint. For the moon?'

'Yes. I need to tell you where I've got to with it. The *idea* never went away.'

'You've been working on it?'

'Yes. I'll try to be brief.'

'I've got as long as you want.'

'I don't… But I want to go through it with you. Bear with me.'

'I'm all ears.'

'Good… When you first mentioned compressing it—'

'Francine's idea.'

'Fine. What it did when you said it back then, was give me an idea. Just an inkling of an idea, but there was nothing I could think of to do with it, as you know. But it brought back some thoughts I'd had over the years.

'As I *think* you know, we're hoping to get some rocks back when we get a man to the moon, but we don't have anything more than photographs of soil samples yet. So everything about the moon's surface – its "regolith" – is conjecture.'

'Regolith. I do remember, Ken, when I used to talk to Ray there, he used the word – when he was speaking about you. But that's all I know about it.'

'It's just the term, coined this year in fact, for the fine-grained soil that covers the moon, made by meteorite impacts over billions of years... Ray's never been an ally of mine... Was it to do with helium-3?'

'Yes. I remember. That's right.'

'Well, that's part of what I want to run by you... We're pretty sure, no matter what Ray may have said, that an abundance of helium-3 is buried very shallowly in the upper layer of the regolith, embedded by solar wind. It's near the surface because that's where the sun reaches most easily.'

'Isn't helium what you put in balloons to make them go up, or you breathe it and get that Donald Duck voice?'

'Yes, that *is* helium. And if you want to know the basic science... It's a very light gas, less "dense" than air. That results in the speed of sound in helium being about three times faster than in air. So when you breathe helium in, you speak squeaky.'

'Like those Chipmunk songs?'

'Yes. They were made high-pitched by speeding up the voices. But helium-3 is something completely different. It was formed in the Big Bang, and also some of it in our atmosphere is from nuclear weapons testing – it's used to "boost" nuclear weapons.'

'OK.'

'Do you remember the Ranger programme a few years ago, Sam?'

'I've heard of it. Was it the one before Surveyor?'

'Yes. What the Ranger probes indicated, is that there is perhaps still a million tonnes of helium-3 on the moon. It's thought that a reaction involving even a small amount of it, could produce a massive explosion. It's only a *theoretical* possibility, but there may be some elements that could be mixed into a powdered paint that could then react with helium-3 – and explode the paint mixture out.'

'Explode the paint mixture out?'

'Yes. On the moon. Explode it far enough out for a giant "splash" of it to be visible from earth.'

Sam was stunned. 'Are you saying that "painting the moon" is *possible*?'

'I'm saying it's a very, very *long* shot, but I think with the right powdered paint it's a *hypothetical* possibility. Mind you, even if this reaction, this explosion, did occur, the paint would need to spread for at least a hundred and fifty miles.'

Thwaite pictured this as about half as much again as the distance from Mount Rushmore to Goodmews.

'The *right* powdered paint?'

'Yes. It would probably look like chalk dust. Though it depends on the paint. It might even look like the top layer of the moon's regolith. Or the powder left at the bottom of a Rice Krispies box. Whichever, I would think it would be easily compressible.'

'And getting it to the moon in the first place?'

'It would be Surveyor 4,' Kennington said.

'You've gone silent, Sam.'

'No. I'm here.'

'Should I go on. We're just about there.'

'I just can't believe that it could happen.'

'It *may* just be possible… But we're getting ahead of ourselves. Let me explain what I need to work out first.'

'Please.'

'To react with helium-3 enough to cause a massive explosion, I think *lithium* could be the element I've been looking for.'

'Is that the same lithium that's used to treat manic depression?'

'Yes. And it's used in batteries too. It's got many uses: it's light and a good conductor of heat. It also has a low melting point and it's flammable. And its metallic lustre would be a great quality to have in the paint. I've been playing with it – carefully; lithium's highly corrosive. I have to be careful of skin contact and breathing the dust.

'The first thing is, you may not be surprised to know that I don't have any helium-3 to experiment with. I might be able to get clearance to source some, but that's an involved process. What I've tried to do is approximate the constituents of what is thought to make up the moon's regolith, where this reaction would have to take place. I've created something *like* a compound, using lithium. I've even given it a "compound" name – "regolithium". My experiments have not been conclusive; that's impossible without helium-3. But I've been able to engineer mini-explosions.'

'OK…'

'But before I can determine if my regolithium will successfully combine with paint, I need the paint, to powder and test. That's the missing link. I will need to be sure – or as sure as I can be – that the mixture with the paint will be able to withstand the reaction with helium-3 and not be incinerated, so it can then be spread over the moon…

'This is where you come in, Sam. We need Francine to create an extraordinary colour.'

'Francine?'

'Yes. And it has to be quick, "in house", without any hint of its real use.'

'What should I say to her.'

'Even if we can make happen all of what I've been explaining, I would consider it a failure in the end unless the colour itself is exceptional. We don't want just "a colour on the moon" – we want a colour that no one has ever seen before. Colour is something easy for the press and the public to understand – "Colour on the moon! And what *is* that colour?" '

Thwaite grasped that Kennington was seeing this event as something far beyond just a science experiment. 'Like "Is it a bird or a plane or—" '

'Hold on, Sam.'

'Sorry.'

'It's vital what you say to her. I need a colour that has an "earthy", natural look, but you need to say to her that we need a bright colour. You'll need to come up with a reason for it. It's her specialty. Then I'll dull it, so everyone can see it.'

'So everyone can see it?'

'On the moon.'

'Doesn't it have to be bright for that?'

'No. The opposite. Do you remember I mentioned that a dull colour would be best?'

'I do now.'

'This might give you some ideas. If not, don't worry. The quick colour-physics is that the moon is mostly a neutral grey and white. That reflection is what we see. We need a colour that will best contrast with the moon's colour, which will still surround the expanse of paint we get up there.'

'Even this big "splash" would have plenty of white around it?'

'Yes. So, firstly, I need her to produce something *exceptional*, that I can work with. We want her to draw on all the colour theory and creativity she can muster, and then I'll dull it. For instance, if she came up with a bright, fire-engine red' – Thwaite pictured a barbers chair – 'I would add black to make it dark enough to reflect as brightly as possible off the moon, but not *too* dark as to lose the colour. A "bitter chocolate", a warm red-brown, would probably be textbook.'

'When would you want the paint by.'

'I'd like it within days.'

'I'll speak to Francine tomorrow.'

'Good. You'll need a cover story. It would be good if you can relate it to NASA – does it still say NASA there?'

'Yes. And inside and on all their papers. As far as Francine or anyone can tell, everything is still "NASA".'

'Good. If you feel you need to phone, I'm extension 445.'

SEVENTEEN

She heard a knock on the church door, and 'Francine?' It was Sam, unusually; but insistent as always.

'Be right there.'

She opened the door. 'Hi Sam. This is a surprise.'

'Are you busy. Can I speak to you.' It was more a demand than a question.

'Come in.'

They sat down on a nearby pew.

'I wanted to ask you. Would you like to take over the Occ?'

'You don't want to do it anymore?'

'I'm too busy.' *Doing what?* she was tempted to ask. 'Mainly, you'd be right for it. And it's "occasional"; you can do it as often as you want.'

The idea of taking over the paper awakened something in Francine. It had always seemed boring, formal, mostly a box-ticking exercise in required information. It could be livelier, at least laid out in a way that made it more inviting.

'Alright, Sam. Thanks.' She wanted to know what had prompted this idea of his, but it wasn't her business.

'Good,' he said with no expression. 'I'll bring you the photocopier later and some other things. You can let me know if there's anything else you need. And I'll leave the Bulletins to you, if you want to keep that going.'

The Beatles' 'From Me To You' had danced across her mind – 'If there's anything that you want…'

'They've been good, Sam. They fit with a Moontown. I'll do one soon.'

He half-nodded.

'Just not *too* soon, Francine. There's something that's top priority.'

So that was why he'd come.

'It will be the Centre's two-year anniversary next month. I want to celebrate it.'

'OK.' She hadn't realized it had been two years. There hadn't been any one-year event.

'It's actually September if you're splitting hairs, but everyone's back at work then, so I want it to be in July… You've produced these *great* colours. I want you – to do something even more special with colour, something that will capture everyone's imagination.'

He hadn't asked her for much of anything since the early days, and always seemed more than satisfied with her Goodmews colours. Now he was asking her for a special colour he wanted, *plus* taking on the Centre publications. She did have other colour ideas she hadn't used yet.

'I want a "coloured moon",' he continued, 'a bright coloured moon that can be the centrepiece for the celebration.'

'Like a poster of the moon? In a window?'

'*I have – no – idea.*' He sounded almost angry, saying these four words like they were in large capitals on a placard.

'OK. I was just wondering, so I could get an idea of the scale.'

'I haven't worked it out yet. I'll let you know. What I'd like you to do, *now*, is come up with a colour that can be the Centre's own "moon" colour.'

'So, not just grey and white like the moon then.'

'*No!*'

'I was just kidding, Sam.'

'I want the *opposite*. That's clear isn't it?'

'Yes.' Though it wasn't. 'Just – I'm sure you don't need to know the technical details, but there's actually no such thing as a "new" colour. Any colour that can exist, already does.'

'I don't need to know about that, Francine. Just make it beautiful, and so it looks unique.'

'Do you have a colour in mind?'

'Do I have a colour in mind. That's your department. I think I've already told you enough to make a start. I want the colour to have an "earthy", natural quality, and a glow – that seems to come from within. I want it to look like something that no one has ever seen before.'

She tried to think of a colour that had looked and *sounded* new when it first came out. Tiffany Blue, from a hundred years before. And there were those colours that caught people's attention with their distinctiveness, like the Le Creuset orange.

Where had he got his descriptions from? It wasn't like the language he'd used when he asked her to create a Goodmews colour.

'That's a tall order, Sam. I don't know if I can do that.' She had no picture of what a colour fitting his description would look like; she couldn't imagine a colour that had all those qualities.

'I know you can do it, uh, Francine.'

She didn't. But if *he* had such confidence in her, maybe *she* should.

'Well, Sam, I'll be finished soon with that exhibition on what moon rocks might tell us one day, then I'll get on it.'

'I need you to start *now*. I've always let you do "your own thing", in your own time, but I need to have everything in place soon.'

Francine felt her heart beating. 'You wouldn't want someone else to get started on it, then I'd come in? There are good artists around that I know. I could brief them.'

'I'm not *in*terested in anyone else. You're *part* of the Centre. It's a project for *you,* and under wraps. Belt and braces that are buttoned up tight. I want it to be a complete surprise when we unveil it. I'll keep things ticking over till you've done the colour. I've arranged for someone to cover your room for a few days. I'd like an update within 48 hours.'

'Forty-eight hours?' It came out sounding close enough to a normal question, though Francine had wanted to screech it out.

'Sam, you know it takes me time.'

'We don't have time.'

But she wasn't someone who just went to her studio and had brainstorms. The room was a lab.

'Can I just ask you, Sam, how you came up with this colour you want? You know I'd have some ideas. Is it set in stone?'

'I've thought enough about it, spoken to people,' he said. *But you didn't speak to* me, *Sam.* 'It's why you haven't seen me around much lately.

'Francine, in some ways it's pretty simple. The Moon Centre is unique, Goodmews is unique. So this colour, this bright colour, has to be. You'll come up with a great one, I'm sure. Get whatever you need – equipment, paint – whatever.'

There was no more room for demurring. 'OK. I'll get on it tonight.'

When Sam had gone, she went back into her room, the old parlour pew she'd made her own, with her bed and dressing table, an easy chair and blue carpet, and some dried flowers in a vase. On the wall were two photographs – one was of the orangewood forest in autumn, its needles bronzed golden by radiant sunshine, and the other was of the phenomenon where the bright crescent moon is nestled at the bottom of a barely visible dark moon. Below it were the two lines said to come from an old ballad:

> Late, late yestreen I saw the new moone
> Wi' the auld moone in hir arme.

What would a 'natural-looking' colour look like, Francine wondered to herself. *A rock? And what would a colour look like that seemed to 'glow from within'? Those prismatic ones that sparkled from chandeliers? Maybe. But paint doesn't do that.*

There was no such thing as a truly 'new' colour. Picasso may have come up with his own cherry-blue recently, and Rothko his 'outdigo' – his opposite of indigo. And there would be others; chemists had been inventing synthetic pigments for 5,000 years, ever since the first one, Blue Frit – Egyptian Blue. But weren't they all simply different shades of what humans can perceive? Colour had an infinite spectrum, and no colour could be beyond that unless the genetics of the eye were to change.

To Francine, it was all emperor's new clothes. Sam was asking for the impossible. Though wasn't the Moon Centre like that – something created out of nothing? Sam had come to town and had pretty much ridden roughshod over it, but he had changed it. He had modernized it. He was one of those people who are driven, to drive the world – unlike most people, stuck in the fishbowl they've always grown up in, content with things as they are.

It had been fun making colours with new Goodmews names, a challenge Francine relished. This was different. It was on a timeline – Sam's timeline. But it felt right, and she felt honoured by Sam's request. He believed in *her*. He was counting on *her*, to use her skill – her imagination – to create something extraordinary for the Moon Centre.

She recalled seeing pictures of the 1933 Chicago Exhibition, lit up by floodlights that had been switched on by the starlight from Arcturus, starlight that had passed through a telescope to focus on a few electric cells which then turned on the lights for the opening ceremony. She nor Sam would have the expertise for anything like that.

But she'd give his colour her best shot. No one had done more for Goodmews than he had; no one had done more for her.

She went to the back room and opened the door to the sudden sharp scent of her work – paint and oil. Her colour wheel – yellow at the top these days, before it moved into green at two o'clock and blue at four – hung on the wall along with torn sheets of paper streaked in experimental colour. Near the window, two pieces of polished amber sat on a shelf, amongst a row of thimble-sized blocks of coloured resin. On the window's middle rail sat her prism, balanced like a skinny skyscraper, a mini monolith.

She looked down at the floor and saw stripes of prismatic colour that had caught the late-morning light, the day's first bright sighting always delighting and surprising her. And she knew she'd be able to get fresh glimpses of the colour throughout the day as it travelled around the room in its sun-guided journey. Sometimes she'd even twist the prism in its position so its gleam would rest on her arm for a while while she worked. Or she'd twist it for a visitor she was expecting, to make sure they got the brunt of its brightness.

Are there paints more beautiful, she thought, *than this rainbow brushed on my floor?*

From the ceiling, two translucent orange dice were suspended along with a peacock feather, its iridescence – its structural colouration, as she'd learned – subtly shifting as she walked around it, dependent on how the light hit it, like oil on water or an abalone shell. *The way we experience colour depends on the quality of light. If I had to choose, I would choose natural colours, that change with the changing light, over synthetic ones – as beautiful as some are – that are created to look the same throughout the day.*

What sunny music could she put on? Julie Andrews, in The Sound of Music. But she didn't have the record.

'I'm on a Beatles kick,' she thought. She always came back to them. They were her taste, like Ritz crackers, that she bought over and over and enjoyed every time; and their songs had so much more to them than just what it said on the tin.

What *was* it about listening to them? She had an image

191

in her mind, of their house on a hill – a pure, clean white gazebo, neatly supported by four perfect pillars – and they'd emerged, spotless and tidy, to drive the world crazy with the exuberance of their songs, now anthemic – touchstones – to her and to so many others.

There were 'sunny' songs by other groups, but none like the Beatles' – their musical palette had always been bright. Even on the Ed Sullivan show, in black and white, their music had been in colour. And they could have driven the world even crazier. But they knew when a song, composed of their alchemy, had reached perfection.

She placed side two of *Revolver* on the turntable and thought about playing the final track and letting her mind 'float downstream', like the song said. But she didn't want a weird song. She wanted Good Day Sunshine, and lifted the needle on to the start.

From the first line, the song shone, glowed, seemingly almost from within, its effortless fluffiness making her feel like running outside into the afternoon. Was it possible to make a colour that 'sang'? Colours in nature made people smile. How did that work?

She was looking at her colour wheel as the song ended. She lifted the needle off, then sat down. Her paint tubes were arrayed on the table in front of her, her beakers and pestle-and-mortar in place, her brushes in tins, her oils in jars.

The room was still. The Cockeyed Optimist song from *South Pacific* came into her head, with its line about the sky being a bright 'canary yellow'. *I* am *an optimist,* she thought, *but I'm not an alchemist. You can't transmute a tube of paint into a colour that doesn't already exist.*

She'd have a play with her yellows. A 'new' one could be called Merrygold.

She squeezed out a few dabs from the tubes, then mixed them together in different combinations. No.

She added some Alizarin red to them. 'Red lorry yellow lorry, red lorry yellow lorry' went through her mind. *Yellow russet. Rusty yellow?* Could that be a colour? Had someone made that already, used that name? That would take time to research, which she didn't have. But artists had always gone their own way to create colours, using anything they could get their hands on; snail slime, glow-worms, earwax. When Victor Hugo painted he'd used coal dust and coffee grounds, maybe mixed with his own blood.

She took her tube of umber and stirred some of its reddish brown into the most promising yellow mix. It lent her vague thoughts of nudging the mixture towards an – 'otherworldly' – Mars colour that – still – had an earthy, terracotta base. She swirled more yellow into it and got an ochre she liked. But nothing unusual. *Yellochre?* Could that be a new colour?

She needed more inspiration. She needed a song that fizzed with energy.

She put on the Stones' 'Paint It Black', and Mick began to sing about a world painted black – black as night, or coal – devoid of colour. She lifted the needle off and replaced it in its holder. A great song. Sam wanted the opposite. Something light as *day*.

She wasn't sure why, but she had the vague sense that as difficult as it was to see her way ahead, she was making progress. Step by step was the only way she knew how to work: probing possibilities, reversing out of blind alleys when she encountered them. Answers for her didn't just snap into place, and she wouldn't have wanted them to. But *was* there an answer? Was what Sam wanted beyond what could be done with colour?

A thought struck her. She had avoided working with brown – as a base. As colour theory put it, it had a 'limitation of scintillation': it was the one colour with no 'endless depth'. But, theoretically – she also realized – a *lustrous* brown, if it existed, would be on the bronze spectrum: it would appear to 'glow' and... it would appear *gold* to the eye. Colours had their 'lustrous' extreme, she knew: silver, for one, was a lustrous white. But a golden glow coming from brown? A lustrous brown? It didn't make sense. Brown was the colour of figs, of Tootsie Rolls. And if a lustrous brown could be created, someone would have done it by now. Joshua Reynolds. Hadn't he made a lustrous brown from asphaltum – 'Jews' pitch' – bitumen from the bottom of the Dead Sea? And what about the Pre-Raphaelites' mummy brown – made from ground-up Egyptian mummies?

She'd seen a bronzy glow in autumnal nature, up near that pond on the way to the orangewoods. There had been a grey pre-dusk backdrop above a thin strip of blue, and the foliage in the clusters of maples had been ablaze with golden bronzes flagrantly lit by the sinking sun. Could she try for that bronziness?

She took her cadmium red – for her the truest, purest red – and her emerald green, one of Van Gogh's favourite, deep colours, and mixed them into a chocolate brown. She wiped her palette knife and added some iridescent white. It brought out the brown's richness. More cadmium red warmed it, but there was still no lustre. She added a fleck of cadmium yellow, another Impressionist favourite, known for its permanence. The mixture looked solid – and remained resolutely muted. She squeezed out a drop of a last favourite, Indian yellow. It was a less pure pigment than cadmium yellow, but it had a clarity, a transparency, and was known to be especially bright in sunlight. As she mixed it in, she could see it overlaying the mixture's dry, red opacity, slowly swelling the paint into a rich yellow. She stared at its depth.

Was she seeing things? Had she been looking at it for too long?

Was she imagining it? No. She didn't know where it had come from, but it was there: a hint of something that looked almost metallic, that was the colour of gold.

Gold! Metal, to make the mix sparkle? Like metal-flake paint on cars or like that drum kit I saw? No. Even if I knew how to do that, it wouldn't be 'new', and it would hardly look 'natural'.

Donovan's *Mellow Yellow* came into her head, with the line about saffron. She remembered the gamboge tree in the orangewoods. It had been two years. And there were the mineral-rich stones she'd always found up there.

EIGHTEEN

In half an hour, she was walking up Orangewood Drive, her heart beating from exertion. She hadn't been up here for months. She stopped and looked back towards Goodmews. There were more rows of houses than she recalled, and ribbons of streets mirrored the sunshine. She could make out the church spire and, at the opposite end of town, the bright yellow Moon Centre. Goodmews looked like a toy town from up here, a riot of roofs in reds, yellows and blues – in bright shades she'd created and named. And she could see the patch of green – the newly named Moon Park, once just 'the park', where the hippies had played chess and bongos and someone had put up that sign that said Welcome, Flower Followers. Was that only last summer?

Now the tables were gone and it was just grass, with a 'Polite Notice' asking people to respect the fact that in October the park was only open to residents over 65, to grant them a period of respite from children's noise.

She began walking again. A family of friendly pheasants skittered across the road ahead of her. *You never know what you'll see round the bend*, she thought. Soon the hills ranged up higher, all around, and the pointy tops of the giant trees began to appear.

It was late afternoon by the time she reached the grove and went through the stile. The daylight had lingered, and a slanting setting sun seemed to ignite the orangewood bark, the complementary blue sky brightening it even more. She peeled off a spongy-orange chunk and dropped it into her bag.

Amongst the trees, she spotted some small, shiny black stones – magnetite, she could tell – and put a few into her collection bag. She picked up some mica and then a piece of garnet. She knew it kept its crystals of ruby red inside, as glowing and transparent as a jar of quince jam.

She'd saved the best – she hoped – for last.

After a couple of wrong turns, she found her way to the gamboge tree. It was more concealed, within more growth, than she remembered. The bamboo cup was still hanging from the trunk.

She looked inside. It was almost full, the insoluble resin that made up most of the sap giving it its rich, amber colour – like mango chutney. It was crucial that the water-soluble fraction of it would be enough to allow the sap to blend into the mixture she was creating. She touched it with her knife. It was hard.

She unhooked the cup from the tree and put it in her bag.

It was quick going down the mountain; did Sam really mean 48 hours? She crossed town to the church. Back in her room, she dumped the rocks and the orangewood bark on to her work table.

She chipped fragments from the rocks into her mortar bowl and pestled them into a powder. She added some mica flakes. Mica of course wasn't a 'trace metal', she thought to herself, but it gave the powder a trace of metallic sparkle. She peeled thin pieces off the stringy tree-bark, then separated each ingredient into its own pile and took out the bamboo cup, cutting it away from the wedge of gamboge it enclosed. Her final action with the hardened yellow fluid was to slice off thin shards of it and put some of the shavings into the mortar bowl. She added water, and as she kneaded the mixture the gamboge liquefied, turning a glassy orange, and resolving into the colour of Buddhist monks' robes, a 'mellow' yellow saffron. What colour would be right, as close to unique as she could get. Could a colour dazzle yet have a warmth, hint at a cold 'otherworldliness' while being 'earthy'?

She added more linseed oil. The concoction verged on gold, close to the colour she loved: the colour of $500 bills in Monopoly. But it was still more matt than shiny, and refused to go gold. It needed more red, or orange. She thought of the bright beta-carotene pink of flamingos. No, that was too loud, like Johnny's moon paintings. It should be softer, but bronzier – Eclipse Orange, she could call it.

Her amber stones! That's the colour she wanted – a glinting, glassy honey, between gold and orange. It wasn't a million miles from gamboge, she realized; and they both were once soft, sticky, tree resin. It all might work together.

Her mortar bowl was a sea of glazy sap now – sap the way she'd pictured it, how she hoped it would be. She recalled that someone had once said that the letters of 'Rubber Soul' on the cover of the Beatles album were supposed to look like sap oozing from a rubber tree. She walked over to the album. Yes. 'Soul' could be that.

Back at her table she looked into the bowl again, then palette-knifed into it a chunk of the golden-brown paint she'd made up earlier. She added more oil, giving the mixture a gloss – a silky depth – that neared translucency, reflecting more light. She added some of the crushed-up garnet.

A little bit of twinkly red peeked out from the gold, like the life-happying coloured bulbs people laced through Goodmews's hedges at Christmas.

A faint metallic sheen lingered near the surface. She unscrewed the tops of two small tubes of paint she hadn't used yet: her orange cadmium, the most intense orange she knew of, and rose madder – her most expensive paint, which had a chalky, granular texture. She squeezed out a globule from each tube. Much too much of the orange. She knifed most of it away, then added what was left and the rose madder to the mixture. She rubbed some orangewood bark between her fingers – the same way she rubbed them next to her ear when she was testing her hearing. She inhaled, holding in the barky scent for as long as she could. Boiling it, she thought, might speed up its break-down process. But it would weaken its colour.

She drizzled the woody shavings into the bowl.

She stirred the gloop, now a twinkling, golden-red, and placed a white enamel dish on top of the bowl to keep the paint moist. She'd leave it overnight, to see if it made any difference, and left the room, closing the door.

A crazy dream woke with Francine in the morning. She had dreamt in colour. Someone had said something about lampshades tinged with 'Tiffany-orange glass' and they had shown her maple trees – or 'caramel' trees – 'lollipop-tipped in Van Gogh's autumn palette'. At one point, in a frenzy, she'd had only three minutes – the length of a great pop song – to do something that no one had ever done before.

She got up and padded across her parlour pew carpet and into the back room. Sunlight shone through the window, some falling on the mortar bowl and the dish on top of it. Would the paint still have that sparkling, amber beauty? Her dream blinked in again. Something about butter-coloured light. She didn't want butter; that was yellow, dense. She wanted a colour imbued with light, like the sea glowing at sunset.

She stood before the bowl and gripped the side of the plate on top, then closed her eyes and slid the plate off, lowering it on to the table. She stuck a finger into the bowl and stirred, blindly, then trailed her coated finger along the table.

She opened her eyes.

It was radiant, the colour of amber, yet grainy, like the pink of the grit on the paths of the park, and it sparkled from its depths, like stardust. She could almost see through it, yet it looked endless.

It was flecked orange, flecked red. It gleamed like a full moon, just risen.

It was Goodmews Gold.

*

'Thwaite here.'

'I've got a colour, Sam.'

'The paint?'

'Yes.'

'Are you happy with it?'

'Yes. I am. Should I bring it in this morning?'

'Yes.'

*

Thwaite watched Francine pry open the tin of paint. 'Let me show you what it looks like.'

She took a small paintbrush out of her pocket and dipped it in, then daubed a stripe of colour onto a piece of paper.

Thwaite said nothing at first, then a tentative 'It's only a thin stroke,' and Francine hoped there was a 'but' to come; 'but it's nice and bright.'

She felt something like a blush inside, the warmth of praise. 'I've called it Goodmews Gold.'

'How do you get the sparkles?'

'Different things.' She took out her booklet and opened it so Sam could see a list of the ingredients.

'Gamboge? Orangewood. Garnet. Cadmium?'

'I've added pigments like cadmium for stability.'

'What's "pigment".'

Sam couldn't really care about that, but... 'It's the "recipe" that lies behind a colour – like chlorophyll is the pigment responsible for a plant's green colour.' Francine suddenly wondered if she should have noted the amounts of everything she'd used, been more methodical in her approach. How would she be able to reproduce the Gold exactly, make more of it if she needed to? She felt she had to check.

'Do you need to know the formula?'

Thwaite shook his head. 'Not now.'

She closed the booklet. Its orange cover reflected off her finger, and her finger in turn cast a shadow on the booklet.

'I'll let you know if I need anything more,' he said. 'Thank you, Francine.'

*

'Ken?'

'Hello Sam.'

'Is it OK to be calling you on this number.'

'Did you get the paint?'

'I have a tin of it in front of me.' Thwaite waited for hearty congratulations on the speed he'd got it done.

'Good. What does it look like.'

'She calls it Goodmews Gold.' Thwaite focused on the business at hand. 'It's very bright, sparkly. I think it fits the bill.'

'I need to see it. A.S.A.P. Is there an air courier near you?'

There was. 'One started up, out of Black Hills Airport last year.'

'Perfect. Use that. Do you have a fax machine there?'

'Yes. A small Magnafax Telecopier. NASA installed it in case we needed it for back-and-forth communications.'

'Good. It's what we have here. I'll fax you to tell you where to have it sent. Your number?'

'It's the phone number, with 8 at the end instead of 9.'

'Got it… And the cover story?'

'I've told her we're having our two-year anniversary in July.'

'Is it?'

'Close enough. And I want to use the paint on a mocked-up moon we'll have "shining" in the exhibition.'

'Excellent. Then the next question for Francine. If the colour's right, I need to know where our explosion should be, to spread it. I don't know as much as I'd like about the moon's surface. Surveyor 4's landing site will be Sinus Medii – Central Bay. It's the point closest to earth and there's optimum lighting conditions, but the terrain isn't smooth; highlands and "rilles" – lava channels probably – are dotted around. Our scientists estimate that there's only a 50–50 chance of Surveyor landing safely, softly – though like always, it's a crucial mission. Another failure will be seen as potentially impacting on our ability to get a man on the moon this decade.

'In any case, as far as you and I are concerned, Central Bay is not flat enough for our "canvas". I need to know where a large, flat plain is, as close as possible to it. Francine will know. She knows her stuff, I've read some of her papers.'

'Really?'

'Yes. Have *you* seen them?'

'No, I haven't.'

'Say that what you want from her might even turn out to be a Moon Centre contribution – who knows? – to NASA's information on landing sites for the manned Apollo missions. She'll be aware that they must be working on that. Actually, no. That might stretch credibility. Just say that you'd like her to begin putting together some information for the anniversary that could relate to future moon landings.

You'd like her first of all to explain where the *biggest and flattest* areas on the nearside of the moon are, for a large target and soft touchdown… She won't be surprised that you know what a good landing site would involve, *will* she? Or question why you're interested?'

'No. But it doesn't matter. She'll do what I ask of her.'

NINETEEN

'Ken?'

'Hello Sam. You beat me to it.'

'This phone still OK?'

'Yes. Couple of minutes.'

'Did you get the paint?'

'Yes. I'm drying it into a powder. But I'm concerned about the colour. It's bright, like you said. But it's an amber, which feels like "caution". Maybe it's my fault for not specifying a colour, and I'm not sure it would have worked, but when I think about it now, *green* is the colour of "go", which is our message: we're *going* for broke.

'But this is what we've got, and I have to make it work… The drying will take a few days, then we'll see what happens when it's blended with the regolithium.'

'You don't want her to go for green?'

'No. We've only got two weeks… Have you spoken with her about "landing sites"?'

'Yes. Mare Imbrium sounds like it could be the best one. I can see it on my moon map. That dark area in the upper left?'

'Yes. Northwest of the centre. It's been my thought too. It's the second largest crater on the moon and one of the least rocky. Though getting the stick to it is even trickier. It's relatively close to Central Bay, but it's still 600 miles away. Do you know about ghost craters.'

'No.'

'They're filled, we think with lava, to the rim. They could be the perfect place to land, but they're almost invisible, only detectable when sunlight is shining very low above the moon's horizon.'

'Should I ask her about them?'

Thwaite waited for Kennington to respond.

'I think not. It would be even more complicated. It will be enough trying to work out how to get the powder – the paint – up there, then getting it 600 miles from Surveyor's touchdown. I think we have to go with Imbrium. It's our best shot. I just need you to ask Francine a few things about the geology.'

'Ken. Can I just ask you. Don't you have geologists *there*? Wouldn't it be easier to ask *them* these questions? And safer?'

'No.' It was the first time Ken had sounded irritated to Sam. 'Do you think I'd be having you ask all these questions if I could do it myself?'

'No.'

'I don't think you realize how much is going on here. First of all, I don't *work* with geologists. There's no plausible reason I could give, while everyone is working flat out, why I'd be going over to a department that I have nothing to do with, to ask them about a *crater* that has no relation to the upcoming mission.'

'Sorry. Tell me what to ask her.'

Ken said nothing for a moment. 'What about doing it this way. Tell her something like: after you'd spoken to her, you spoke to someone on the science team at NASA to get more information for her, or for the Centre files even, about landing sites.'

'For the future.'

'Yes. Say that when you mentioned her telling you about Mare Imbrium, they said they'd like to have a short summary of her knowledge about Imbrium specifically, as it's been mooted as a future landing site.'

'She'll be glad to offer her expertise.'

'Good. Tell her to focus on Imbrium's soil, its regolith, and whether it's likely to be firm, but penetrable enough for a spacecraft to land. I want her confirmation of what we think we know. We've only got *orbital* observations. It looks like the top layer is loose, like powder, but we don't know how it changes as it deepens. The surface, at least, seems to have a high porosity.'

'Porosity?'

'The amount of empty space in the regolith – how easily compressed it is, how far in a lander's legs will go. High porosity would allow for it to support a lander... Can you get the summary by Monday morning?'

'I'm sure I can. I'll tell her NASA wants it A.S.A.P. I just hope she can give us what we need.'

'Have her fax it.'

'You want *her* to fax it?'

'Yes. I think it would be good if she feels like she's directly involved. Does she use the machine?'

'She hasn't yet. I'll show her how to connect it to the phone line. It's easy enough to operate.'

'Have her send it as close to 10 A.M. Monday morning as she can, addressed to... "The NASA Science Team" – which doesn't exist. The fax is in a central area and everyone can hear when it's going, but I'll be there to pick it up. And even if someone else happens to see it first, it's not sensitive information, and I can always say it's for me. You have our fax address?'

'Yes. I'll give it to her.'

*

To the Science Team: I have included a bit of history, which I'm sure you don't need – and other basic information – but this will also be a good fact sheet for the Moon Centre.

Mare Imbrium

For the NASA Science Team, Cape Kennedy, Florida.
Prepared by Francine Robb
NASA Thwaite Moon Centre Geologist.
Goodmews, South Dakota.
July 3, 1967.

Mare Imbrium (MI) is a dark plain on the Moon, easily visible to the naked eye from earth. If the moon were a clock face, from the earth's Northern Hemisphere MI would be the roughly circular patch at 11 o'clock. To those who see the Man in the Moon, it's his right eye.

Dark patches like MI were once thought to be vast oceans: Mare Imbrium, named by the 17th-century Italian astronomer Giovanni Riccioli, means 'Sea of Rains'. Although we cannot be sure until lunar soil samples are brought back to earth, it is now believed that MI's dark appearance is due to the lava that covers it. (Moon watchers who have observed Imbrium through a telescope know that its colour depends on the angle of the sun: its surface has a silvery lustre at 'noon' but looks a dirty yellow-green at sunrise and sunset. Its soil, they speculate, may contain a universe of colour that we can't see from earth.)

Mare Imbrium, itself, is a vast, three-mile-deep crater surrounded by three rings of mountains thousands of feet high, some of the loftiest on the moon. By May 1967, 99% of the moon had been mapped; we know that MI is the moon's second largest mare (a Latin word, pronounced 'mah-ray') and one of the largest mares in the solar system. At around 700 miles in diameter, MI is large enough to hold Great Britain and France.

MI was gouged out in minutes by a rain of meteorites left over from the formation of the solar system – an impact more powerful than billions of hydrogen bombs. These effects, known as the 'Imbrium Sculpture', are still visible today.

MI is dotted with smaller craters, but is relatively flat. April's Surveyor 3 mission took photographs of the soil. They confirmed this smoothness, first indicated last year by both Surveyor 1 and the Soviets' Luna 9. Mare Imbrium is very smooth for the moon.

*

Sam,

I have received the fax.
I am having this note (below) wired to you

immediately. Give me a call at noon (exactly) today. I have a brief window then.

Mare Imbrium will be our target.
The paint has been dried.
I have been able to initiate a chemical reaction – a small eruption – with the regolithium.
I have made some further calculations.
We're almost ready to go.

Ken

*

Banno went up the yellow paving stones, round to the front of the Moon Centre and through the revolving doors. He nodded to Jan and walked down the corridor.

In his Songs and Poetry room he turned on the light. The rubber doorstop, as always, was where he'd left it, and he pushed it over to the open door to prop it in place. He turned on the record player to a low volume, dropped the needle on to *Moonlight Sonata,* and sat down on his stool, against the wall and next to the open door. The end of the *Sonata* had come to sound like a frenetic Charlie Chaplin film score, but this early gentle part is what he listened for. It lasted about six minutes and always tugged at his heartstrings, bathing him in its tenderness.

*

'... Good timing, Sam. Thanks for phoning. Let me bring you up to speed. This won't take long...

'Last year, before Surveyor 1, NASA asked me to design a temperature probe they could use on a mission, to measure the heat in the lunar soil. We never got to the probe, as other priorities came up, and none were used on Surveyor 2 or 3. But I was asked to design a probe for Surveyor 4, and that is the crux of our plan.

'I'm developing software that I've told NASA I will be using to receive and crunch the data from this probe. I'm also working on a large cylinder – that looks like a miniature rocket – that will contain the working temperature probe. I've told NASA that I will attach this cylinder to a leg of Surveyor in a way that when Surveyor lands, this cylinder will be imbedded in the regolith so that temperature readings can be taken and relayed back to me here at the Cape.

'What I'm also doing is building another, identical-looking cylinder – I've called it the "moonstick" – one word.'

'OK! Did you get it from the *leaflet* I sent you back in January?'

'Yes. It struck me when I first read it. It will connect our rocket to Goodmews, if the history comes out later. It brings the concept of a moonstick into the future.'

'I like it, Ken.'

'I thought you would. It's not dissimilar to the way you've brought *Goodmews* into the future.'

'Thank you.'

'What matters now is that inside *this* moonstick will be our compressed paint mixture, and some fuel and a small battery, and this is what I will actually attach to Surveyor's leg.'

'You're able to build this?'

'Yes. NASA has supplied the materials, including the aluminum frame, which is the same as for an airplane. So it's light and durable. And the moonstick is small, as far as rocket cylinders, or even small rockets go. It's shorter than an average man's height and about a foot in diameter.'

'And why does it look like a rocket?'

'Because it *is* a rocket. It has to be a rocket shape so it can be launched to Mare Imbrium. Unless it was shaped like a rocket, it would just be an outer shell that would have to fall away after landing to expose the moonstick, which would then have to be fired. That wouldn't work for us.'

'You're confident they'll agree with your "temperature probe"?'

'I've been told on the q.t. that they have, unofficially. And time's getting short now. They're not going to have me going back to the drawing board. The probe isn't crucial to the mission, and it's seen as *my* baby. I've convinced them that it will work for their purposes. That's what matters.'

'But won't they wonder why this "probe" looks like it could be *launched* to somewhere?'

'I've explained to NASA that the rocket shape is for aesthetics as much as anything else. They want Surveyor 4 to look good and as Space Age as possible for the world's cameras before Surveyor's placed inside the main rocket. It would be ugly to have something attached to Surveyor that looks like a silo or a giant can, even if that shape made sense, which it doesn't for our plan.'

'So, it's happening, Ken.'

There was a pause. 'Let me explain what else we need to do. As quickly and simply as I can... *You* need to put together a report, say ten pages or so. After Surveyor has landed safely on the lunar surface, I will make the report public.

'Surveyor's landing is the last information anyone on earth will get about its flight. The results of our moonstick will only be known after Mare Imbrium has been painted, and it can be seen – by everyone on earth.

'I'll describe now what should happen after I've attached the moonstick, but what the report needs to be about is what will happen after it embeds itself in Mare Imbrium. It should also include some technical aspects of the project, so we can explain to a press, and a world, how we did it. I'll summarize those features and wire it to you.'

Sam fiddled with the handkerchief that peaked from his breast-pocket. 'Are you sure you want *me* to write this report?'

'Yes. I don't have the time. And you know the history of the whole colour idea better than anyone. It *was* your idea… For now, you need to take some notes, so you can begin to put together at least the bare bones of this report. Do you have a pen?'

'Yes.'

'I want it to be in plain English for John Q. Public – what people will be seeing, as well as – in understandable ways – how this new colour and regolithium were integral to the project. I want people to be able to understand, if they want to, how we did it. Can you do that?'

'As long as I've got the info I need.'

'Good. So here goes.

'After everything else has been weighed, I will secure the moonstick – by brackets to Surveyor's leg. Then, like all previous Surveyors, Surveyor 4 will be placed in a capsule in the top part of the rocket that will carry it to the moon.'

'There'll be heavy security everywhere when you attach the moonstick, *won't* there?'

'Of course. This time there's a wide exclusionary "box" surrounding the entire site, with surveillance cameras at the perimeter and buried motion-sensors off base to alert NASA to anyone approaching, but you mean *me*. Will anyone be watching me.'

'Yes.'

'There are always people everywhere, and there will be people assisting with the fixing of the moonstick to Surveyor and then the lifting equipment to get it into the rocket, but I have a top level – Level 4 – "special-sensitive" clearance, and I'm in charge of what is believed to be the temperature probe.'

'OK.'

'Then – just so you know how the flight will work, step by step – this is what should happen. There will be the last-minute checks to make sure everything about the rocket is in place and ready to go. Launch day will be confirmed... And as long as the weather holds on that day, the rocket will launch. On the way to the moon, stages of the rocket will fall away, and finally Surveyor will separate from the rocket as it's orbiting the moon. Then Surveyor's legs will open and it will descend to the lunar surface.

'When it touches down in Central Bay, the attached moonstick will be compressed by the impact: the brackets will fall away and, inside the moonstick, a battery will ignite its fuel, propelling it towards Mare Imbrium. It should take about two hours to get to Imbrium.

'I estimate that, on the moon, the moonstick will travel at around 300 miles an hour. According to moon maps, there shouldn't be large mountains in the way, that would interrupt the moonstick's journey to Imbrium. It should finally crash nose-cone-first into Imbrium's regolith, destroying enough of itself to force the paint out.'

'How loud a crash do you think that would be?

'Sam, as I think you actually know, there will be no sound. There is no air to transmit sound waves on the moon.'

'That's right. Sorry.'

'That's OK. Questions – John Q. Public, remember? – are good. Anyway, what happens next is what the whole plan revolves around. The paint should react with the moon's helium-3, and the mixture should catch alight. It will begin to burn slowly, just below the surface.'

'Is there a way to picture that?'

'In my mind… If you were on the moon, you'd see it building to a fiery ball of gas, feeding on itself, getting larger and larger. It might look something like the inside of the sun.'

'The inside of the *sun*?'

'Maybe. But whatever this superheated gas-ball looks like, it will build up until it bursts like a giant firework.'

'Like fireworks?'

'Remember, the paint, and now the regolith, will be imbued with lithium. Lithium's a pyrotechnic – its salts cause flames to burn brightly, in fact we think certain orange stars contain a high concentration of it. What should then happen is that this blazing mixture will spread like lava until it runs up against Imbrium's surrounding mountains. Then it will stop, and this grey crater will be left coated in our transfigured Goodmews Gold.'

'Sounds incredible. Will we see the moon being "painted"?'

'I'm afraid not. Even though our gas-ball of colour will be incredibly bright because it's so hot, at the same time it's

215

spreading, Imbrium will be in shadow – from the earth's vantage point. There's no way getting round the timing.'

'That's unfortunate.'

'Well, that's the universe. But it's how I picture it, how I think it will happen. I'm burning the midnight oil to get the moonstick finished. Enough prototypes. I've probably done 50,000 drawings of the damn thing.

'I'm going to wire you now some more information on the moonstick and on the spread of the paint. It's a bit long, and it's complicated. You just need to have a general understanding of what we're doing, for your report… You need to speak to the public's imagination as well as the technology, otherwise no one besides scientists will have any idea, or take much interest in how we did this. You're explaining something that's never been done before, that no one's ever seen, and I want people to be able to picture it.'

'We're going to do it, Ken, aren't we.'

'The stick's got to be attached, the flight has to go precisely, the explosion has to happen like I predict… but, yes. I believe it's going to happen.'

'And I take it you're not bothered that when NASA discovers the truth about the temperature probe—'

Kennington laughed. 'The probe will be the last thing on their mind. They'll read the report along with everyone else, and they'll be desperate to know how we did it. Painted the moon, under their noses.'

Thwaite needed to ask. 'And are people going to say that since the technology exists to… do what we're going to do, couldn't something more useful have been done with it?'

'It depends what you mean by useful. There will always be people who say things like that – that's what they said about Goddard and his rockets. Look what *that* led to. I have no idea how, or even *if* what we're doing may contribute to science, or space science, in the future, but who's to say what shouldn't be done if it *can* be done. And of course what we're doing might fail, but we will have been the first to try.'

'Could it go horribly wrong?'

'The whole thing's 50/50, maybe 60/40.'

'Will it destroy anything?'

'All we're doing is altering the appearance of one crater, beautifully in my opinion. Maybe originally it was just to steal a march on NASA, but it will be something much more. Of course there'll be that lunatic fringe like always – hippies probably – saying we're besmirching something pure. But if I didn't think most will marvel, and be impressed by what we've accomplished, I wouldn't have stuck with it. I would have dismissed it all as a loony idea from someone loco in the cabeza. The frosting on the cake will be that it will encourage people to look at the moon again. That's what NASA should also be for. Did *you* even look at it, before the Moon Centre?'

'Not really.'

'And why *should* anyone? It's been the same dull rock that's always been there and always will. We're going to change that, for the better.'

'The paint will be permanent?'

'For all intents and purposes, yes. First of all, erosion on the moon is extremely slow – about one centimetre every twenty million years. There's no atmosphere: paint in a vacuum doesn't deteriorate, and on the moon would be like storing it in an air-tight container, as airless as the most complete man-made vacuum. Also, I've created a paint that

217

should be able to withstand the moon's extreme temperatures and not contract and crack. The moon can go from minus about 300 degrees Fahrenheit to hotter than boiling water.'

'Really?'

'Yes.'

'Just to ask... Will the colour confuse future landings?'

'No. My understanding, to begin with, is that a list of 30 potential sites has been narrowed down to 5 for the first Apollo landing. It might well be the Sea of Tranquillity, which you may have heard about in the news, but whichever one they decide on, they're all near the lunar equator. None of them are anywhere near Imbrium. Besides, NASA – and Russia and anyone else – will know all about what we've done, well before then. We're going to publish all our info, and they'll be able to make any decision to avoid the area if they feel they need to... Sam, I have to go. I'm wiring the notes you need now.'

'Thanks.'

'When you've done the report, phone me before you send it so I can be at the fax to pick it up. Put "Private. For Kennington Varnen" on it.'

'Will do.'

'Are you open tomorrow?'

'We close at 2, and for the rest of the week. Fourth of July in Goodmews is celebrated as Independence *Week*.'

'Didn't know that. Phone me though, if you have questions.'

TWENTY

It came 20 minutes later.

<u>From the desk of Kennington Varnen</u>

July 3, 1967

1. <u>The moonstick</u>. We can get away with a small amount of fuel for the moonstick – just enough to propel it 600 miles – because both it and its payload are light. (The fuel itself, liquid hydrogen, is both light and extremely powerful and has been one of NASA's most significant technical accomplishments. In fact the Soviets' lack of this technology has proved a serious handicap for them.)

   With the fuel and battery, the stick will still be within weight tolerance, and should not affect Surveyor's flight or landing. (The stick can't weigh much more than the 'temperature-probe' rocket, which NASA has now officially approved.) At apogee, the stick's greatest height – and its slowest speed – it will run out of fuel and loop down to Imbrium, pulled by gravity, until it crashes.

I'm still working on the angle that I need, to orient the moonstick to the leg of Surveyor so when it's launched it will hit Imbrium where we need it to. Imbrium's a large target area, so we have a wide margin for error as far as getting the stick near to its centre, but we don't want to be too far off, unless the spread of the paint, in at least one direction, will be stopped too early by the mountains around the outside.

(The stick doesn't need a guidance system or steering capabilities. As you may know, the Soviet's Luna 2 – the world's first man-made object to land on another celestial body – had no propulsion systems on it. Like our stick, it was an independent spacecraft.)

Externally, the stick will look like a rocket, with fins for stability (and to keep it pointed in the right direction) and a pointed nose-cone to reduce drag. (Our 'warhead', or payload, at the top is the Goodmews Gold mixture.)

The stick will no doubt be at an angle that might look a bit strange, but I have been entrusted to attach it how it needs to be for the temperature probe. There's a lot to consider to get this right, but I am a trajectory specialist and I'm confident I will.

I based the moonstick itself on the German V2s from World War II, which were designed by rocketry enthusiasts who are now working on the Saturn V rocket to be used for the Apollo launches. Missile designs that worked during the war have been improved technologically, so the range I will be able to get with the moonstick will exceed the 600 miles (617 to be exact, by my calculations) we need. By the way, the first rocket to ever reach space was a modified V2 rocket.

The key thing is – as I've said above – we're able to keep the size and the amount of propulsion fuel needed way down; as you know, gravity on the moon is about 1/6 of earth's. To put it in 'earth' terms, the Germans fired rockets from France to hit London during the Blitz – a distance of over 100 miles. So at gravity 1/6 of earth's, a small rocket of our moonstick size would be able to fly six times that distance with our small payload.

2. The spreading paint. Serendipitously, our timing is right for the reaction to build as it needs to. Touchdown is July 16, around the start of a lunar dawn; and as the sun gets higher, the moon's regolith will heat up, enhancing the reaction. This 'gold turmoil' may last for a full lunar 'day' (about 340 hours). Then, as the sun sets on the moon, the moon – as always – will cool, as will our mixture, and the reaction will stop – unless, which is more likely, Imbrium's crater edges have already caused it to stop, as the mountains are where the moon rock rises well above the helium-3 strata.

    And my speed estimates for the spread are very conservative. Over these 340 hours, the paint will only have to spread at about $1/5^{th}$ of a mile an hour – a thousand feet an hour – to finally be visible from Earth. (A leisurely walking pace is about 15 times that fast.) It will spread faster, I'm sure, as it will be the product of a massive gas explosion.

    Also fortuitously, the timing of our first 'Moonshow' will be perfect. In fact, I think history will look back on it with some amazement. The end of the paint spreading should just about coincide with the new moon in early August, as we see it from earth. Several days after the new moon has appeared, enough of the moon will become visible so that we can begin to see our painted Imbrium.

Then, what should happen is that, each night, the colour will expand, from right to left in the Northern Hemisphere from earth. We'll see a little more of the gold each night as the moon waxes – we'll be able to see our gold Imbrium completely about 11 days after the new moon, through to the full moon. Then, as the moon wanes, the reverse will happen, until the moon disappears. Then a few days later, there'll be another new moon, and the cycle will start again.

Ken

Thwaite sat down. It was real now. He was part of something that would change the world.

Now he needed to put it into words for John Q. Public.

By late morning he had a ten-page report that felt nearly complete. It didn't 'speak to the imagination and technology' as well as Kennington would have liked, but Thwaite wasn't a scientist, and hardly a poet. He'd give it some last thought over the next few days, when the Centre would be quiet.

With his red pen he titled the paper The Red Report and wrote EMBARGOED across the top of each page, then signed his name at the end and tapped the sheaf into a pile. He took it over to the file cabinet and stuck it into the back of a drawer between some other papers, and locked the cabinet.

*

Banno liked sitting in the calmness of the *Sonata* at the end of the day, watching the light beginning to fade through his window, as slowly as snow melting.

He turned the record player off and went down the corridor.

'Come in,' Mr. Thwaite responded to his knock.

'Hello Banno. Haven't spoken to you for a while.'

Banno nodded. 'Could I ask you something.'

'Yes. Go ahead.'

'I happened to come across Goodmews Radio a couple of months ago, and *The Moon Quiz*. It's fun. I even knew some of the answers.' He half-expected Mr. Thwaite to congratulate him.

'You like quizzes.'

It sounded like an automatic response. 'Some of them,' Banno said.

'Why don't you try for it?'

'What, be on it?'

'Why not. It would be good PR for the Centre.'

'I could only answer a few of the questions.'

'We've got *sheets* of moon facts filed away. You can borrow them.'

It wasn't what Banno was ready for. He was still getting used to everything. And he wasn't there to do PR for the Centre.

'I'll show them to you. You'll be able to tell if you want to go for it.'

'OK.' He could at least borrow the papers, and ask his question later if he still wanted to. 'Should I get them from you at some point?'

'If I don't do it now, I never will.' Thwaite went over to his file cabinet and unlocked it, and took out a chunk of A4 paper.

'This should be more than enough to start with,' he said. 'See how it goes... I'll see you tomorrow.'

When he got outside the revolving doors, Banno set off on a post-work walk, crossing Copernicus Broadway into the quiet streets – the UNADOPTED streets, said the sign – where the pavements seemed to be a second thought, each one soon petering out into a mown green verge.

It was the end of one of those perfect Goodmews summer days of blue sky and mild breeze – a beautiful afternoon, beautiful neighbourhood, beautiful people. Banno scanned the sky and found the moon, just beginning its journey westwards, a waxing afternoon moon, as he'd learned. *It's how it should look. A half moon, mottled, with a bit of pink.*

Lately Goodmews had begun to feel less foreign to him. People-watching had become more interesting as the people became more familiar. He still enjoyed the purposeless pleasantness of passing strangers, but he mostly knew now where he was going.

'Woke up this morning, feeling fine…' he sang in his head. He knew the words; and though he knew he wouldn't get the tune right, the Hermits buoyed him to lightly traipse. He floated his arms over a stair rail, then when no one seemed to be watching he tried a couple of Gene Kelly leaping heel clicks.

He took out his radio, untwisted the cord and stuck the earpiece in his ear.

The transistor made walking life worthwhile. Even though the music that came out of it was tinny and in mono, the songs were the same, and in ways enhanced: with the sound in his ear, beginnings and endings were clear.

He found Goodmews Radio. He'd heard that it played people's suggested compilations, without ads, from 5 to 6. The Tin Woodman's 'If I Only Had a Heart' came on, lifting

Banno into longer strides but at a more relaxed pace, more suitable for after work than a fast song like 'Rebel Rouser' or something thumping that made him want to only walk soldierly. Even worse was a song that made him plod along, like the Temptations 'My Girl', whose lead-in always sounded to him like 'In *back*pack, in backpack, in *back*pack'.

What any music in his ear did, though, was lend even the most familiar houses or sights a new lease of life, so when he passed them he could view them from his world inside a soundtrack, almost as if he was invisible. He didn't know why, but this separation by sound made him feel the opposite: he felt more connected to the world. It was a less threatening place. He was unafraid of eye contact. Nodding along to songs, he could feel that he had that pursed-lip eye-squint look on his face, like he'd seen on other music-nodders, and it didn't matter if people stared back at him, even beggars. They weren't going to bother him; he was sorted, protected.

It all made for a happier world, one he felt more in tune with, and he'd stop to stare up at buildings, smell flowers, watch people's playful interactions – without having to listen to them: not their conversations, not the school kids, or parents talking to their kids. He felt as happy as a thirsty plant being watered.

Today, with few people around at first, he had felt the freedom to sing aloud to A Whiter Shade of Pale – off-key no doubt, but no one to worry about. Now, the pavement was getting more crowded. He moved aside to let a group of girls pass, four abreast with linked arms, a giggly gaggle that sounded like pigeons gurgling. Then a man passed him from behind, seeming to be humming harmony to Banno's music.

Copernicus Broadway approached, the constant car wheels loud on the tar. 'It's only nice to hear a road when you're lost,' Banno thought. He turned off his transistor and took out the earpiece, and put it all into his backpack. 'I can tell a polluted road when I smell one,' he said to himself, the fumes in his nose, the exhaust in his lungs.

GOODMEWS RADIO
CHANNEL 267.5
MEDIUM WAVE

He hadn't known where the station was, and went up to the building and turned the doorknob. It was open. He stuck his nose in and could see nobody. It smelled musty, like a second-hand bookshop with too many books. He saw a handwritten sign above a door:

WE ONLY PLAY ORIGINALS

The letters were written in psychedelic shapes filled with a paisley-patterned jumble of colour, like on the Byrds' *Fifth Dimension* album cover.

Banno realized that 'originals' was one reason he liked the station so much. Cover versions were almost always worse. How could they ever sound like they came from the heart, when the heart of the original was of a time as much as a voice.

He suddenly thought of the moon facts he'd shoved into his pack. He hadn't felt the papers when he'd put his radio in. Could they have come out? He checked. They were there.

A worker was talking to someone at the back of a van. Banno could see a smile budding on the listener's face, in anticipation of the deliciousness of being about to speak to someone who would listen and converse. He approved of that type of smile. It wasn't like a pasted-on one that he sometimes watched, to see how long it would remain on the smiler's face after the smilee walked on.

He turned back. He wasn't ready for the main road yet. He headed into the suburb – Cashew Quarter, as it had been nicknamed.

He felt out of place, like he was somewhere where people didn't use small change anymore.

The whole area smelled sweeter than the rest of Goodmews. The streets were tree-lined and with proper kerbs – sole-scrapers if need be, though he didn't see any mud around. There were wider, more beautiful front doors here – freshly painted, with their stained-glass window squares more ornately curlicued. The domino addresses were on bright blue backgrounds, except many of the houses had no address on them at all, only a name on a nameplate, like ORANGE WOOD COTTAGE. And most of the roads themselves had short, non-moon names, like Apple Walk, though there was an absurdly long one – KEPLER DRIVE TERRACE CRESCENT LANE ALLEY GROVE – and as he walked down it he heard piano drifting out of a house. What could be nicer than hearing that, or a floating violin, or sax.

He popped in to a shop – THE MEWSPAPERMAN. He'd done a double-take, but that's what it said. The man standing behind the till was, to Banno, 'of a certain age' and had a beer belly. Did he remind him of someone, like a teacher he once had? He wasn't sure.

He bought a small bag of roasted salted cashews, 'in the spirit of the place,' he said to himself, 'like Tris's shop sign.' Outside, he tore the packet open with his teeth and stuck his nose into the bag for that cashew smell. 'Feel hungry, like Johnny's sign.' He wolfed down the contents. To him, cashews were his happy food, the perfect blend of salty sweetness. They soothed his soul, like the doughy deliciousness of a fresh croissant or the healthy-candy taste of a good raspberry.

He tried to picture the mewspaperman's face again. It was distinct – sort of flattened or smashed – and he tried to re-evoke its features. Had he seen the man at the Moon Centre? Had he introduced himself to Banno? Maybe not. Maybe he'd never seen him.

For now, Banno needed to find a bathroom. He felt he'd developed a 'liquidity problem': pit stops – or 'piss stops' – seemed to have become the story of his life. Like a cyclist who gets to know a town's quieter back streets, he'd found the rubbish bins, the benches and the old mailboxes that still worked, and he'd also found Goodmews's free public toilets, though he'd made some mistakes: the occasional quirky symbols used for the men's or the ladies' sometimes defeated him; and one time, seeing BOYS on a building, he'd almost gone in before realizing it was a school and BOYS was just an old sign for the boys' entrance. He was sure there must still be undiscovered toilets, but who would be the sort of person to tell him about them? Other toilet searchers? He couldn't have asked anyone – he would be 'the guy who pees a lot', or 'Mr. Leaky'. What he knew, would have to do. He'd come to rely on the toilet map in his head he'd developed over his year in Goodmews. It was perhaps like the colour-coded Tube map that someone had once described as Londoners' collective unconscious. As a back-up, he'd discovered the bars he could nip into most inconspicuously, even though that usually meant threading his way through the patrons to use the toilet, if he could find it. He could never tell if there were unwritten rules about doing this, and he would never lie and say he was going to buy a drink. And why did they drink so much beer in Goodmews anyway?

He arrived outside what he'd read was the best public toilet in Goodmews, built around the same time as the church. He went down the stairs, bordered by black-iron handrails, into the large washroom, where he was unexpectedly greeted by the pleasing smell of fresh paint. It must have been water-based, as it simply smelled clean. Everything about the toilet felt welcoming – it was public, free, and even the black and white floor-tiles looked spick and span.

It was getting dark. 'It's Late' came to him – Ricky Nelson singing, 'Is that the moon I see... Can't be... Looks like the sun to me.'

A bus shelter appeared, a few hundred yards away. *Pollution-ville*, Banno thought. But to feel invincible, just for a day, was worth it, and he took his breath anyway.

He got to that key last stretch of pavement where some people might run, so as not to miss the bus. *Bus riders are punctual; they have no choice.* But he wasn't in a rush, and he knew Goodmews buses were frequent – sometimes he just jumped on one that wasn't going exactly where he wanted, because he might find a discarded copy of *The Occasional* to read.

The people sitting in the shelter looked, to Banno, as sad and intent as people who line up in a station, waiting for their train. As the bus approached, they rose to the road like a ballet troupe and waved it down, then began to board. He was about to follow them on, when he realized that he wanted a bus going the other way. He saw one across the road, indicating to move out. There was traffic in both directions but he judged that it wasn't going fast, and broke into a stop-start run, picking his spots between cars, looking up to see if the bus driver had seen him, finally getting in front of the bus so it couldn't move – as long as the driver saw him, which she did.

He boarded, to sudden noise. The world of the bus. Was it designed to annoy? Did babies cry more on buses here? Transistors louder than they had to be.

He placed the correct change on the driver's money tray and went down the aisle until he found a seat on his own. So many times in the past he had politely endured a seatmate's verbal onslaught until it felt like it was his turn to talk, only to realize that he'd got it wrong again: the person next to him couldn't stop talking, like someone who craves more food after eating something tasty. They hadn't been talking to him because they were a fan of conversation, but because they were a fan of their own voice.

Three people got on, one after the other, each with a cat box, probably going to the vet.

Everyone sat glued to their seats, with no choice but to wait. Then the bus was on the move. Banno saw that the passenger poles were white. He was pretty sure they'd always been yellow. The white made the bus feel brighter, fresher. Would the arrival of the first colour TVs next week have the same sort of renewing effect? He'd never seen one before.

High up at the front were signs: INSIDE VOICES PLEASE and NO EATING ON THE BUS.

It was a smooth ride at a decent clip – a one-banana-er probably, if one had been allowed to eat. It was so much more relaxing than needing to get somewhere on time then seeing that you might be late, the bus becoming your nemesis each time it stopped to pick someone up, always including the stop before you needed to get off.

Was the baby across the aisle looking at him? What could he do but half-smile back. Some days on the bus he felt like he was surrounded by strangers and not *of* the place; but today it felt good to be with people – Mewsicians of all stripes, going about their business, just trying to look presentable, and who would probably all help if anyone needed it.

He took out his book, thinking he'd never seen anyone get to the end of one on a bus.

'*Li*brary. *Gal*ileo Court.' The driver's voice sounded like a stadium announcer's – booming, with no emotion.

The woman across the aisle who'd been talking non-stop got up. As she got off, the man behind Banno, who had maybe been subdued, began to fill the vacated airspace. One of the new riders, an older man, sat down next to Banno.

'Next stop *Moon* Church.'

Banno could sense that the man was reading over his shoulder. He waited a while, then nonchalantly closed his book. Was it possible that the man had been reading at the same pace *he* was? He did recall seeing it happen at a museum, where the person behind the one pushing the NEXT button on a display seemed to be reading the information at the same speed as the button pusher.

'*Moon* Centre and *Fire*man's Cottages.'

Back home, Banno flipped through the first few pages of what Mr. Thwaite had given to him about the moon; it looked like about a hundred sheets of paper. He randomly spotted a couple of facts:

> If you drove upwards, at 60 miles an hour,
> it would take 6 months to get to the moon.

> More than half – about 60% –
> of the moon can be seen from earth.

This is fun, he thought, not like homework, not something I have to study. It's facts I can choose to look at if I want.

About halfway through the pile, Banno came to a page that said EMBARGOED in red at the top. He felt a gentle pulsing in his throat as he read the words in the middle of the page:

The Red Report
For distribution to KV only.
This report to remain classified until further notice.

What is *this? What is it doing in these moon facts? And who – or what – is 'KV'?*

What would someone else do, he wondered, if they came across this. Would they have a look, out of curiosity, even if it wasn't for them?

It didn't matter. It wasn't meant for him. However it had got into these papers, Mr. Thwaite had entrusted him with them. He owed it to Mr. Thwaite to do the right thing.

He flipped to near the end of the pile of papers, hoping he wouldn't see EMBARGOED.

He was safe; it was just another page of facts.

The moon is about one percent of the mass of the earth.

What's mass. Weight?

The full moon is about 500,000 times fainter than the sun.

He couldn't comprehend that.

What if he read the embargoeds?

He wouldn't. He didn't do what he wasn't supposed to do.

He turned on Goodmews Radio. *Five Everyday Enigmas* was almost over. He cursed himself for forgetting about the programme and missing the part where the Enigma Jury of three – a local comedian, psychiatrist and builder – discussed the most interesting responses to last month's posers. But he was just in time to write down this month's. He always enjoyed hearing them even if he never sent in any answers – what would he have to say?

As usual, this month's enigmas were read out, slowly, and the audience given their three weeks to mail in their thoughts.

'1. Would you rather sit next to a smelly person on a plane but still have your chosen window seat, or sit on the aisle where there's no smell?

2. What do you *not* do when you are out with your spouse?

3. On an evening that you're due to go out for dinner, would you rather have a headache and be hungry, or have no headache but no hunger?

4. If it was in your power, which regulation would you enact: eliminating small print in contracts, or outlawing prices that include 99 cents?

5. Would you rather stay home with worry and self-pity, or go out and be smilingly false?

6. Would you rather spill water over something electric and short it out, or have a mouse in your house?'

TWENTY-ONE

The week off had meant late to bed, late to rise for Banno. Every day, like today, he just lay there, post dream or post–drifting epiphany. *We want change,* he thought, *progression in our lives, so as not to be bored. But mainly, we want to wake up every morning at least as healthy as the day before, secure in the knowledge that our body is still OK.* It reminded him of the consistency of Big Ben in London: even during World War II, at designated hours, it still pealed live on the BBC.

The Moon Quiz was about to start. If he was going to try for it one day, this was a good way to learn. He liked the fact that the audience wasn't a whooping one and there were no prizes. And listening to the programme, instead of studying the facts he'd been given, meant he wouldn't have to think about avoiding the embargoed pages any more.

It sounded good. It would only mean a slight shift in his lunch hour once a week.

He'd confirm it with Mr. Thwaite.

*

It seemed to Sam that the inspiration for his final report-thoughts had been his recollection of an article about the Bulgarian artist Christo – if that was his real name. Sam had read it the year before, around the same time as he'd come up with his Moontown idea. There'd been a photograph of one of Christo's so-called art installations: ten giant inflated research balloons sitting on someone's lawn. At the time, Thwaite hadn't known whether to laugh or cry, but the incongruity of the construction had struck him.

Perhaps it was the memory of those balloons that had now engendered a number of phrases he might use, and over the week he'd whittled them down to four.

> A true new moon.
> A watershed in human history.
> Art on the lunar surface.
> A marriage of science and beauty.

He wasn't convinced about the history and the new moon ones; but what he and Kennington had masterminded would be at least a magnificent work of art, far grander than someone like Christo's.

He'd let the list sit on his desk for a while to decide which ones fit. Then he'd read the report for a final time and send it.

*

Francine was glad to have time to think about how she could give *The Occasional* a more homegrown tone, make it more small-town friendly. There could be a crossword about

Goodmews, rather than just the Mooncross. There could be interviews with Mewsicians, along with a photograph of them, giving their thoughts about the Goodmews moon like Sam had originally said he'd include. Maybe there could be a section on local crime, though not even mail in plain sight got stolen in Goodmews, and the only untoward incident she'd ever heard about was a policeman chasing someone up an alleyway who'd taken a piece of hose.

But it wasn't only the Goodmews paper that Sam had lost interest in. And had he ever been interested in Goodmews itself?

She was glad he had chosen it for his Centre and that he'd recognized the value of adding her scientific knowledge – not to mention her colour expertise – to it. But she wished he would have included her in his plans for what sounded like the Centre's most important event yet.

TWENTY-TWO
Tuesday, July 11

Thwaite answered his phone.

'Sam. How's the report.'

'Ninety-five per cent there.'

'OK. I take it you didn't need to phone after you got my fax.'

'No. It seemed to all be there. Thanks.'

'I do need it soon. This week. Noon Friday would be the latest. I'm intending to make it public when Surveyor lands on Sunday night.'

'Will do. I just need to slot in some final thoughts, information.'

'OK. If I need to see it sooner for some reason, I presume it's to hand.'

'Of course.'

'Where is it now?'

'Here in my office, locked in my file cabinet.'

'OK. Now, I also need you to do something else – a press release, to drum up interest before the landing. I need that by noon Friday too.'

'Alright. What should be in it?'

'Use the anniversary cover story – that's perfect. Take a few ideas from the report – some teasers to whet the press's interest. Say there will be a special colour, but nothing about it. I think the colour bit will be what attracts the most attention – as much as how we did it. The truth is, it will be unlike anything anyone's ever seen, and people should feel like they have to witness it, be part of history. But don't go overboard. The facts should speak for themselves.'

'Is the launch still scheduled for Friday?'

'Scheduled, yes; keep your fingers crossed.'

There was a hint of concern in Kennington's voice. He had always sounded cool-headed to Thwaite, even detached.

'Are there problems?'

'Not *problems*. But it's always a manic week before a launch, making sure everything's right. And I do still need to attach the moonstick. I have to decide which leg. There may be other instruments attached to one of the legs, though I'm not sure about that yet. There'll be a camera mounted somewhere, and also a soil-sampling scoop. It may be best to use one that nothing's on.'

'But the stick itself is ready?'

'Yes. And of course no one wants a delay. But things have cropped up in the past when the rockets were going through their final checks. Short circuits have been found, and there've been other snags, and they've had to take the rocket apart at the last minute to get at the faulty wiring or whatever else was wrong... But I do expect that Surveyor 4 will launch on Friday. It should be confirmed on Thursday.

I'll phone you then. For now, you need to do the press release.'

'I'm on it.'

Should he try to get a quote from a famous person? Someone from TV? Like *Star Trek*? Or *Bonanza*? Or a singer – Nancy Sinatra? But he had no contacts. And even if he did, no one would take the chance to endorse something he had to be sketchy about.

He wrote: Moon to be Greatest Show on Earth. Not a bad title, he thought. And a subtitle? International – inter<u>cosmic</u> news. No. A pivotal event. That sounded OK.

He should get it done before the day got busy. And it should sound more natural than the report, be less 'listy'. The best way to do that was on the fly, and without all the rigmarole of going into his file cabinet and digging out the report.

As he began to write the release, he realized just how well he knew the information. It was just a matter of stringing together the main ideas.

But was it all a leap in the dark? *Would* the stick get attached? And would the paint spread like Kennington said? Would he himself see it? And even if everything went as planned, what would happen to them? It was more than illegal to 'hitch a ride' on a NASA rocket. No one did that.

Banno closed his door for the day and went up the corridor. If Mr. Thwaite had gone to lunch already, he'd just remind Jan that he was going now, at noon as planned. But he hoped Mr. Thwaite was still there, so he could ask him his question.

Banno knocked at the half-open door, his heart pounding

lightly. Is he tired of my questions, seen me enough already?

'Yes?'

'Mr. Thwaite?'

'Come in.' Banno could see he was busy – his desk was strewn with paper, and his lamp was shining on his typewriter. Thwaite took his glasses off, which Banno hadn't seen him wearing before.

'Thanks for the papers you gave me to study,' Banno said. Thwaite cocked his head. Banno reminded him: 'For *The Moon Quiz* maybe one day?'

'Yes. Is that all.' There was no smile in his voice.

'I just wanted to ask you, Mr. Thwaite. Besides the papers, I've found that I can learn by *listening* to the quiz on the radio too—'

'Do we need to talk about this now?'

'Should I ask you tomorrow?'

'No, go ahead. Take a seat.'

As Banno did so, he watched Thwaite move some papers around on his desk, not even looking at him. 'Would it be alright if I took a different lunch hour on Thursdays? At 12 instead of 1? so I can listen to it? It doesn't seem very busy then.'

Thwaite's lip had snarled up, like it had got caught on a tooth. He looked back up at Banno, with a look of hate. His face relaxed. 'It's an odd request.'

'OK. I just… Does it really matter when my lunch hour is?'

'Everyone here works the same hours,' Mr. Thwaite shook his head.

'OK. Sorry.' He'd thought Mr. Thwaite would have been fine with the idea. Now he felt like he was being suspected of trying to do something underhand. Had he asked for something he should have known he wasn't entitled to?

He stood up.

'Before you go.' Mr. Thwaite looked hard at him. 'I don't really have time now, but as long as you're here, I need to say something to you. Sit down please.' Thwaite's voice was like a small battering-ram on the ear, and Banno inwardly cringed.

'I hear you chatting too much to visitors when you're supposed to be guiding them. Chatting is not part of your job. I can hear you from my office! How professional do you think *that* sounds? Do you want *every*one to hear you?'

'No.'

'You've learned the script, right?' Thwaite raised his eyebrows.

Banno felt like mimicking his words back at him. He wasn't a child, he'd done nothing wrong. 'Of course.'

'Good.' Thwaite's face had soured again. 'That's what you're supposed to do; not *chat!*'

Banno's throat felt hot. He felt he should at least half-concede something.

'Sorry.'

'Do you chat in public toilets?'

'No.'

'In public locker rooms?'

Had he ever been in one? 'No.'

'Well, that's how chatty you should be *here*.'

Banno felt like saying to Mr. Thwaite that he was sorry, but he wasn't perfect, but neither was the Centre – his window didn't open fully, the walnut cake in the café wasn't always fresh…

'I won't do it again.'

'That older couple you saw yesterday, from just over the border in Wyoming?'

'Yes.' Banno remembered them.

'After they saw you, they came to see me. You know why?'

Banno recalled that they had asked him if he'd recommend the Centre as a place to work and he hadn't known what to say. His job was OK, but he wasn't sure about Mr. Thwaite's occasional belittling of Francine over her 'hippie' church, and he didn't like the way Mr. Thwaite asked him the same thing twice in a row, as if he didn't trust him. The couple's question had reminded him of one parent–teacher evening when he'd taught at a difficult school. 'Would you send your own son here?' someone wanted to know. He wouldn't – if he'd had one – but he'd answered yes, probably in the same way he'd given this couple a noncommittal 'it's OK'. Had that made them wonder if something wasn't quite right at the Centre – or with *him*, and they'd gone to Mr. Thwaite?

'No.'

'When you asked them if they knew who Johnny Mercer was – which is fine, if you *know* how to ask a question – and they said they didn't, why did you tell them they should know? Do you remember that? Why would you say that?'

Banno shrugged. 'I thought they could tell I was just being friendly. Why didn't they say something to *me* if it bothered them?'

'People don't want confrontations – in a museum! You must know that from – ' his eyes widened – 'your "experience". I thought you had a lot of that!… I don't have to teach you how to *talk* to people, do I?'

'No.'

'And apparently they asked you if "Song to the Moon" – from *Rushalka*, they said – was part of the exhibition.'

'I'd never heard of it.'

'I understand that. Neither have I. But you don't have to tell them that you can't bear opera. They were offended. I was embarrassed for you.' Thwaite's voice tightened: 'But I'm more concerned about the Centre than about you. You are not here to make people feel stupid. Or to make *me* feel like a damn fool for hiring you.'

Banno couldn't think of anything to say. How could it be so terrible that he'd been a tiny bit honest with someone. It couldn't really bother Mr. Thwaite *that* much – *could* it?

'Do you need me to give your visitors a form to fill in? About how their visit went with you?.. Actually, I don't *want* your opinion on that, or on anything at this stage.' Thwaite took a breath. 'If I get another complaint, you're going to arrive at work one day and find someone else sitting in your stool. Do you understand?'

'Yes sir.'

'You *pos*itive? You know you work or you're gone?'

Had he read something about that? 'From Goodmews,' Banno said.

'That's right.'

'I'm not sure.'

'Have you been asleep for the past nine months?'

'No.'

'Have you heard of *The Occasional*.'

Banno barely nodded. 'I don't always look at it.'

'You better get a copy. Pronto. Last November's. You ever seen the library?'

It wasn't a real question.

'Never mind. If you could clean that stain off your lapel first. And close the door please.'

Thwaite looked again at what he'd written.

... and finally, when the Centre's second-anniversary celebrations do take place on Monday, they will feature an astonishingly beautiful colour. It has been created by the Moon Centre exclusively for the occasion. All will be revealed on the 17th.

It felt like a good ending. The whole thing seemed complete enough and, he was sure, had a more 'popular' feel than the report. The release could always be checked against it if he felt he needed to; later in the week he'd have to get the report out anyway to finish and send on to Kennington.

Was this good enough, though? Should it be checked for spelling mistakes and things like that?

It was something he couldn't have asked to be done with the report – that was detailed and confidential. But this was much more general, and it would soon be public anyway.

Was that proofreader around? Would he be available at such short notice?

Tris was making his bed when the phone rang – 'in mid-slipcover,' he said to himself.

'Hello?'

'Tris Palman?'

'Speaking.'

'Sam Thwaite here.' His voice sounded sharp.

'Yes. Hello, Mr. Thwaite.'

'Sorry for the short notice.' He spoke quickly. 'Can you come in tomorrow and do some proofreading.'

So soon? Maybe Francine's messages was enough work for now. But he was needed, by Mr. Thwaite.

'Do you have an idea of how long it might take?'

'The morning at most.' There was almost a snarl in his voice, but maybe it was just urgency.

'You want me to come *there*.'

'It's required. It's an official document.'

'Sounds fine. What time?'

'Nine.'

Tris knew that, like always, this would mean that his focus for the rest of the day would be on staying healthy and then getting a good night's sleep, so that when he presented himself at the Centre in the morning he would be able to concentrate.

'Fine. See you then.'

Maybe he *should* check the press release against the report, Thwaite thought, before having the release proofread in the morning, and he should stick that 'science and beauty' line into the report.

He went over to his file cabinet, unlocked it and reached into where he'd put the report. It didn't seem to be there. He went through the files one by one. It wasn't there.

It made no sense. Had he taken it out?

It had to be somewhere. It couldn't have just disappeared.

*

The lunchtime air smelled to Banno like chicken soup or Chinese food, or Chinese soup or chicken food. He smelled. His body was dirty. He was a weirdo, with stained clothes, like one of those bent old men searching gutters for cigarette stubs.

He didn't feel like going straight home, and walked the other way down Copernicus Broadway into a breeze that had felt invigorating that morning but was now a raw wind. He *tried* to do the right thing. Why wasn't that good enough?

People passed by. He crossed the road to where there were fewer of them and no shops, then turned up a side street that was empty and felt even more windblown, but felt right. The buildings were shabbier. He'd crossed some sort of undefined boundary and was on the wrong side of town, 'down in the boondocks', like the song said. It was a blacker street. Yes, there was the normal blackness of the parked cars' tyres, the lamp posts, the roof gutters, the drainpipes. But were there more black cars and black-painted doors than usual and more creosoted fences? Banno saw black roof tiles and black-smudged houses with their bricks painted black. The dogs were black; the cats; even the flowers. What were they, irises? He thought of the Los Bravos song 'Black is Black' – 'I want my baby back' – that had come out the year before. He'd seen in the paper just last week that their lead singer had committed suicide, at the age of 23, after his new bride was killed in the car he was driving. *The brain can't be repaired*, Banno thought; *the body often can.*

He turned round and walked quickly back towards the main road, taking his wallet from his casual back pocket – 'the mug's pocket', as someone had called it – and put it into a secure front one. He wouldn't be able to take it if another bad thing happened now. And if a third one happened…

The magnitude of power that people like Mr. Thwaite had over people like him was too great. He would never understand it. *Could I really show up at work one day and find someone else 'sitting in my stool'?* He'd thought that Mr. Thwaite trusted him, liked him.

He *had* heard something about having to work in order to stay in Goodmews, and he didn't need further confirmation; Mr. Thwaite wouldn't kid about something like that. *Were* there other jobs around? Would he be suited for anything else?

Down Galileo Court he saw the library. He walked the short distance and went in, and over to the Reference desk.

'Do you have the current *Occasional*?' he asked the seated woman. He thought he detected a look of concern as she handed him the paper.

He plopped down with it into a large brown-leather chair.

It was noisy; certainly not the library quiet he knew from back home. Older men sat at a table not far from him, chatting loudly enough to fill all the space around them, speaking English, but more like foreign babble. A group of teenagers, in an area shelved with colourful paperbacks, were talking almost as loudly. And little children were laughing, shouting – piercing the air like parakeets – in the *CHILDREN*'s section, a designation he'd never come across before and was sorry to see in a library. They weren't *singing* were they?

There was even a coffee machine in the corner. *Why?* It felt more like a place where people went if they wanted to meet up, or play, not a place to read and study or look for a job. It wasn't fair. Should he ask the librarian to tell people to be quiet? Or was that not the done thing for Goodmews librarians – none of them saw it as their job? Maybe they knew it was a losing battle. Maybe libraries were different here, and there was no Quiet rule, even unwritten.

But amid all the noise, it was warm. He flipped to the half page of Classifieds near the back. There were no jobs for Visitor Assistants, though why would there be? He'd never seen anywhere in Goodmews, besides the Moon Centre, where VAs might work.

In one ad, the word 'guard' caught his eye.

> DO YOU HAVE WHAT IT TAKES TO BE
> A SCHOOL-CROSSING GUARD?
> Can you help ensure that our children cross
> the road safely before and after SCHOOL?
> A bright orange crossing needs a bright crossing officer.

Banno had seen that crossing outside a school. He thought about having to deal with shrieking children every day, having to argue with motorists. No.

There were also cleaning jobs. Under HELP KEEP GOODMEWS SPOTLESS, there were vacancies for taking down notices stuck on trees, and there was an overnight kitchen-scouring job at Johnny's. But these were all part-time, not enough to live on, and they sounded like community service.

There were a few more jobs, including one to work in the 'stacks' in the basement of the library, to help sort and shelve books. They were all below his station, but who knew what the future held? He went over to the photocopier. As he was about to insert some coins, he saw that someone hadn't used their allowance up, and there was enough credit left to make a copy. Should he use their money? No one would ever know, and it was such a small amount anyway. Or should he tell the librarian?

He walked back and spoke to the woman who'd given him *The Occasional* and told her he wasn't sure what to do.

'Don't worry about it,' she laughed. She had that ratchetty voice of a smoker. '*Some*one's going to use it. It might as well be you.'

Banno retraced his steps to the photocopier, made his copy and went back to the woman at the desk. He looked again at the advertised library job as she was finishing her phone call. It was full-time. She hung up and looked at him. 'Yes?'

'Is this job still available?' He pointed at the ad.

'Preliminary interviews close tomorrow.'

'Could I do that?'

'Have you read about how that works?'

'I didn't quite get that far.'

She nodded. 'We interview prospective candidates to screen them before they make a formal application.' She looked at a list on her desk, running her finger down what looked like a class attendance sheet, then said to Banno, 'Would later today be possible for you?'

'OK.'

'Can you return' – she checked her watch – 'at three?'

'Yes.'

'See you then, Mr.—'

'Culdrun.' He spelt it out, with brief pauses between the

letters. 'C U L D R U N. Banno Culdrun.'

'Thank you. See you at three then.'

He passed the church and read the message on the signboard: TRUST DOCTORS, THEY'RE USUALLY RIGHT, and found himself on a road he didn't recall. He saw the street sign: METEOR AVENUE (LEADING TO METEORITE CLOSE). An 'Occ-hawker', he'd heard them called, was selling the paper up ahead – she must have been saying 'Occasional', but it sounded like 'Alume' or something else. Banno approached her. He knew they didn't like being asked directions, but he was hungry.

'Do you know if there's a place to get a hamburger or something, nearby?'

'It'll cost you if I tell you.'

He didn't understand.

'A dollar,' the woman said without a smile, 'or you can buy the paper—'

Was it a joke?

'—Or just the sports section if that's all you can afford today.'

It had to be a joke. Banno smiled, pretending he understood. 'I thought I'd heard there was one on Tidal Lane.'

'Yep. About halfway down, on the left.'

'Man!' he heard as he was walking away. 'Man!' It was somebody else, approaching him from behind. Banno stopped and turned round. It was a young guy.

'Do you know where G-Mall is?'

Banno felt he wouldn't be able to explain it – or couldn't be bothered; he wasn't sure which. 'I don't know.'

'Excuse me?' It sounded threatening to Banno. 'You

know where it is, man.'

'I don't.'

'How can you live in Goodmews and not know where G-Mall is?'

'Don't know.'

The young man stared at him. 'I need to get there and you know where it is.'

'I don't. Sorry.' Banno walked away. He wanted to look back at the guy, to see if he was looking at him, or following him, but it would be a too obvious show of concern. He kept walking till he found the hamburger place, but decided not to buy anything; he didn't want to be late for the library. He sat down on a nearby bench.

There was nothing he needed to do to prepare for the interview. Every couple of minutes, he looked at his watch, which confirmed, like always, that if two minutes had seemed to have gone by, about two minutes had. *'Time moves like a crab'*, he thought – *but don't they move sideways?* And were they *his* words or something he'd read? He got up and walked towards the library, then turned back and went up another road. It was like pacing back and forth, the same whether you were inside or outside, and he stopped.

He felt a tap on the shoulder and turned round. It was an older woman, a stranger.

'Are you lost?' Had she seen him walking aimlessly, and sidled up to him? Where had she come from?

'No.' He felt like crying. Her kindness had made the time-wasting walk worthwhile.

He was back at the library ten minutes early and caught sight of himself in the glass as he went in. Did he look scraggly? Would they be able to tell how dirty he was?

The Reference woman was still at her post. Banno stood in front of her until she looked up.

'Hello,' she said.

'I've come for the interview.'

'Yes,' she glanced down, 'Banno.' She noted something down. 'You have a few minutes, if you'd like to freshen up a bit first—'

'No. I'm ready.'

There was a pause. The woman stood up. 'If you could follow me, please, sir.' She pointed to a corner. 'If you could leave your bag there for now.'

He was led through a side door and then along a corridor that opened out into a large, bright, maze-like room. Doubles of desks faced each other in groups of four, the workers seated with stacks of files in front of them and separated from their colleagues opposite by make-do dividers. One or two looked up and smiled as Banno passed; most worked silently, looking down.

A telephone here and there pierced the air. Except for laminated notices the walls were bare. The whole room was fluorescent, without any shadow, and felt temperature-controlled. The windows were closed, to the world. '*Offices, cars and stores,*' he'd read somewhere, '*we spend too much time indoors.*'

The woman took him into a room where he was introduced to a man and a woman sitting behind a desk. He sat down in a chair facing them. Behind them, the wall was a window. He could see the desk-workers in the next room, but also a vague reflection of himself and the cloudy backs of the interviewers' heads. It was sort of an interesting halfway-world, but he didn't like it, didn't like having to stare at himself. But, he felt, they shouldn't need to ask many questions; this was only a preliminary interview, and he was obviously more than qualified for a job like this. Though what would he say if they asked him why he wanted the job? He hadn't thought about that.

The man smiled. 'How are you today, Mr. Culdrun?'

Banno looked down. Why do I have to answer that question? They want me to say I'm fine, but I'm not, I'm never fine. But they don't want the truth. Nobody does.

He nodded his head. *All I can give you.*

The next five minutes were nearly a blur. He answered their questions and then it was over.

Outside the library, Banno couldn't remember exactly what they'd said, except at the end they said they'd be in contact. And he couldn't remember all *he* had said, but somehow he knew he hadn't lied. He would never have let himself lie. Lying was being untrue to his heart. It was *using* his heart.

TWENTY-THREE

The sun had risen and the fog was dissolving over Goodmews. Scads of bright white webs spun in the night sat in still-dewy trees, as the last of the mist swirled about. It was so quiet it made Tris think that there shouldn't be cars here. *Such still streets are worth their weight in gold, worth the wait in gold.*

He recalled that the most pushed-out-of-shape person he'd ever seen in Goodmews was a neighbour honking his horn at someone who had double-parked.

It brought to mind his abiding memory of his first job, at the car wash, watching the inside-back-window-washer rounding off yet another eight hours of boredom. At the end of every day, the guy would be reborn, and with the skill of a bartender twirling bottles on high to pour out cocktails, he would prestidigitate his spray bottle and vacuum hose back onto their hooks.

Tris passed a hedge, shivering droplets in the wind, filled with so many – too many – twittering birds that they sounded almost electronic, then saw a bright flash of swooping parakeet-green. He rhymed to himself, 'Summer is coming, the birds are here, but I've lost my binoculars.' And he thought about the fact that, even with binoculars, he could almost never see those birds in a tree that people pointed out, because they were looking from a different angle.

A bunch of little birds flew out from the hedge and away. Tris stood and listened as the twittering faded. It wasn't quite the same as the farmyard noises fading out at the end of 'Good Morning' on Sergeant Pepper, where each animal is capable of eating the previous one. But not a million miles away.

He sat down at the bus stop. An airplane passed overhead, masking the occasional car but burying the birdsong. He caught a glimpse of the bus's reflection in a building's glass frontage as it rounded a bend a second before coming into view. He decided to walk. Most people wouldn't; they'd take the bus because it was easy and cheap. As always, he'd given himself plenty of time. He liked to be fifteen or twenty minutes early for appointments so he could just sit and wait, or walk around when he got there. His world was 'built 'round punctuality', as the Kinks song went.

He stopped at a sign in someone's front garden.

PLEASE <u>DON'T</u> STOP AND SMELL OUR ROSES

It sounded like an example of what could be on a list in a tongue-in-cheek guide to Goodmews: '15 Things Not To Do… 1. Smell the roses.'

Why would anyone have a sign like that? Tris said to himself. He was constitutionally unable to cruise by a rose without wanting to inhale its fragrance. The worst-case scenario for him – besides being shouted at for disobeying a

DON'T SMELL sign – would be a rose that had no scent. There was no point to such a flower.

He had a 'sig-nif sniff', as he called it; boysenberry?

At the Moon Centre he picked up a Bulletin, which he saw had come out that morning.

<u>Occasional Space Bulletin</u>
July 12, 1967

This is my first Bulletin as editor.

Tris looked at the bottom. It was Francine. She hadn't mentioned she was doing this, though he didn't think he'd seen one for a while.

To bring Goodmews up to date, in April two important Space events occurred. Firstly, NASA's Surveyor 3 landed safely on the moon. This was a great boost for NASA morale following the Apollo 1 tragedy in January. Secondly, NASA announced the astronaut names for what is again hoped to be the first successful mission in the Apollo programme to carry a crew into Space. This will be Apollo 7, the precursor to a future Apollo mission that is expected to put a man on the moon.

This Friday, the 14th, Surveyor 4 is due to be launched to the moon. Live television coverage is not anticipated, as no crew will be on board, but there should be TV reports later.

Mr. Thwaite emerged and led Tris to the room where he'd taken the test. He noticed that Mr. Thwaite was wearing black and white spats-like shoes. *Were they spats? Why would he wear them?*

The door, as Tris recalled from before, had TO KNOW THE MOON on it like the others.

He sat down at the table and could see there were only a few sheets of paper piled in front of him.

'Is it OK to use proofreading symbols? It's quicker, and neater. I can write down what they mean.'

'No it's alright. I'll work 'em out.' Thwaite headed to the door. 'Should I close it.'

'Please.'

The temperature seemed OK, and it was quiet. Tris laid out his ruler and pens and turned on the desk lamp. He counted the sheets – six – and placed them in a neat pile to his right, then took the top page and put it directly in front of him. *Do I go into my 'moon' phase now?* he thought.

Red pen in hand, he placed his ruler under the page's one line of text, which was in large letters. He repeated to himself a proofreader refrain:

'Oversized letters, must be checked better.
In books, they get overlooked.'

He read the five words carefully.

FOR DISTRIBUTION TO <u>KV</u> ONLY

The line was centred correctly and there were no misspellings. He didn't insert a comment, accepting that the 'all-caps' and the underlined KV were intentional. He had no idea who or what KV was, but that wasn't for him to know. He turned the page over and placed it face-down to his left.

At the top of the next page was TO KNOW THE MOON. He got up and opened the door to make sure the motto on it conformed to what he was reading, which it did – the same words, capitalized exactly as on the page. He closed the door and sat back down, and began reading.

Press Release
The Moon Centre's second anniversary
To be held Monday, July 17, 1967

There were five pages of text, besides the cover sheet – a pretty long press release. Tris let his eye wander down the page. It didn't look like it had anything to do with the moon, which would have been more interesting.

This Press Release produced by
The NASA Thwaite Moon Centre
Copernicus Broadway, Goodmews

In the right-hand margin, next to the first underlined line, he wrote a query – enclosed in a circle to indicate it was a query, not a correction.

Do the P and the R in 'Press Release' need to be capped? (as you have them). (They look OK and do conform to the caps in the title.)

He also felt obliged to query one other thing on the same line. He drew a slash mark after the first query in the margin, to indicate this was another one, which he also enclosed in a circle:

Suggest 'is' after 'Release'

A bit below this query, he drew an arrow to a vertical line he made next to the three lines of text and queried whether they really needed to be underlined.

Whether Mr. Thwaite would care about any of these finer points, he had no idea; most people probably thought that proofreaders only corrected spelling. But it was his duty as a professional to also suggest improvements. Like any client, it was up to Mr. Thwaite to accept or reject his suggestions, but that was of no concern to Tris; he had no investment in the release, no responsibility for it. Whatever the job – a book of trivia, a murder inquiry – he abided by the proofreader's credo: focus, without emotion, on clarity and sense. He'd never lost any sleep over the subject matter of something he'd proofread.

With deliberate concentration, he began reading the release – checking spelling, grammar and punctuation and that certain smaller things were correct: two spaces at the start of a new sentence; one space after a comma in numbers one thousand and above; and capital letters used only where they were needed, not randomly sprinkled about.

Over the first two pages, a brief history of the Centre was given and it was explained that there would be anniversary celebrations on Monday the 17th and that they would involve a special colour created by the Centre. That sounded intriguing. Tris had never heard of a new colour being created. He wanted to talk to Francine about it if he could; it would be *her* creation, wouldn't it?

On the final, half page, there was mention of a full report – The Red Report – that would 'expand on the above information'. The release ended with some words about how spectacular the celebrations were going to be.

Tris looked at his watch: just past eleven. He scanned the completed pages, a final check to see whether he'd missed anything, though he knew it was more for self-assurance – that he'd done all he could. Mostly, it was an excuse to dote on all his corrections again, so he could admire how many mistakes he'd found. The grammar and spelling had been pretty good, though; just the odd typo. And Tris doubted whether Mr. Thwaite would do anything about the couple of sentences where the meaning could be clearer, as Tris had pointed out. But it didn't matter. It was good enough. Most people just want the gist, quickly.

He gathered up his proofreading implements and the press release, and dropped it off to Jan in Reception before walking down to Songs and Poetry. He felt excited about seeing Banno again. They'd had fun talking about music that first time, and somehow he'd even understood Banno's 'cheeve me a chone'. So why had it been so long – months – since they'd seen each other?

Would they still have that connection he'd felt?

Tris had his piece of paper in his pocket with a few things he could ask him. And he could music-pun some more, like 'I hear you coughing, but you can't come in', if someone was waiting. *A friend is a person you can have pun with*, Tris said to himself. Would Banno cringe at something like that – or cringe at *him* when he took out his questions, like doctors do at 'patients with notes' or talk-show hosts at 'callers with material'?

Tris stuck his head in. Banno was eating from a small packet. Should he say something like 'How's it goin' Rowan'? Would that compute after all this time?

'Banno.' No one else was there.

'Tris. Good to see you again.'

'Cashews?'

'Yeah.' Banno put the packet in his pocket and stood up, glancing past Tris. 'How're you doing?'

'I'm OK. How are you, Banno?' Tris felt that he could almost have said, 'How ya been, Gunga Din?' But there was no need for that. The connection still seemed to be there, and normal was fine.

'I'm alright… Have you heard Goodmews Radio?'

'Sure.'

'The *Moon Quiz*?'

'No.'

'It's a programme on there. I might try for it someday. Mr. Thwaite's given me a stack of moon facts to study if I ever went for it… Let me show you the poem.'

Tris followed him as they walked across the carpet, wondering which poem Banno meant.

'Have you heard that Bee Gees album, Tris, that's just come out?'

'It's great.'

'I agree. "There's a light…" ' Banno half sang. 'Pops into my head. It's the beginning of one of the songs. I can only remember the early part.'

They'd picked up from where they'd left off. 'Like only being able to remember those first seven words of *The Declaration of Independence*. Me too.' Tris raised his eyebrows about a tenth of an inch. ' "To Love Somebody".'

'That's it,' Banno smiled. 'I can never remember the words leading up to that bit.'

Tris nodded. 'And the one with "I walk the lonely streets"? – "I Can't See Nobody".'

'Beautiful voice.'

'Indescribable. Though—' Tris took his wallet out and the piece of paper he'd stuck into it – 'someone said, "It's a voice that's been aged in the depths of emotion, and now on tap for us – a voice that goes from plaintive to 'plaintiff' ", if you can get that. I'm not sure which Bee Gee it is though.'

'Robin.'

'The one with the big overbite?'

'I think so.'

When they got to the far corner, Banno cupped his hand above his mouth. 'Mr. Thwaite,' he whispered, 'told me he could hear me chatting to people when I was supposed to be showing them around, and it wasn't professional.'

'When did he say that?'

'Yesterday.'

'Oh.' The way Banno said the word jumped out at Tris – he'd pronounced it without the 'r', like the Beatles sang it. Was it an affectation he'd picked up from the song? Maybe he'd just heard it around – some Midwesterners said it like that – but Tris couldn't recall Banno having dropped the 'r' in other words. It made Tris think of something else, but he couldn't remember what.

'You better not stay too long,' Banno said. He was looking towards the door.

'OK,' Tris kept his voice down. 'I can see Mr. Thwaite sounding *irr*itated. Was he angrier than that?'

'He was pretty het up about it. But it's no big deal.'

That sounded a bit too off-handed to Tris, and he wondered if he should ask Banno more. 'Where's he coming from? It can't matter that you were chatting, can it?'

Banno's answer was a grumble.

'Banno. Do you think he was serious, that it was that bad?'

'He didn't like it. I even checked out a job at the library afterwards. My name's mud.'

'Your name *can't* be mud. You didn't do anything.' Tris couldn't know this for sure, but he wanted to let Banno know he was on his side. 'Maybe he's just so busy that he doesn't want to have to think about anything else.'

'That's not how Mr. Thwaite sounded. I'm sure I'm not even supposed to have told you what he said. The oath, you know.'

'I'm sure it's alright. But he'll never know.'

'So, were you seeing Mr. Thwaite again?'

'I guess I'm not supposed to say this either... I've just proofread a press release about the Centre's plans for the anniversary?'

'I don't know about that.'

'You don't?' Did that make sense, that Mr. Thwaite hadn't said anything about it to Banno?

'Nope. Maybe Mr. Thwaite's going to tell me later.'

'Can I just tell you? You're not going to tell anyone.'

Banno said nothing. He wasn't saying no.

'It's on July 17th.'

'Hmm.'

'And it talked about this Red Report that said more?'

Banno looked at him, then spread out his hands. 'You better go before Mr. Thwaite comes along.'

'Yeah. But that doesn't sound so nice, about what happened.'

'I'm OK. See you later.'

Tris emerged into a changed day, T-shirtible sunny. The sky's declouded, he mused, the trees' mist deshrouded. Something was off. Banno had seemed much more distant than when they'd first met. Had Mr. Thwaite said more to him than he'd let on? It must have been bad enough, for him to check out a library job. Had Banno kept his own counsel – like an injured baseball player who maintains his tough façade by refusing to rub – because he and Banno weren't close enough to confide in each other?

But they'd connected the time before, hadn't they? Maybe Mr. Thwaite hadn't said anything more than what Banno had told him. But why hadn't he asked Banno to tell him more? He tried again to recover the thought he'd had when Banno said 'Yesterday'. Did it start with a 'T'? Did it have something to do with 'Yesterday'? It was a short phrase, a few words. But it was no longer on the tip of his tongue. It felt like it had gone into a spider web in his head, or maybe to the back of his tongue, and he knew if he didn't get it soon, it would be gone, as if swallowed into a point of no return. *'Things We* Didn't *Say Today'!* That was it. Like a Beatle song reversed.

He passed the hedges wainscotting the pavement, fronting people's houses – *houses cosied up,* he thought, *private with their privet hedges.*

He saw that familiar hedge ahead. He neared it, as always, in anticipation of its sweetness; but as often as he'd passed it, he still hadn't identified its scent. In the same sort of sense-preparing way that he primed his ears for an upcoming rock concert – by lying between speakers that were blasting out music – he flexed his nostrils with deep nose-inhalations. It was like sniffing at someone as they approached, though with a person there was no certainty they'd smell sweet. He got alongside the scene of the scent. It was still there, Olympically sharper, stronger, tarter – than a daffodil?; but as he walked past it, savouring the nose-mecca nectar, he still didn't know what it was. He passed a corner shop with its name on a bright pink hoarding above it: SORRY FOR ANY INCONVENIENCE. In the shop window it said YOUR LOCAL CONVENIENCE STORE. *No need to apologize,* he thought. *Thank you for spelling it right.*

Francine would want to know that he'd got the job and what it was about, and she'd no doubt know more about the anniversary than Banno did. And the colour.

Tris could see that the church scaffolding was gone, even above the doorway.

He saw the week's message –

THE ORANGEWOODS: TOOTHPICK BEHEMOTHS OF SILENT GRANDEUR

– and climbed the church steps. He hadn't asked Francine what the message meant or where it came from when he'd proofed it; he didn't really care, and that wasn't what he was being paid for. But he liked the sound of it.

Dropping by should be fine.

The door was open; wonderfully, church doors were always open. Tris walked in, and down the middle aisle. He remembered the church as being dark and dreary. Now it felt light and airy. The ceiling was a sky blue, and there was a black and white chequerboard pattern on the floor that he didn't recall having seen before. *Was the church this quiet?* he wondered. *I think I prefer complete quiet to birds, the next best thing. But is that like death?*

He went over to some round orange plaques on the wall. Like on many of the road names, they had birth and death dates, and here also what the person had been remembered for – teaching, nursing, hod-carrying. Locals, he assumed. Commemorative stained-glass windows were at a low enough level to read. None of the words needed correcting, but the messages were boring – words of praise for founders. There was nothing about becoming a Moon Church.

On one wall he saw a couple of photos. One looked like a black hole, with furry whiteness around it. It was next to an information sheet in a frame.

SOLAR ECLIPSE

A <u>solar eclipse</u> can only occur on the night of a <u>new moon</u>. A solar eclipse occurs when the <u>moon is between the sun and earth and blocks the sun</u>. A <u>solar eclipse</u> can only be viewed from a relatively small area of the earth and lasts for a few minutes.

Next to it was a photo of what looked like an orange full moon.

LUNAR ECLIPSE

A <u>lunar eclipse</u> can only occur on the night of a <u>full moon</u>.

A <u>lunar eclipse</u> occurs when the <u>earth</u>
<u>is between the sun and moon</u>.
A <u>lunar eclipse</u> can be seen from anywhere on the night
side of the earth and lasts up to two hours.

'Let's see,' he thought. '*Solar* eclipse is when the *moon* is in the middle. *Lunar* is when the *earth* is. So, when is which in the middle. "SMiLE"?: Solar – Moon; Lunar – Earth?'

He saw a poem on the wall.

CHURCH GOING, BY PHILIP LARKIN, 1954.

Tris had never heard of him. He read, down to

WHEN CHURCHES FALL COMPLETELY OUT OF USE
WHAT WE SHALL TURN THEM INTO...

Into moon churches? – like this one

> *with its church spire*
> *Its hurt spire*
> *Once* his *spire, to inspire*
> *Now* her *spire.*

Tris glanced at the walls. There wasn't a clock anywhere, and he wondered if that was so people couldn't keep glancing up at the time when there used to be sermons. Maybe *she* gave sermons and, like in his Claite class, it would seem longer if there was a clock you could keep checking to see if the sermon was nearly finished.

'Tris!' Francine's clear, strong voice startled him. Did it

mean 'Are you supposed to be here?' She must have come out of a back room.

'How's it going?' she said.

'Fine. How's *colours* going?'

'Good, thanks.'

'I wanted to ask you. You know the pedestrian crossings around town? You did them, didn't you?'

'Yes.'

'And other colours.'

She nodded.

'I was wondering what colour you would call the crossings.'

'I'd say it's poppy red… Do you know about minium?'

' "Minium?" '

'Yeah. I've always liked it. It was a poppy red colour used for the paragraph signs and capitals in medieval manuscripts?'

'I never heard of that.'

'I thought you were a proofreader,' she smiled. 'They're in those beautiful colours with those beautifully shaped letters.'

'I do current stuff?'

'I know. I'll just tell you. One of the things I learned in my colour course was that the people who applied minium were known as "miniators".'

'OK. Can—'

'And,' she interrupted, 'these miniators also ornamented the manuscripts with small illustrations that were known as…?'

'I don't know.'

'Miniatures.'

'Oh!'

'So, what were you saying?'

'Can I ask you something.'

'Of course.'

Tris followed her and they sat down on a pew. Hung on the back of the row in front of them were blue cushions embroidered with different moon phases.

'I just finished some proofreading for Mr. Thwaite?'

'Great! You passed the test. How'd it go?'

'It was alright… Can I ask you something about it?'

'Are you supposed to talk about it? You took the oath, didn't you?'

'Yes. I'd never tell anyone that we spoke about it.'

'Do I need to know?'

He wasn't sure if she was irritated with him or if this was simply that pleasing, scratchy-throated female–Jim Morrison voice of hers.

'Can I just ask you?'

She was either internally frowning at him or thinking about what to say.

He thought of adding that – according to its date – it would soon be public knowledge anyway.

She shrugged. She wasn't saying no.

'It was a press release – about the anniversary on Monday?'

Francine looked surprised. 'I knew Sam was planning it, but I didn't know it was happening already – or there was a press release about it.'

'You're not involved?'

She shook her head. 'Why are you so interested? It's just a proofreading job, isn't it?'

'Yes. But it talked about a special colour created by the Centre for the anniversary, and I was just curious, and you've done all these great colours around Goodmews… I've never heard of a colour being created and it sounded fascinating, so I just wanted to ask you how that's actually done.'

Francine looked down, then back at Tris. 'I haven't heard about this press release, and I think you know that I can't really talk about how I've created the colours, because they're trademarked, by the Moon Centre.'

Tris felt his heart fluttering. Why he had the bit between his teeth he wasn't sure, but why wouldn't Francine know about this press release to do with a Moon Centre colour? He searched for some non-committal words to camouflage the mini-debate inside him.

'It sounds like *Banno* didn't even know there *was* an anniversary,' he said, and scrunched up his nose. *Yes, I told Banno too.*

She looked contemplative.

He had to ask.

'Francine,' he said, almost obsequiously, 'I also asked Banno if he'd heard about this Red Report that was mentioned in the press release.'

She spoke steadily: 'Tris, I feel uncomfortable that you're breaking your oath with me. I'm sure you know that you're not supposed to talk about anything that goes on at the Centre – with anyone.'

He felt slightly wounded, but he knew he'd overstepped his bounds. And Francine was the sort of person who was so far above board that it wasn't fair of him to have said anything.

'I'm sorry. I think I was asking about this Red Report because it sounded like it might turn out to be more work.'

'Not your favourite thing.'

271

'Well, at least not that sort. I'd rather proofread solid objects.'

She nodded.

'And I've known proofreaders who've retired, but because they'd worked on some ongoing project earlier, they were still expected to be on call if more work had to be done on it. And some of these projects have gone on for years afterwards… Anyway, Francine, I mainly wanted to say thanks for getting me the job, but I also wanted to see the church. It's interesting what you put up about eclipses.'

'Find any mistakes?'

He half-snorted. He was thankful she wasn't angry with him. She'd opened the door to normal chat again, and they could now leave behind the negativity he'd brought into their conversation. He thought of the words to the Keith song '98.6': *'Hey, ninety-eight point six, it's good to have you back again.' Square one, as dull as it might be, is fine if you've been on minus square one.*

'Can I ask you one thing,' he said.

'Course-ya-can,' she rushed out.

'You're not also a vicar or a rector or something, are you? You don't give sermons, do you?'

Francine laughed – loudly, sounding in the church almost as raucous as one of those sudden, chorused guffaws you hear bursting out from a table of people who've drunk too much. 'No,' she said. 'You know there's nothing religious about it, don't you?'

'I guess so. But would you call it the Moon Church if it wasn't in a church?'

'No. I'm not sure what I would have called it, but it would have been something to do with the moon.'

'But it *is* sort of churchy, with your messages, isn't it?'

'It's a tradition I've kept up. They're just quotes I like. I like quotes.'

'So do I. I like aphorisms.'

'They're good, yeah. Do you know Thomas Huxley's one, about natural history?'

'No. I don't know anything about natural history. I don't even really know what it means. Is it knowing the names of things in nature?'

'That's *some* of it.'

'I never tried to learn it. I know the names of a few plants and flowers. I like colours. That's about all I can relate to. Sometimes I can't tell the difference between real flowers and fake ones. I probably couldn't even tell if a green tree was a painted one or a real one.'

Francine made a slight groan. 'Well, *I* don't know how to proofread properly. Anyhow, Huxley said something like, "Not knowing natural history is like walking through an art gallery with half the pictures turned towards the wall." '

'Like Johnny's should be.'

She laughed. He was glad he'd been able to tap her funny bone. 'Or,' he said, 'like walking through your neighbourhood and not knowing the names of your neighbours?'

She nodded. He could hear the humming sound she made when she was thinking.

'So, since you liked the stuff about eclipses, do you want a few more moon bits?'

He *might* remember. 'Sure. I *am* in Goodmews.'

'Well, we see the moon, like the sun, rising in the east

273

and setting in the west.'

'OK.'

'In reality, the moon only *looks* like it's doing that, because the earth is also turning eastward, but much faster.'

'OK.' It was too complicated for him to picture. He looked beyond Francine and could see into the back room and lots of little paper-squares in different shades stuck on the walls. They reminded him of the multicolours of jockeys' jerseys or those of snack packets one sees inside overstocked corner-shops.

'So,' she was saying, 'even though the moon is moving eastward around the earth each day, it has a "net" motion – as my teachers put it – towards the west each day. So, for us here on earth, it "rises" in the east and sets in the west.'

'OK.'

'Do you know what the moon is tonight?'

'You mean, like full or not?'

'Yes.'

'No.'

'Have you looked at it recently?' she smiled. He'd noticed before that her smile was slightly pained.

'No.'

'Well, you wouldn't have seen it for a few days because it's "new". Tomorrow should be a – beautiful – sliver if the sky's clear. Do you know when a new moon happens?'

'Once a month?'

'Yes. And it rises at sunrise and sets at sunset. Do you know *how* a new moon happens?'

'Not really.'

'Should I tell you?'

'Sure.'

'It's when the moon is aligned between the sun and earth, and the nearside – the side facing us – is totally dark. It's invisible to us because the illuminated side is facing away.'

'OK.'

'Last fact.'

Tris nodded. He couldn't take much more moon information.

'At a new moon, if you were on the moon, you could see a full earth, which is eighty times brighter than a full moon.'

He thought about how bright a full moon was, especially in Goodmews. 'Are you sure?'

'Yes. And in two weeks—'

'It'll be full?'

'Yes.'

'I liked your latest message,' he said. ' "Behemoths". What *is* that?'

'I don't know. Somebody had written it on a piece of paper I found when I first came here, tacked onto an orangewood. It might have been one of the hippies before they got kicked out. I like it too, whatever it means.'

'I haven't been up there. What are they?'

'They're giant conifers, and their needles turn a coppery pink in the autumn.'

'Sounds beautiful.'

Francine seemed to be leaving him space to say more. When he didn't continue, she asked, 'So what else have you been doing besides checking my messages for me?'

'I also play this game I invented,' he let drop.

'You invent games? To make money?'

'No no. Just something I play against myself.'

'OK… What *kind* of game?'

'It's a dice game. Two teams take turns. I roll the dice for each of them and record their scores, and the highest total wins.'

'Is that a "game"?'

'It's fun,' he shrugged. Should he tell her more, give her a sense of who he was – how he liked adding up the numbers, and losing himself in familiar statistics?

'You don't play with anyone else?' Francine's voice had gone harder, like burnt toast, and it sounded almost judgmental.

'There wouldn't be any point,' he said, like it should be obvious; but he was defending himself – he didn't want her opinion, it was *his* game.

He tried to sound unfazed by her comment. 'It's just for me. It's relaxing.' But he knew that his game did more than just relax him.

He waved his arm around. 'I see the scaffolding's come down. Someone will have to change the Welcome sign.'

'That's true.'

'I better go. See you later.'

'See you soon.'

Francine creaked the wooden door shut and leaned against it. Why hadn't Sam told her that the anniversary was in a few days? She'd been involved with just about everything else – at least she thought she had. He'd asked her to make the colour – the 'centrepiece', as he'd said.

It wasn't right, her being kept out of the loop – even if the 'loop' was only Sam.

But what bothered her more was the feeling that now niggled at her, the feeling of thinking less of someone. She tried to dismiss it. Maybe he'd forgotten to mention it and was going to tell her. She didn't want the situation at work to become like what sometimes happened on her road, when someone said something inconsiderate to her and she felt she should force herself to stop smiling at them. While it could be a relief not to have to continue feigning a friendly smile, she always found it too stressful, and preferred to out-nice the neighbours, even if it made her feel 'over-communitied'.

She'd ask Sam about it soon, and about something else she now realized – Surveyor 4 was due to land on the moon the day before the anniversary. If there was some connection between the two dates, why wouldn't he want to use the knowledge she had about the moon in planning the celebration?

She tried to forget about it and whatever this press release was, that Tris had mentioned. Big deal – why should Sam have to include her in everything. She'd made the anniversary colour, yes, but it was just part of her job.

Without Tris though, she realized, she would never have known about the press release. So when he'd told her about his game too, should she have shown more interest, been less dismissive? But he seemed OK.

TWENTY-FOUR

Banno made his way through the revolving doors. The sky was clear but it had gone surprisingly cold for summer, and he'd been caught out. Like most of Goodmews, because there had been the promise of sun breaking through the thinning morning fog, he'd dressed lightly. That seemed to be the way here – people judged how warm to dress not by checking the temperature but by looking to see whether there was sunshine or the promise of it.

He turned up the yellow walkway to his cottage. *I'm glad I told Tris about Mr. Thwaite. I should have told him more. He would have wanted to know.*

Inside, he switched on the TV. A terrible programme was on. He went through all the channels. Kid show after kid show. The only thing worse was animal programmes. But mainly there were ads.

He went back to the first programme, just as it was finishing, but before he could turn off the TV, the ad came on and he heard 'Colours come out bright, whites come out white, as white as your baseball team's home uniform.'

He didn't want these false promises, these false smiles, the fake lilt in the voices in TV ads, in his head. Why would anyone want them? They seemed like something that should have been relegated to the past by now. Wouldn't people look back on this era and wonder how they'd still been such a TV staple? Just like someday TV might only be something for children.

He turned the sound down and flopped onto the sofa with *The Occasional*. He turned the pages quickly, though it was hardly worth the time.

He would have liked to fall asleep, then wake up and have dinner, but his thoughts returned to Tris. *Yes, it was wrong that he broke his oath. Should I have told him that I'd seen the report? No. That would have broken* my *oath.*

But Tris had confided in me, even if he wasn't supposed to. Was he maybe a new friend? Did I owe it to him to at least have a look?

Banno went over to the dining table and sat down and pulled his chair in. He flipped through the sheaf of moon facts until he got to the first of the pages he'd ignored before, with EMBARGOED in red at the top.

The Red Report.

He turned the title page over so it was blank-side up and looked at the next page.

After a journey lasting 62 hours, NASA's Surveyor 4 touched down on the lunar surface just after 8 P.M. Eastern Standard Time tonight. This soft landing was a crucial step for NASA in its quest to put a man on the moon by the end of the decade.

So that's what's happening. Must be for national security that this is embargoed until it happens.

But this mission also carried with it a spectacular surprise. As the culmination of a year-long project directed by the Goodmews Moon Centre—

This was about the *Moon Centre*?

—and known not even to NASA until now, a radiant paint was hidden inside a 'Moonstick' affixed to Surveyor by NASA rocket engineer Kennington Varnen. This paint, a powdered mixture of gold colour and 'star spangled' minerals, is now being spread over one of the moon's largest craters, Mare Imbrium, that many see as the Man in the Moon's right eye.

What?

In two weeks, soon after next month's new moon becomes visible, something never before seen in human history will begin to appear – a glowing, golden,

'Painted Moon Desert', that will be visible with the naked eye from earth.

What was this? Was the Moon Centre *painting the moon?*

This exceptional sight will become part of our new night sky. Every month, everyone on earth will be able to watch a golden moon waxing and waning before their eyes.

He looked at the next page. It was the end of the report. At the bottom was a signature. It was Mr. Thwaite's.

Banno's mind had turned up its own transformer, like a toy electric train pushing itself faster and faster down a runaway track, no brakes, wind at his back.

Was this real?

He forced himself to focus, slowing his mind down until, like steady puffs of smoke, it returned to normal thoughtspeed.

He looked back up to the top of the page.

Each night for two weeks, the colour will expand little by little until the moon is full. Then, as the lit part of the moon decreases each successive night, so will the gold.

Why had Mr. Thwaite written this? And why would he put it in with the moon facts? Was he testing my trustworthiness, to not read it? No. It couldn't have been put there deliberately; he gave me the facts spontaneously, after we talked about the quiz. So, it was a mistake. But why would he want to paint the moon? Is that possible? And isn't the Centre all about appreciating it? All those songs. All those facts. Have they just been a cover? It seems crazy.

Banno couldn't recall if he'd even heard about this upcoming launch on the news. He made himself look through the pages of the report, and he was pretty sure he got the main point: a unique paint, created by the Moon Centre, had been secreted inside a 'moonstick' by a *NASA rocket engineer* – he mouthed the three words – in order to get the paint up to the moon.

He read further.

When the Moon Centre was founded two years ago, few people outside the Space programme could have envisioned what was about to be realized in Space exploration. Many incredible events have happened in the last two years, including the first spacewalk and, last year, the first soft landing of an unmanned spacecraft on the moon. But until now, there has never been man-made colour on the moon.

At the end, it said that it was the Moon Centre's hope that their achievement would inspire new wonder at the heavens, especially in the minds of the next generation.

Banno's eyes wandered to the wall, to the corner where the paint was peeling, with faults running up to the ceiling like cracks on a dried-out bar of soap. Then he looked at his Cezanne calendar, in the middle. He'd often thought about replacing it with just a picture, something he didn't have to flip every month. Though somehow, without a changing calendar, it would be a deader wall. He looked at today's square – July 12th. Wednesday.

He slipped The Red Report back into the stack and straightened it up.

Why had he read it. Why had he broken his promise to himself not to, to not do what he wasn't supposed to. If he couldn't trust him*self*, why should *any*one trust him? He was as bad as the rest of them. A liar, to himself.

So, what was he supposed to do now? Could it just go away? Could he forget he ever read it and not say anything? It was like when someone doesn't apologize for doing something wrong – because that would just bring up the incident again.

He didn't *have* to tell anybody, *did* he? No one would ever know he'd read it. But he had; how could he *not* tell someone. And how could he *not* tell someone that the *Moon* Centre was planning to paint the moon. Was it?

Who could he tell? NASA? Could they be in on it? Thwaite was part of NASA. So was this engineer. Was the Moon Centre a front?

Which is more right? Keeping one's oath – one's word – and not saying anything? Or telling someone what the world might need to know, now – before it happens.

An image of Cinderella's coach turning into a pumpkin at midnight came to mind, then Jackie DeShannon singing 'What the World Needs Now'.

He grabbed his jacket and went out.

He passed the Centre; dark, closed for the evening. *Tris would want to know, and he'd want to do something about it if it's really happening.* Banno sang to himself, *'Five to two, I feel blue. Has anyone seen my pal.'*

He turned down Crescent Crescent and stood outside Tris's flat. *We are the only people we've met who seem to like to have met us. He'll be glad I looked at the report. He'll know what to do. He broke his oath to tell* me *something; I can do the same for* him.

I can't. I'm not him. I keep my word.

I have to get away.

What would I do if he came out of his flat? Maybe he's out and on his way back. Is that him? Is that *him? Should I go up or down the road? Against or with most of the walkers?* Banno knew it didn't matter; either way would get him back to Copernicus Broadway and on his way home. But which way? It was like being in a department store and not knowing which escalator went which way.

He doubled back up Crescent Crescent and turned the corner into what was usually that warm bath of the familiar shops of his everyday walk, then passed the Centre again. Ten to seven. *Tidiness* would be starting soon. He felt tired. His cottage would be cosy. But at his yellow pavement, he continued walking, west. He passed the last shop and he was the only walker. He zipped his jacket up and turned right, up Orangewood Drive. A car passed him from behind, then one came from ahead, the driver giving a small-town wave. Banno didn't return it. Who was it anyway? He'd never seen the man anywhere – as well as one can tell who someone is through a car window – certainly not in Songs and Poetry. *Why should I wave back to every tomdog and harpie?*

As he walked, the looming gloaming cast a gloomy light on the low cloud bank; slipping up from behind it, the moon made a surprise entry into the fading blue. It was bigger and brighter than he had wanted, or expected – it bulged like a hernia, hanging in the heavens. He stood still and stared. He could easily make out the grey splotches of the Man's face –

he was lying on his right side, sleeping, or snoring. His eyes were vacant but he was open-mouth carolling, or choralling. Banno sang, to the tune of the Teddy Bears' song, 'To know, know, know-ow it…' 'To paint, paint, pa-int it…'

Was it possible? The moon being painted. The moonbeam painted. Tainted. Why would anyone want *to? Why* should *anyone?* The Centre's slogan came to him: 'To Know the Moon'; *'To* Own *the moon'?*

Greed springs eternal. Can Mr. Thwaite – Mr. Paint; Thwaint? – really be planning to paint *it? Do I care? I should. It's not right. Should I ask…* Thwaite *if it's real?*

I can't. I'm not supposed to know.

It must be, if it was embargoed. Should I do something about it? About the liar?

No plane, no more cars, Banno thought, as he stood there. *No noise is good noise.* The breeze whistled through the trees. *There isn't wind on the moon, is there. But if there was, is this what it would sound like? Like that instrument – a harp, that the wind played? A lyre? Liar! What did the moon ever do to you, Thwaite? What right do you have to paint it?*

The music had disappeared; besides the easy breeze through the trees, Banno's pulsing tinnitus was the only familiar sound he could hear. *You can close your eyes,* he thought, *but even with earplugs you can't close your ears if you have tinnitus.*

He listened to the silent frequency his ears dialled as the clouds coalesced into a monkey face, staring skywards, puffed against the blue. Banno saw it was his own face, and a dark cloud of hair drifted over his deep forehead. He lay in state as his features emerged – his pointy nose, pointing up, his eyes closed to the sky. His mouth was opened in *The Scream,* then disappeared in the cloud.

His stomach was clamming up and he felt queasy, like he was below some horizon. It reminded him of the shallow nausea he sometimes felt in a mechanized car-wash, when he was stationary in his car but felt like he was moving forward.

The nausea passed. The blue was fading. He tried to visualize the speed of its fade; it was as slow as a moonrise behind a tree in full leaf.

The moon went into its swirl of clouds, then came out again. *Mister Misty Moon Blight.* Banno pushed on; he had to walk. *Azure; as you're walking.* Or cooking – *What's a pinny for; What's a pinafore.* Could he smell bacon, then sweetness in the air? Did that betoken senility, he wondered. Or was it some plant he'd never heard of? Like a 'pork 'n' taffy' bush? And when would it ever be moondown?

Suddenly some orange trees towered up ahead. He stared at them. They were unlike anything he'd ever seen – behemoths, with their limbs etched in soft twilight, sloping down like a witch's cap. The ear-buzzing he'd been hearing grew intermittent. The wind came up, then died, the louder wind gone.

The trees were beyond a stone wall. He walked step by step towards something iron in the corner and saw it was a stile. *That's a good thing,* he thought. *To cross a bridge when you come to it.* He went through the stile and into the darkening grove. He could smell some moist decay.

A piney orange peace descended on him. He walked off to the left, singing… 'Where seldom is heard, a discouraging word, and the sky is not cloudy all day.' He went down a slope to one of the giant trees, and stroked its feathery bark, so unlike the scaly alligator bark of other trees he'd stroked. The girth of the trunk was massive, too big to hug, but it contained a hollow, large enough to hold a human. He peered inside. Was it fire-blackened? He couldn't tell. It was empty. It was tempting. 'Orange tree, oh so pretty,' he sang, 'and the bark is oh so sweet, but I just want to get back home and have some thing to eat.'

He went quickly back to the stile and through it to the road. The clouds had gathered again, but the moon still kept them light, at least for the moment. He began walking. He wasn't sure, but as far as he knew this was the only road. Up here, where he'd never been, felt like some alien world; but he was going downhill, so it should be the way he'd come. He walked faster. He had to get back before the clouds went heavy and it got too dark.

When he saw the lights of Goodmews, Banno realized that his back was wet. He reached his yellow path, night-bordered in turquoise cat's eyes, which he didn't recall ever noticing. There was a comfort in being back in his cul-de-sac, his 'cluddy-sac'. He didn't know the people but he knew the contours. *It warms the cockles of my feet*, he thought, and was soon inside his cottage.

He'd left the TV on, with no sound. *Lucky Choice* had just started! He'd watched it enough to know that the ad break always came after a certain number of rounds; he'd be ready to switch off the sound when that happened, and keep it off until the type of ad came on that would be the last one before the show resumed. He turned up the volume and sat down on the sofa.

The pace of questions, as always, was lullingly calm, the presenter pleasantly chatty with the panellists – the sort of quiz show one could nap to. But then it all seemed to accelerate. Before Banno could try to answer the question, the presenter said the answer, and before he had a chance to consider the answer he'd just heard, the next question was being asked. He found that he couldn't tell which panellist was sitting to the left of the presenter. It was a physical blind spot – the person was like an upper-body illustration without a face. The questions and answers continued to pile up, foaming into a tsunami that began to roll towards him, growing even larger, then towering over him like the Japanese painting he'd once seen of a giant wave; and his need to sleep began to leave his engaged brain behind. He got himself up and turned off the TV and slopped back onto the sofa. He thought of those times he'd done something stupid, like bending the wrong way and hurting his back, or inhaling too much dust, and in one second his whole world had been turned upside down, in a way that couldn't have been thought of 24 hours before, when life was fine. Was it too late? Had he entered a halfway house, like books do when they're stored in a room after being read, a room that their owner doesn't always realize may be their last before they're taken away?

It felt too warm but it wasn't so warm. He was sweating, then he felt cold and made sure his jacket was zipped up, making him sweat more. He wiped his wet forehead, and closed his eyes. He needed sleep, but he knew he'd rather be up all night worrying about what might happen in the morning than have whatever it was happen without his having thought about it. But he'd decided. He couldn't work for a liar.

Which is the higher truth? Being honest – telling Mr. Thwaite what I read, but that I will keep my oath and never divulge anything? Or saying nothing.

TWENTY-FIVE

The sun had materialized. Banno recalled a dream thought – 'Before the words filled the bottom of the bath, I stopped reading.' He could make no sense of it but it proved to him that he'd slept. He still had some sleep left in him and tried to climb back into the dream, but he couldn't. His open eyes burned. He closed them and tried to find their sweet spot to stop them burning, but that didn't work either.

*

Thwaite let the phone ring. It would be Kennington. Maybe he should have told him he hadn't been able to find the report, but it didn't matter now. The rewriting was almost done.

He swivelled in his office chair and picked up the phone.

'Sam? Moonstick's attached and authorized secure. Launch is confirmed for tomorrow.'

'Great.'

'The report?'

'Is tomorrow still OK?'

'It's not finished yet?'

'Just about. I've got the press release too. I just want to finish checking it against the report. I'll send them together. And I've got the names and num—'

'Junk the release.'

'Oh. OK.'

'So much going on. Too much. But I realized we don't need it. Since we'll be publishing the report Sunday night, all will be revealed then. I should have told you earlier. Hope you didn't spend too much time on it.'

'No.'

'So, tomorrow at noon.'

'Yes. Noon.'

'Good… NASA's almost there. There's still the rocket trajectory they've got to be sure of because it's similar to the upcoming Apollo flights. Like always, there will need to be a mid-course correction, probably sometime Saturday night. Surveyor's got to be at a particular speed at that point – 2,630 miles an hour – and on a direct course to the moon.'

'Is that expected to go smoothly?'

'Yes. Everyone hopes they learned from Surveyor 2. Its mid-course manoeuvre failed, and it spun out of control and crashed.'

'Yeah.' He recalled Ray at NASA saying something about that.

*

Keys in pocket, feet in shoes. Can't work for a liar. I'm better than you.

Banno was out of his front door, tightly clasping the

sheaf of moon facts, with the report in the middle. *Have to give it back. He won't know, he won't look.*

Banno's stomach froze. *No job means no Goodmews. But I want to be here. I can't. I can't work for him.*

No turning back.

If he tells me I can't resign? I'd have to run. To where?

*

'Morning Banno,' Jan greeted him.

'Is Mr. Thwaite in?'

'He'll be here' – she looked at her watch – 'in ten minutes.' She said it like a dental receptionist who tells you what your check-up and X-rays just cost with a straight face.

He took a seat, and let his eyeballs shift up and down, right and left, in time to the ticking clock on the wall. His front teeth were clamped together and he felt like he was in some sort of frozen narrowness, needing to wait in stillness. *I shouldn't take the sheaf of papers in. What if Thwaite leafs through them, or remembers he put the report inside? Then what could I do. Would I have to tell the truth, and say I read it?*

He had to get to his room. If Thwaite asked about the papers, he'd tell him they were there. But by the time Thwaite looked, he'd be gone, free.

'I'll just be a few minutes.'

He saw Francine's back as he passed her room, and kept moving down to Songs and Poetry. He closed the door behind him, then went over to the desk, knelt down and shoved the stack of paper under a pile of folders in the bottom drawer. He whispered to the room: *Thank you for my time here, and for meeting Tris.*

He walked out, and back down the corridor.

'Francine.'

'Hi Banno. How are you?'

She was so normal. He wanted to be normal, in the comfort of her normality. 'Can I close the door?' he managed. 'Thw— *Mr.* Thwaite's not here yet.' He felt like he was sitting on a box in outer space, cut off from the world.

'Sure. You OK?'

'I want to apologize for smiling with him when he mocked your church that first day.'

'Oh. Don't worry about that. That's just Sam.'

'I'm quitting.'

'What? Why?'

His bladder of truth he'd been holding in was full. He had to let its honesty – his confession – gush out, for Francine to receive. He had to tell her what he knew about Thwaite, that the evidence was in his room. *Don't I have to be honest? Without that, I'm nothing. Don't I want to live the way I would want to be on my deathbed? – honest, no longer needing to protect people by not speaking the truth?* But he couldn't get the words out, like that time in the hospital that he couldn't pee and they wouldn't remove the catheter and let him go home until he did.

'It's not right for me,' he said. '*You* love the moon. Nobody else here does.'

'Nobody else loves the *moon*? Do you want to sit down, Banno?'

No. I want someone to know me.

But if you're not honest, how can anyone really know you?

'I have to see Mr. Thwaite. I hate liars. Mr. Thwaite—'

The door opened. Banno snapped his head towards Thwaite in the doorway.

'You wanted to ask me something?'

Banno nodded.

'If you could come to my office – now.'

He got up and followed Thwaite out of the door, not looking at Francine.

They sat across from each other.

'What's up.'

Banno kept his eyes down. Could he do as he'd planned?

'I'd like to resign,' he mumbled.

'What?'

Banno raised his head. 'I'd like to resign.'

'That's what I thought you said. What are you talking about?'

Banno's heart was pounding but he said nothing.

'You putting me on?'

He felt like a criminal in a police interview who would refuse to answer any question.

Thwaite pushed his chair back from his desk and stood up. 'Why. I'll give you five seconds to explain.'

He jabbed his finger towards Banno. 'I don't have time for this.' His voice was rising like an announcer's in the last furlong of a horse race. 'Get out of my office! Get out of your cottage!' Thwaite looked at his watch. 'By 10 A.M.'

Banno stood up and walked to the door, Thwaite shouting after him, 'You're in trouble. No one's going to give you a job in *this* town. Goodbye Goodmews for you.'

Thwaite's voice was near his back as he walked from the room.

'What a goddamn waste of space you've been, you useless oddball. Get out! Francine!' Thwaite stormed into her room. 'Banno just walked out. He just quit… Who does he think he is?'

'Something's wrong,' she said quietly. 'Just before you saw him, he told me he was going to.'

Thwaite raised his eyebrows.

'I don't know why,' she said. 'All he said was that no one else here besides me loves the moon. I don't know why he would say something like that.'

Thwaite shrugged his shoulders.

Francine decided not to mention what Banno had said about liars. 'Did he tell *you* why he was quitting?'

Thwaite slightly shook his head, but he didn't seem interested. 'What are you doing this afternoon?'

'Nothing special.'

'Good. I need you to fill in for Banno. Can you do that?'

'OK.'

'And till I get somebody. I'll get the script to you.'

After Sam had gone, Francine tried to think why Banno hadn't wanted to say more about why he was quitting. Then she wondered vaguely if Sam was planning to replace him before the anniversary. It was only four days away now – though she still had no idea what it entailed.

*

Banno crammed what he could into his backpack and tied his sleeping bag to it, then swept the kitchen floor and closed the windows. *Hope has moved out on me.* But he had nothing against his cottage. He would leave it tidy.

294

He picked up his guitar case and walked out of his door and up the yellow path. What would he say if someone asked about his overstuffed pack or where he was going; questions were stabbing probes to his soul. No one ever seemed satisfied with his answers, but he couldn't sugar-coat them with white lies: the god of whole-truth-and-nothing-but-the-truth could be waiting to smote him.

No one was around. Goodmews felt like some abandoned place in the middle of nowhere. He felt rudderless, like in the song, like 'some ol' engine that's lost its drivin' wheel.'

Where was he going? He had nowhere to go, nowhere he *had* to go.

Then, what was the point of being here? What was the point of being anywhere? What was the point of anything?

He was alive, yes. But so what? So he could wander, and beg?

He sat down on a bench and closed his eyes. 'Many manys ago,' he thought.

Why should he ever open his eyes? He'd seen everything before.

He got up and walked. A bearded man in a baseball cap who looked around 40 was walking towards him. Banno wondered if either of them recognized the other. The man made a hand motion to his mouth, and Banno instinctively touched his own mouth, thinking a crumb might be there, but he didn't feel any. The man reached Banno and said something like 'you look displeased', in a slightly aggressive way. Banno continued to walk, faster, turning around after a minute or two. The man was far away now. He looked back at Banno. It was unnerving, and Banno turned back to continue in the direction he'd been going. Nothing looked familiar. It was like being in a taxi in a city he'd never been to. He had no idea where he was.

TWENTY-SIX

Tris finished proofing Francine's four 'F'-initions, as he called them. He'd drop them off after saying hi to Banno. He wondered if his run-in with Mr. Thwaite was still bothering him. Perhaps Tris had read too much into it.

He went through the revolving doors and down to Songs and Poetry, and peered into the room. Francine was sitting on Banno's stool. Tris felt a shock run through him.

'Francine!'

She turned towards him and stood up.

'Tris! Hi.' She had that pained-smile look. 'I'm glad to see you.'

'Is Banno not around?'

She raised an index finger to him to say Just a minute, then moved to the door and looked quickly up the passageway. She turned back to him and said in an almost conspiratorial voice, 'He left this morning. I'm filling in for him.'

'Did something happen?'

'He quit – this morning.'

'Why?'

'I don't know.'

'Did you see him?'

She nodded. 'Just before he did.'

'He didn't say anything?'

'Nothing about why he was quitting. He sort of mumbled something about nobody here loving the moon except for me, and something like "he hates liars".'

'What does that mean?'

'I don't know… Then Mr. Thwaite came and they went off. Did he say anything to *you* when you saw him?'

'Not really. He did tell me about a disagreement he had with Mr. Thwaite, but it didn't sound bad enough to make him *quit*… Did he tell you about that?'

'No.'

'It was just that Mr. Thwaite had spoken to him about chatting too much to visitors.'

'Why should that be a problem?'

'I don't know. But it didn't seem to bother Banno *that* much, at least as far as I could tell.'

'Still not nice for him.'

'No. Should I see if he's home?'

'I've checked.'

'Which is his cottage?'

'Number 2. But he's not there. I could see through the window that his stuff is gone.'

'Already?'

'You can't live there if you don't work here.'

Tris nodded. 'Will you let me know if you hear from him?'

'Of course. And vice versa. For him to quit, and give up his cottage – and his job…'

'Where could he go?'

'I'm not sure.'

'I've done your messages. Should I leave them with you?'

'Yeah.'

'Your handwriting's nice. I have to make sure I concentrate on the actual words.'

Francine laughed. 'OK. I don't think you've missed anything.'

'No, really. It's beautiful. Do you know where you got it from? Is it just natural? or were you taught it like that in school.'

'Calligraphy was part of my Colour Science course, and I suppose I've just kept it up.'

'And you *are* an artist.'

'I don't know about *that*, but thanks.'

People were wearing coats just because it was cloudy, but to Tris it felt warm. A woman looked like she was wearing a tent. It was a raincoat, but it wasn't about to rain. Far ahead he could see someone from the back in a long black coat. He didn't recognize the person, as he didn't know anyone who dressed like that, but he'd always wanted a long black coat.

What could have happened? he thought. He didn't know Banno well, but who knew what went on in someone else's life, in someone else's mind. Mr. Thwaite couldn't have said something so awful that made him quit, could he have? That couldn't be it, could it? Was Banno that sensitive about what people said?

*

Banno had wandered for hours, a guttersnipe, a slug, leaving an aimless silver trail of slime on the pavement. The job! He found his way to the library.

A different woman was at the desk, filing some index cards in what looked like a shoebox.

'Hello,' Banno said to her.

She looked up. 'May I help you? We're closing soon.'

'I was interviewed for the basement job last week?'

'OK.'

'Can you tell me when I'll hear back.'

'It normally takes two weeks.'

'Can you let me know now? I'm not sure where I'll be then.'

'I'm sorry, sir. We won't have a decision until next week.'

'I need to know!' He heard his voice booming out in the hush.

'Please keep your voice down.'

'Why! Everyone else shouts in here!'

The woman glanced to her left and right.

'What does it *mean*?' Banno pleaded. 'They said they'd be *in contact.*'

'I will have to ask you to leave, sir.'

'Why!'

She looked at him as if to say, 'If you don't leave now…'

He was beaten.

He went up the steps to where he knew Francine lived. I'll be welcome here, like at the library. He tried the locked door, then put his things on the ground and crouched down to look through the keyhole.

'Banno?' came a voice from behind him. His heart pinged like a tiny sledgehammer and he didn't know whether to look round or run; he was a rat caught in headlights. He was off limits.

He stayed half-crouched, frozen, coiled to spring at whoever it was if they got closer. He looked back slowly. It was Francine. She was dressed in orange, in some striped bedsheet. A muumuu, he realized. Why wasn't she wearing her uniform? He'd always had to. 'A moo moo here,' he said to himself, 'a moo moo there. Here a moo, there a moo, everywhere a muumuu.'

'Are you alright?'

He thought of the Bee Gees' words: 'Can't you see what I am?' Why does she have to ask?

He slowly stood up, but spoke looking at the ground. 'I need a place to stay.'

'Let me let you in.'

He moved aside as Francine took a large key from her bag and unlocked the door. 'Come this way,' she said, too smoothly for Banno's liking, and led him down the aisle. There were moon maps on every wall, like pictures of Christ, watching him. At the end of the aisle they got to a small corner room, and Banno put his pack and guitar on what looked like an army bed.

'Can you use your sleeping bag for tonight?'

He had no words for this woman. *I've just arrived. I don't like questions. And what's with that stupid dress. Does she think she looks sexy in her stripey clothes? Or they make her look young? Does she think she owns the place? Standing there guarding me like a priestess?*

He knelt down and began to unroll his sleeping bag, watching her at the open door out of the corner of his eye.

'Too much discussion,' he mumbled.

'Banno… I can try to help you.'

He stood up and moved towards her and took hold of the doorknob. 'I'm going to bed.' Francine backed out of the room, letting him push the door closed. A few seconds later he opened it. She hadn't moved. He backed back into his room and shut the door.

*

Francine dialled.

'Tris. Banno's here, at the church.'

'Oh! That's good.' He wondered for a moment why Banno hadn't come to *him*. 'Did he come to see you?'

'He just needs a place to stay.'

What would he have done if Banno *had* come to him?

'How's he doing?'

'He looks scruffy. I think he'll stay here tonight.'

'It's good of you to take him in, Francine. Thanks for letting me know.'

'Can you come here tomorrow, if he's still here?'

He *should*. They'd been getting closer, *hadn't* they? Banno had confided in him – only yesterday? – about being chewed out by Mr. Thwaite. And he'd told *Banno* about the press release. So why hadn't Banno spoken to him before quitting? – this morning.

'When would be good?'

'Call me in the morning. I'll know more what's happening.'

Francine heard shouty singing and guitar chords being strummed – slashed – echoing out of Banno's room. She

302

thought he'd gone to sleep. Quietly, she moved to his door. The music stopped. She waited a few seconds, then knocked tentatively.

The door was thrown open, back towards Banno, giving her a start. He had a quizzical look on his face and a pen and piece of paper in his hands.

'I just wanted to see if you were OK, Banno.'

'Sure!' There was a hint of a smile on his face. 'I'm writing some songs about what's been happening to me.'

How could he suddenly be so bright and positive, she wondered.

'Are you feeling better?'

'I'm fine!'

'Did you want to play anything that I could *listen* to?' It had sounded rough – wild – both his voice and the playing, but it was clear that music had been a tonic for him.

His half-smile vanished. 'Can't you tell I'm practising?'

'Sorry. Yes.' She took a step back in her mind, but then she had a thought.

'Banno. If I could suggest something. Would you want to do some busking of your songs outside the church?'

Banno cocked his head, like a questioning dog.

'It's church property. You'd be allowed to do it there.' He was listening. 'I've never heard you sing – your voice sounds strong.'

'I know.'

'You could probably make some money.'

Banno stared at the – priestess, the princess, the goddess, who'd pulled something rare and beautiful out of a hat. *My new songs. For the recognition I deserve. And the money.*

'That's a great idea,' he said. 'When?'

'You could give it a go – tomorrow.'

'When.'

'After work might be best – about five?'

'Someone from the Centre might see me.'

'Mr. Thwaite?'

Banno nodded. 'Eleven… I have to practise.'

'Are you hungry?'

'No.' He felt like shoving her out of the doorway, but began to close the door instead. She stepped back, and he closed it.

He sat down on his bed. What could he say?

Then he got the greatest idea he'd ever had.

He began to write the song, to the tune that had been swirling round in his head all day.

It will all be between the lines, and only for those who stop and listen, and only for those who want to understand. I won't be revealing anything. I won't be breaking my oath.

I will astound and enrapture, with the sound of a master.

Tris's phone rang. '… I heard him playing his guitar,' she said quietly, 'and told him he might want to try busking tomorrow, outside the church.'

'Was he playing for *you*?'

'No no. He was in his room. He didn't want me there… It didn't sound good, maybe it was out of tune, but I think it would give him some confidence, maybe even be a way to make some money.'

'I hope you didn't push him too much. He sounds fragile' – *probably more than I thought.*

'I didn't. He wants to. He said he'd written some songs about what he's been going through… It's the first time I've seen him even coming close to a smile since he got here.'

'That's good. Maybe it'll help. Maybe we'll find out why he quit. It seems crazy. Did you know he was thinking of trying for this *quiz?* Do you know about *The Moon Quiz,* on Goodmews Radio?'

'Yes. Banno wanted to be on it?'

'He was thinking about it. And he said that Mr. Thwaite had given him a stack of moon facts he could study.'

'Mm… ' she stretched out the sound, then completed the phrase: '… hm', transforming her reaction, in Tris's mind, from 'I'm not sure about that,' into 'That sounds sort of interesting.'

'Anyway,' she said, 'I think this will be good for him, but also a friendly face would help. I haven't seen anyone busking in Goodmews since the hippies. I don't know who would stop and listen… Can you make it tomorrow? I think around eleven he'll be there. I'm working.'

'Sure… It seems like a long time since I saw him. I hope Mr. Thwaite doesn't come by.'

'Me too. But he's usually here for most of the morning.'

Tris stared at the flaking patch of paint on his windowsill. It looked like Banno's face, fissured, like a Mount Rushmore head.

Maybe he'll sing 'To Love Somebody' and I'll join in, show people I'm his friend. Stick in a couple of my lines for fun? –
'There's a bench, a certain kind of bench, that never sat on me…'

Should I have tried to look for him after he quit, see if I could help?

There's so much more to the world – people, sunshine – than sitting in a room and playing a game. Friends matter, you realize when you get out.

TWENTY-SEVEN
Friday

Thwaite grabbed the phone on the first ring.

'Morning,' Kennington said brightly. 'You saw the launch?'

'Yes.'

'You're sending the report at noon.'

'Yes. And the phone numbers of the radio stations and wire services. To "Private. For Kennington Varnen".'

'First-rate. If I think you need to know anything, I'll tell you right away. Otherwise I'll phone you when they do the correction, to reassure you that everything's on course.'

'Thanks.'

'It *will* be tomorrow night, but I don't know just when yet.'

'I'll be here.'

*

Tris stood leaning against a wall. He glanced up now and again to make sure he didn't miss Banno. He'd taken out his notebook and held his pen. He could see himself looking like a gunslinger of words, poised and ready to write, his notebook deholstered, his pen drawn. There was no one else around, but he could also imagine a bunch of scribbling note-takers standing alongside him, targets of an anti-intellectual firing squad. But how can anyone remember anything without writing it down?

Banno picked up his guitar and left his room. He went down the aisle and out of the door and sniffed at the air. Goodmews smelled like dirty potatoes, like a foreign city. He knew he looked cool, in his shades and baseball cap, like someone about to jump into their woodie and drive down to the ocean, like the Beach Boys on their album cover, like he was a surfer.

He saw Tris.

What are you doing? Taking notes so you can tell the world that I know about the report and I lied? I'm not lying anymore. Cheeve me a chone.

What should I start with? The Beatles.

He saw Banno coming down to the last step and sitting on it, his feet on the ground. Banno took his cap off and placed it next to him, upside down – for coins, Tris assumed. He wanted to let him know he was there, but Banno was already strumming, his head down, and he didn't want to interrupt him. Would he be any good? Tris had seen so many singers busking back home and they were almost always too young, or too loud, or too derivative. But sometimes a good one came along.

Some of the people walking by stopped. The strumming grew louder, and most people walked on.

Banno began singing, booming his voice out.

'Listen… Do you want to know a secret?
Closer…'

He broke off and looked around, his lips pursed, his eyes wide and smiling, as if he really had just revealed a happy secret.

Most of those who had stopped were drifting away. Maybe they'd thought that the music would be relaxing. Others passing by didn't even look at Banno. Tris had wondered if he would be as bad as Francine had said. He was. He was like a support act that isn't good enough to be a support act. But Tris felt proud of him. He was brave to face the world like this.

He began strumming again, then slashing at his guitar and launching into a shouty, off-key rendition of 'California Dreaming'. The tune was pretty close but the words were different.

'Stopped into a libe
that I saw in town.
Got down on my knees
and they chucked me out…'

Tris wondered if that was what had happened at the library.

Banno had stopped again, in mid-flow.

Tris saw a young girl with her parents drop some coins into Banno's cap as they left.

'Thank you!' he shouted; then to no one in particular as far as Tris could tell, he announced, 'A couple of moon tunes now', and began singing Moon River, then stopped, and stood up for the first time.

'Some of you may know. I used to work at the Moon Centre.'

He began to sing again, a different song.

> 'I was weak
> as a breeze
> and I never
> saw it coming…'

– the tune, Tris recognized, was 'Till There Was You' –

> 'No I never
> saw it at all
> till there was Moon –
> Centre.
>
> There were trees,
> orange trees,
> but I never
> saw it coming.
> No I never
> saw it at all
> till there was Moon –
> Centre.
>
> There was Mo-oon
> and wonderful whiteness…
> till, one day
> all of the brightness…'

He broke off again and seemed to look around, nodding

here and there. It hadn't sounded too bad to Tris, but why was he changing the lyrics to all these songs?

He was humming, then in a plaintive, flattish voice he sang,

> 'What if you hated the moon
> and couldn't look at the sky
> or see the Man in the Moon
> or the Man's right eye…'

What was he talking about, Tris wondered. Who would hate the moon? And what was with not being able to see the Man's right eye? Just to rhyme with 'sky'?

> 'There's a light…'

That sounded like a song…

> 'A certain kind of *moon* light,
> that never shone on me…'

Banno trailled off, from his own beginning of To Love Somebody.

'You don't know what it's like.' He said the words, not singing them. Then he shouted 'This is it!' Did that mean this was the end?

He began to fingerpick, as best he could, the classic double-bassy introduction to 'Stand By Me'. Tris remembered once seeing a decrepit-looking man who was grudgingly allowed to join a park basketball game, emerging like a chrysalis, outplaying everyone. That was what came to mind as Banno began to sing, caressing the words with a gentleness he hadn't heard before.

The song, everyone knew, was about the moon being the only light in the dark night. Banno finished a verse, and continued strumming in the same rhythm without the words, and then began to sing again…

> 'When the moon, was white,
> and people, didn't lie
> and send, their colour up above.
> No I won't, be afraid
> when the moon they paint…'

Those were the strangest words yet.

> 'Blue-oo Mooon…' –

he launched into, in tune –

> '… and when I looked,
> the moon had turned to gold.
> Blue-oo Mooon…'

He began singing bits of the Beach Boys' 'In My Room', about being alone in the dark but not being afraid to 'tell my secrets', until he trailled off and sat down, to a smattering of applause.

Tris walked over to him, wondering why he had kept chopping and changing, singing half-songs and jumbling everything up, when he could have finished each song, holding his audience with that voice he'd found.

'Banno?'

Banno looked up at him, but Tris couldn't see his eyes under his sunglasses and couldn't decide where to look. Maybe Banno thought he was looking at his lips, which he didn't want him to think because he was trying not to. But, he thought, what else can you focus on besides someone's eyes?

Banno looked back down. 'I can't listen to you,' he growled.

'Banno—'

'Don't follow me!' He grabbed the coins out of his cap and put it on. *His brim of protection*, Tris thought – *'The Eve of Destruction', the song that had defined 1965. Did it define Banno now?* He was up the steps and back into the church.

*

Thwaite fed the ten pages of the report into the fax machine, one after the other.

*

Tris could see the Moon Centre up ahead. Even if Mr. Thwaite saw him come in, he couldn't know Banno had just busked. And he probably didn't even know that Tris had ever spoken to him.

He was through the doors and waved to Jan as he walked by. 'I'm just giving something to Francine.'

She was standing near the Songs and Poetry window, looking out.

'Francine?'

She turned round. 'Tris!' she said, then dropped a grape on to the floor.

'Whoops!' It was his Pavlovian reaction, like 'gesundheit' to a sneeze; he'd even once started to reach through a shop window when he saw a tray inside falling down.

He watched her pick the grape up – a green one; he'd thought in the last week the reds had begun to outsweet, outcrisp them. She walked over to him, rubbing it, and put it in her mouth.

Brave Francine eats a grape, he thought. He would never have done that; he couldn't recall ever having eaten anything after dropping it. A corn nut once? Maybe it would depend on how valuable something is; he'd probably pick up the world's best cherry.

'The floor's not dirty?' he said. He was reminded of a friend he'd travelled to Europe with who'd defied the odds by having ice cubes in his Coke in a town where the water was said to be dicey.

She gave Tris an *Are you serious?* look.

'How did it go?' she said.

'Well, he did it. He seemed almost in his element. But something wasn't right. I tried to talk to him afterwards but he just went back into the church.'

'That's too bad. I hope I can see him when I get back.'

'Good luck… He sang OK. But the whole thing was confusing. He sang some moon songs he must have learned here, and some other songs, and some he must have made up, that didn't make much sense. But he didn't finish any.'

'Maybe he was trying different songs to see how it went – a collage or something?'

'Naa. It didn't sound like anything as planned as that. He stopped in the middle of *lines*.'

'Were people listening?'

'Not many.'

'Because of his singing?'

'Could be. But after he warmed up he sounded OK. But I don't think anyone knew what he was singing about. It was all mixed up, even something about not being able to see the Man in the Moon – or the Man's right *eye*.'

'Maybe he was just sticking in one of those moon facts he got from Mr. Thwaite – that the man's right eye is a giant crater.'

'Maybe. *I* think right "eye" was just to rhyme with "sky". The weirdest song was his own words to "Stand By Me" – which he sang pretty well. At least I wrote down some of *these*. I think I got most of them.'

'Good.'

'Do you want to hear?'

'Yes.'

Tris half-sang:

' "When the moon, was white, and people, didn't lie,
and send, their colour, up above,
I won't, be afraid, when the moon they paint…" '

'Sounds like a children's story or something,' Francine said. 'Maybe it's just a pastiche of the song he's done.'

'Yeah. Maybe it's just a story about painting the moon, but I don't know why it's about people lying or not being afraid.'

'No. Can I have them for a while so I can think about them?'

Tris handed her what he'd written down. 'Then he started singing some of the Beach Boys' "In My Room".'

'I don't know. But it's still good you saw him.'

*

Banno lay on his bed. The room was so small, so old, so dank. The tiny window was too high up. Why didn't she ever open it? He needed fresh air.

He sprang up. It was getting dark, he had to go.

He stuffed his few belongings and his sleeping bag into his pack and grabbed his guitar. There was a knock at the door, sending his heart pounding. Had someone – Tris? – worked out what he'd said, and told Thwaite? Thwaite would know what he'd done: 'He's read the report. He's broken his oath.' Was he here to get him?

'Banno?'

It was her, the priestess, or whatever she was; she knew too, and she'd heard him clanking around, packing his stuff.

He slung his bag over his shoulder, ready to run.

'Banno? How did it go?'

It was a ploy, but he had no choice. He opened his cell door.

She looked at his bulging backpack and back at him. 'Are you leaving?' She sounded surprised.

He rushed, brushed past her, then opened the door and turned round. 'Stop trying to save me. I need peace.'

*

Tris answered his phone.

'… But he was leaving,' she said, 'with his backpack when I got home.'

'To go where?'

'I don't know. He said he needed some peace.'

'What's that mean?'

'I don't know.'

*

The day was disappearing, but it was clear and warm, and the road into the hills was familiar enough, even though – maybe due to the rain – it seemed rougher than the time before. It was dry now, but more like a corrugated track.

The orangewoods loomed, their greens and browns, like that painting in Johnny's window, welcoming him. They closed in on him. His steps slowed, to a treacle, in time to a sad blues song in his head. *Lord have mercy.*

He went through the stile and into the grove. He walked aimlessly, up and down and circling round until he came upon something he'd never seen before. Was it a teepee? He walked up to it. It was a shelter made of branches and plastic bags. He peered in. Nothing. He went inside and slipped his pack off, and sat down in the dirt and sang…

> 'I risked it, I rasked it,
> no green and yellow basket.
> I wrote a song about the moon
> and in the way I sang it, I sang it,
> maybe someone got it,
> maybe they will find it.'

A robin landed just outside, and Banno smiled at it.
I want to be happy like this, all the time.

TWENTY-EIGHT
Saturday

Francine made her way out of the church, her head zinging with questions.

Johnny's was thankfully empty. The radio was on – 'Red River Rock': Johnny and the Hurricanes. I'm at Johnny's, she thought. Here in this red rock valley. Updated classics were some of her favourite music, like this rockabilly-ish 'Red River Valley'. So were boogie-woogie modernizings of cowboy songs.

She could hear Johnny's knife on wood in the kitchen – morning 'chopping hour', as he called it.

She was glad she didn't recognize the tall, young waitress coming over to her table; it was less intimate, no need to make small talk. Francine ordered a cup of tea.

It was the right place to be, nodding along unnoticeably to the rocky song while staring out the window on to Copernicus Broadway. It was nothing like looking at the orangewoods or anything like that, but it was a never-ending view of people's five-second walk from one end of the window to the other, with another person or not – their different strides, their smiles, maybe looking up, or even into the café. And no one would wonder what she was doing here alone, watching the world go by.

The music stopped and a commercial came on.

Did my telling him to busk mess everything up?

She took out Banno's lyrics about the moon being painted that Tris had given her. It helped that they fit a familiar tune.

She sang them again in her head.

> *'When the moon, was white,*
> *And people, didn't lie,*
> *and send, their colour, up above.'*

It fit the rhythm of 'Stand By Me' well enough.

That childlike but ominous guitar-intro Francine knew well – the opening notes of 'Paint it Black' – came on the radio. Then came the words about darkness, about wanting the sun 'blotted out' from the sky and everything painted black.

The song ended and another came on, one Francine didn't like, and she tried not to listen to it. She repeated Banno's words to herself. *'When the moon was white, and people didn't lie, and send their colour up above…'*

He'd closed the door on her at the church like he couldn't wait for her to leave. Did that mean he was writing words that mattered to him and he wanted to get them right? But why sing about a world 'when the moon was white'.

The young woman brought the cup of tea.

'Thank you. Did you say "yum yum"?'

'No; "enjoy your tea".'

319

Was it a story? Suggested by something in Songs and Poetry? Maybe a nightmare he had? – about people sending colour up to the moon to darken it? Like his life had become?: black; dead?

Francine, it's only a song, a nonsensical one. That's all he was doing: singing a song. Stop trying to read something into it. You've spent enough time on it.

She'd give it two more minutes while she sipped her tea. It would come to nothing; and maybe it was just a way to keep Banno in her mind. But she felt she owed it to him, or maybe it was just that she found the process interesting.

She thought of the Beatles' 'Strawberry Fields'. There were lines she never understood in that, like the one about being in someone's tree. But, like other songs, she thought to herself – other great songs – the words might sound like gibberish, but they could mean something, and it might be possible to 'grok' them if you listened to them enough.

What if she stuck the moon into Paint It Black and it became a song about the moon – not the sun – being blotted out from the sky? And *painted? – black?* She looked at Banno's other words.

> *'No I won't, be afraid*
> *when the moon they paint.'*

A rhyme, girl, and not a very original one; you know, like moon/June, love/above.

Focus, Francine. In reality, how could one be 'afraid' of the moon being 'painted'. That sounds like some primitive eclipse-belief. And what was with the Man in the Moon's right eye? Nothing. 'Eye' just rhymed with 'sky', like Tris said.

Enough. She shook her head at herself, and wondered if

the waitress had seen her trying to puzzle it all out.

I just hope Banno's alright, Francine thought as she rounded the corner.

Her eye was caught by a different view of the church than she remembered. A pale moon, three-quarters full, had drifted down from a Corsica-shaped cloud to sit on the steeple. Yes, in Goodmews the moon is beautiful, as it's beautiful anywhere on a clear night. She recalled once seeing the Bay of Rainbows crater through a telescope. It had been sunrise on the moon, and the mountain peaks on the crater's border were lit up first, with the floor below still in darkness. For a few minutes, the peaks had looked like they were detached from the moon – the phenomenon known as the Jewelled Handle.

And maybe one day she'd see that other lunar beauty, the Imbrium Sculpture, though what a 'sculpture' meant on the moon she wasn't sure. It would wait for her; it had waited for almost 4 billion years. It was wonderful that the moon was an unspoiled world of rock.

Or, still unspoiled. She recalled hearing, in her course, about a secret government plan – Project A119, from the late-fifties – to explode a nuclear bomb on the moon, which would have produced a flash of light bright enough to be visible from earth. It was cancelled. For Francine, a successful Project A119 would have constituted a crime against the solar system. *I'd go to great lengths to save the moon*, she said to herself. *The orangewoods? Yes. Johnny's? I suppose so.*

When she got back to her parlour pew, she phoned Tris.

'Tris. Have you heard from Banno?'

'No. Is he back?'

'No. Tris, I was thinking about what he said when he left, that he needed some peace.'

'And?'

'I think he meant the orangewoods.'

'Why?'

'He had everything with him – his backpack, his guitar. Where else would he go?'

'*I* don't know. Somewhere else in town? Why the orangewoods.'

'I don't know, Tris. But that's my guess… Could you go up there and check. See if he's there, if he's OK?'

'You want *me* to go?'

'I think you'd have a better chance to talk to him than I would.'

'He didn't want to talk to me. I don't think he wants to talk to anyone.'

'Tris. I don't think he knows *what* he wants.'

She was probably right, like she'd been about *him*. She'd made him realize he was wasting his life playing his dice game just by the slight look of disapproval she'd given him, and now he hadn't for a week. So, why was he talking to her this way? She'd helped him. The song 'Anything You Can Do (I Can Do Better)' came into Tris's head. *Whatever I think I know, I think you know better.*

What was there to lose. Just time. And energy. 'OK. I'll go this afternoon… How do I get there?'

'You know Orangewood Drive.'

'Sure. But it's a long ways, isn't it?'

'It's not that far, just a few miles up.'

'And the orangewoods?'

'You'll see them off to your left. And the hills are spectacular.'

She turned on the News at Noon. It was Vietnam, like every day, and again those murky phrases – 'collateral damage', 'friendly fire'. And more reports on Agent Orange. *That* was hardly murky. It was a chemical spray that destroyed crops, and eliminated forest foliage to 'increase the enemy's visibility'. She'd heard it described by those on the ground as history's latest example of a scorched-earth policy.

The only thing that seemed murky to Francine about Agent Orange was its name. It was colourless, named after the orange stripe on the barrels it was stored in. She'd even come across the fact that it came in a range of toxic strengths: Agents Pink, Green, Purple, White, Blue and Super Orange, all named after the coloured stripe on their barrels. Was it really making people go orange, she wondered, and would there be pictures one day of them that would look like the after-effects of napalm? Or thalidomide? There's so much going on in the world, she thought, that we're never told about, or are misled about, and find out later the harm it caused. Nuclear weapons testing came to mind. Reports had come out after meltdowns at plants in the Soviet Union, and Francine remembered reading about the Windscale fire in England, maybe ten years before, that had burned for three days and spread radioactive contamination across Europe.

She was glad the church had served as a refuge for Banno, at least for a night. But had encouraging him to sing, in the end been his downfall? No. She couldn't blame herself for that. He wanted to sing. He needed to sing. About colour and the moon, for some reason. She thought for a moment about moon shadows. What would a shadow of a moon in orange eclipse – or a coloured moon? – look like?

Had what Banno said meant something?

She'd once read that code breakers were 'linguistic alchemists' who conjured sensible words out of meaningless symbols. But Banno's words weren't meaningless, were they? And she wasn't a code breaker anyway.

But what had he said? That there'd been a world where the moon was white, where 'people didn't lie', until something, or someone, sullied the moon, by 'sending their colour' up to it? She'd decided it was gibberish, hadn't she? So why was she still turning it over in her mind?

What didn't feel right? What hadn't felt right since Tris had told her about her colour being used for the anniversary? The colour. Why hadn't Sam told her the date, or how her colour – made to such exacting, unusual specifications – was going to be used.

Why hadn't she asked him?

Can it really have been created for something as basic as a moon poster? For this anniversary, in two days. The landing. Tomorrow. Is there a connection?

The landing. Sinus Medii. Its coordinates: 2.4 degrees north, 1.7 east. Mare Imbrium: 32.8 degrees north, 15.6 west. Not that far from each other, probably less than the width of Mare Imbrium itself. Mare Imbrium; so smooth, you could almost paint it? So visible...

What had Banno said when he quit? That he hated liars. That Sam had lied about something? The moon? Could that have made him quit? Was that possible?

Is he telling us that someone – Mr. Thwaite? – is planning to send my colour up to the moon. To Mare Imbrium? Can that be done?

Francine knew she would drive herself crazy if she kept going over what Banno had sung. But, she thought, it was that lesson in life that kept recurring, and is never answered: when to be concerned about something, and when one's being overly concerned. She wasn't a panicker, but, When to panic, and when not to.

Her brain was so engaged she could barely contain it. Could her Goodmews Gold be Thwaite's Agent Orange – his scorched-*moon* policy?

The jangly guitar and the Byrds singing 'Don't Doubt Yourself, Babe' floated into her head, with the words about 'knowing where it's at' and the truth being found.

She had the feeling that her jigsaw puzzle of questions had suddenly solved itself.

I'm right, as sure as I can be.

But my Goodmews Gold will be the stain on it, for everyone to see.

And the evidence, the 'truth'… Where can that be found?

*

It was late afternoon by the time Tris got fully into the hills. *I'd rather use my brains than my legs*, he thought. *I know my limits.* He stopped. *Do I really have to become your search party, your crusade, just because you think Banno might need us and you think you know where he might be? 'I'm Your Puppet', and not in a good way. It sticks in my craw. And it's* far. *And the hills aren't 'spectacular'; 'tacular' is about as much as I could say – they aren't much different to what I've seen in other places: they're pretty, but no dramatic features. I think locals revere their hills, or dales, or whatever, because*

325

they're familiar. For me, it's a view I could get tired of.

Was she a local now? And is the moon so beautiful to her because it's familiar?

He was off again. *Keep going, keep going.* It sounded like what a policeman would say while breathalyzing someone for drunk driving.

He walked steadily up the road, a riverbed alongside – more a shallow, silted-up waterway, dotted with white, full-moon-round rocks. Was this mission of his as sad as that of poor sods who go up a mountain to watch an eclipse – or shooting stars – and it rains?

He heard a guitar, then some singing, in the distance. It was Banno's voice.

Giant A-shaped trees – they had to be the orangewoods – began to appear to the left. The singing was coming from the trees.

Should he leave. Report back to Francine that he'd found Banno but felt he shouldn't disturb him?

He saw something that looked like a stile, and went through it. He should try to talk to him.

> 'Mistererererr Mooooooonnlight.
> You came to me, one summer night.
> And from your beam you made my dream.'

Tris remembered talking about the song the first time they met. He walked towards the singing until he saw a shelter of sorts. That was where it was coming from. Who had built that? It couldn't have been Banno in so short a time, could it?

He thought about joining in, to announce his presence, but Banno would have jumped out of his skin.

Tris waited for him to finish, but Banno kept going. He walked up to the shelter, as gingerly as he could, but the needles pine-chillingly crunched underfoot. He stopped. The playing had stopped. He watched a leaf that kept riding up and down on a branch and felt almost ill, though he knew that 'almost' ill was not ill.

'Banno?'

There was a sharp screech from another bird.

Banno came out of the shelter, hunched, then straightened up most of the way, still looking at the ground. He had on a waspy-looking, yellow and white striped rugby shirt, and Tris could smell its sweat, or Banno's sweat, or urine, thicker than the fresh air. 'P.U.' he thought.

Banno was still looking down. He rubbed his chin. 'Who told you I was here. Who are you to bother me?' He raised his hands to just below his eyes, in a vertical, almost prayerful, palm near palm, looking at Tris, then sliced down with a breathy 'tyou!'

Tris wondered if he should be afraid of him. Even though Tris was a bit taller, Banno probably weighed more. But he'd try to answer. 'Francine—'

Banno looked up. 'The old muumuu bag!' It was a menacing voice and his eye looked wild, rather than distant. His face had gone brown, like he'd suddenly lapped up whatever sun there was. 'Why'd you follow me!'

He felt Banno had said this only to show his anger; it was clear he didn't care how Tris responded. But Tris felt he should. 'I *didn't* follow you. We just wanted to see if you were OK. Francine thought you might come up here. She was just trying to help.'

'Did you bring money?'

'I brought some cashews and raspberries.'

'You idiot! Get off my land.' Banno turned and went back into his shelter.

Why am *I here*, Tris said to himself. Were they even in the same world anymore? *Leave him to his unhappy existence, let him stew in his own curmudge.*

But. 'Banno? Is there anything I can do?'

'You can leave me alone,' came a muffled voice from inside.

'Is that what you want?'

'*Don't ask me* the same thing again. I've told you already. Stop making me repeat myself!'

'Sorry.'

'You've messed me up, man.'

'Sorry. I'll go.'

'You're so *stu*pid' –

Tris thought about tossing the song title back at him – 'Stupid Cupid', and Banno rejoining with a light-hearted 'Stop pickin' on *me*'.

– 'Why'd you tell me to read that re*port*?'

Report… Was Banno talking about that Red Report, that Tris had mentioned to him and Francine?

'I didn't tell you to read it, Banno.'

'You've ruined my life!'

'*I* ruined it?' *By mentioning a report?* But it blocked everything else out of Tris's mind. 'Was something in it?' He said this to keep the conversation going, as much as anything else.

'*You* know.'

'I don't, Banno. I don't know anything about it, except it

was called that in what I was proofreading. But I'm sorry. I shouldn't have brought it up.'

There was silence. Tris looked around. It was beautiful there; the orangewoods were clothed in a downy rust, a fuzz of needles. And Banno had made them his home.

'Do you want me to leave?'

'Cheeve me a chone.'

Tris understood. And was Banno telling him he was the only one who did? Was he telling him, in his cryptic way, not to give up on him, not to leave him?

Tris had once heard that a real friend was someone who told you their personal yoga mantra. Even though it was the same one doled out to millions, it was theirs. He grabbed the lifeline: 'Thar's poetry in thum thar words.

'Banno?'

He waited. There was only the sound of breeze – a steady cricketwhistle of wind swaying the treetops – and a bird call, and another. Tris felt that his stance was different, as if he was being filmed, or watched. He felt like he had the patience of topiary.

He took his bags of fruit and nuts out and put them on the ground.

'Goodbye, Banno.'

Banno listened, relieved that Tris's footsteps were growing fainter, then gone. What had Tris said?: 'I didn't tell you to read it.' *You think someone else did?*

Banno cast his mind back to the conversation they'd had at the Moon Centre. What *had* Tris said?

As he played the scene over in his mind, a film of heat rose to his skin. He recalled being unable to respond when

Tris mentioned the report. He hadn't lied – he hadn't said he'd never heard of it. But he'd only seen the first page. He'd read the report after they'd spoken, yes, but it was his own decision. *Tris* hadn't told him to.

He felt his throat catch. *Why have I been blaming him? Am I crazy?*

He walked out of his shelter, kicking aside rocks and broken twigs, and lay down on his back, staring up to a small clearing of sky. He watched the white clouds file away, as sombrely as Moonlight Sonata, leaving a pastel blue in their wake. *That's where colour should be,* he thought. *In the sky, not on the moon.* He closed his eyes and let the gentle breeze fan his body.

He could tell that the light was fading. He opened his eyes, expressionless. Had his life been like the moon? Light he would never reach, surrounded by darkness.

That hollow tree he'd seen. He could walk down the slope to it, find a stick – a moonstick – and gouge three holes in his chest, one at each breast and one at his belly button, then smear something into the hole, the crater, on the right. He'd climb inside, the Old Man in the Moon.

Thy key be hummed. I will be done.

The quiet settled in, hopefully for the centuries.

Banno began to lullaby himself, stretching the words out.

> 'Silent night, lonely night
> All is black, moon is white
> Round yon light from your manly face
> All is bright in eternal space

I will sleep in peace
I will sleep in peace.'

*

The sun was setting, round and big like the moon. Tris had been walking towards the sun's brightness. He turned round for a moment to treat himself to the pleasure of looking at the softer, powder-blue sky.

When he reached the silty riverbed again, it was bathed in gold dusk. Birds were chirping-in the end of day, in stereo: a sparrows' echo? – or 'sparrowzecho' as someone had dubbed it.

Was it his fault? How could it be? How could mentioning a report ruin someone's life – even if he *had* told Banno to read it. But he hadn't. But that's what Banno believed, and there was nothing he could do about it. He'd tried. But what could be in a report to cause someone to quit their job – and disappear into the hills?

By the time he reached home and got inside, it was nearly ten. Francine would be expecting him to phone. He was exhausted. He'd phone in the morning.

*

'Sam? Mid-course correction completed.'
    'Great.'
    'The report's good.'
    'Good.'
    'Just so you know, I'll be incommunicado here at the

Cape until the landing tomorrow night. I won't even have access to the fax.'

'OK.'

'I'll phone after I have confirmation of the landing, and just before I make the report public.'

Thwaite's brain fizzed with a soothing calmness. He'd done all he could. It was out of his hands now.

And the report was good, though it still made no sense that he couldn't find it. He'd locked it away. He hadn't even opened the drawer…

Thwaite's heart was suddenly thumping: he'd taken out those facts for Banno. Had the report been inside them? That had to be it. He'd given the report to Banno. Would Francine know where Banno was, or what he'd done with it?

But none of that mattered. In 24 hours Surveyor would be on the moon. Kennington would make the report public, and the world would be in awe.

TWENTY-NINE
Sunday, July 16

He went downstairs after having some breakfast. He'd phone Francine after having a game. He'd already proved to himself that he could go cold turkey if he wanted to, but playing was easier than not playing.

He sat down and spread out his charts on his desk, took the two brown dice out of the drawer, let them fall, and recorded a seven.

A knock at the door jostled him back into Goodmews. Through the pane, he could see it was Francine. He wasn't ready for her yet, but he had no choice, and opened the door.

'Francine!' he forced a welcome. She was even more of a let-down than he'd anticipated. She wasn't beautiful, and she had those birthmark-type blotches high on her cheek, like his mother.

'Did you find him?' She looked excited but her voice was dull, almost mechanical. He hadn't noticed that before, and wondered if it ever embarrassed her.

'Yes.' He didn't feel like saying more. Was he turning into Banno – not wanting to talk to Francine, like Banno hadn't wanted to talk to *him*? He'd already confirmed she'd been right about finding Banno; why should he have to listen to her droning on in her wise words. *Drone, baby, drone.* But he had to say *some*thing.

'Like you thought.'

'Thanks for going up there.'

'Did you want to come in,' he knew he needed to say. He wished his game hadn't been on show.

'Thanks.'

'You were right,' he said, walking back to his desk.

He pushed his dice and charts to the side, and looked back at Francine. She was looking at him, not at his game, but he wondered if she would say something about it. *Don't! play your game alone*, he sang to himself, to the tune of the Searchers' 'Don't Throw Your Love Away'.

'There was this makeshift shelter that he was in,' Tris said. 'Someone must have left it.'

'Oh. I think I might have seen that. A ways off to the right of the main path?'

'Yeah.'

'It's good you found him.'

Tris nodded. He could tell he had that wry, Lee Harvey Oswald closed mouth. But Francine hadn't even mentioned his game, and he should be thankful for that.

'Can we sit down?' she said.

He motioned to his armchair, and sat down at his desk.

'How'd he seem?'

'Not great.'

'Did he say anything?'

Tris didn't feel like saying anything himself. But what was the point of that?

'He told me to go away; what right did I have to come looking for him.'

'Are you saying it's *my* fault?' Francine said.

'No… It was the right thing to do…

'He did say one thing. He told me he'd read that report.'

' "That report". Which *one*?'

'The Red Report? – that I mentioned to you, that was in what I proofread?'

'OK. Yes.'

'He said that reading it ruined his life.' Tris winced. 'And that I told him to.'

'Did you?'

'No. I just asked him about it, like I asked you.'

'Because you didn't want more work,' she smiled.

'Yeah.'

'Tris. It's not your fault that he read it. You shouldn't blame yourself. Anyway, how could this report be enough to make him quit?'

'I don't know, but it sounded like he meant it.'

'Did he say anything else?'

'No. He'd probably already said more than he wanted to. He just wanted me to leave.'

'And you *did*.'

'Yeah.'

'He didn't say anything about what was in this report?'

'That's what I've just said. That's *all he said*. Does it *matter* what was in it?'

Tris wondered why he was being like this. Hadn't Francine just taken a load off his mind by telling him he wasn't to blame?

'Tris, just relax,' Francine said calmly. 'I think it's important.'

'Sorry. I just don't know what else I can say.'

'It's alright.'

Thank goodness, he felt, that she had given him the space to apologize, and had accepted it. All could be OK again between them.

'I think I might know what was in it.' She said this with a straight face, in her straightforward way, her head held straight.

'How.'

'From what he sang.'

Tris could feel his irritation rising again, or was it more just bracing himself against what she might be about to say?

'I think Mr. Thwaite is planning to paint the moon.'

It took Tris a few seconds to react. 'Where did that come from?'

'Banno's words, that you told me.'

'Franci-ine.' Tris could hear himself whining. Why did he whine so much? Because he could? Because he didn't have children who would have done his whining for him?

Is this what he'd come back to – Francine's 'brainstorm' about Thwaite, and *Banno*? After all Tris had done, as she'd told him to – gone all the way up there, found Banno, tried to talk to him, told her what Banno had said – this was what she had to say?

'Why do you think his words mean *any*thing? And what do you mean Thwaite's planning to paint the moon.'

'Do you want to hear?'

Not really. 'OK.'

'I was in Johnny's yesterday. I heard "Paint It Black" on the radio.'

'Yes, it's on all the time.'

She paused a moment. 'Do you want to hear.'

'Sorry.'

'Do you know the words?'

'Think so.'

'About the sun being "blotted out" from the sky, and everything being painted black?'

'OK.'

'I thought I was an idiot—'

'You're not an idiot, Francine.'

'—to waste my time comparing the Stones' words to what Banno was singing. But I think that, somehow, they filled in the puzzle for me...

'I think Banno's words mean what I said they meant.'

'You *think*.'

'I'm pretty sure.'

It wasn't a real thing she was talking about, was it?

He said her words back to her as deadpan as he could, to see what it sounded like – to her too: 'Samuel Thwaite, the man who founded the Moon Centre, wants to "blot out" the moon, by painting it.'

'Yes. When I gave Banno the idea to busk, it seemed to remind him that there was something important he had to tell people about.'

'Francine. He sang a song about somebody sending their "colour" up to the *moon*. And you're saying that means that the moon is actually going to be "blotted out" from the sky? – *painted,* by the Moon Centre?'

'Yes.' She sounded impatient, but not as impatient as *he* was. Why was he even talking about this? But he could be as sure as she was, about what she was saying.

'Francine, it makes sense that Banno had the Moon Centre on his mind after quitting; he even sang a bunch of moon songs. But from what I saw, I don't think he was singing about anything. You know what state he's in. You told me how he was when he quit and when he came to the church. I think everything's just become jumbled up for him. Maybe he did need to sing about these things to get them out of his head. But how can you possibly deduce from his songs – draw a straight line – to the Moon Centre *painting the moon?*'

She looked up at the ceiling behind him, like she was in deep six. Had he landed a blow? Did he have her theory on the ropes?

'Tris, you know Banno probably as well as I do.'

'I don't know him very well.'

'I know. But do you think he's the sort of person who would go out and busk, perform for strangers, just for "fun"?'

'Maybe to make some money?'

'But it didn't seem to you that what he was singing mattered to him.'

'I don't know. But if he felt *compelled* to tell people something, why in the world would he do it in a way that… made no sense? How would he know if anyone was even going to listen? – let alone be able to work out his "message".'

'Maybe he didn't care if anyone heard him, or, If someone gets it, fine.'

It still didn't make sense. 'What if you hadn't given Banno the idea to busk? What would he have done?'

'I've thought about that. I don't know.'

Had he won? Had he proved her wrong? 'And what if I hadn't seen him busk, and told you about what he sang.'

'I know. That's the only way I would have found out... But you *did* see him. And you found him in the woods, and he told you that he read that report – and that it ruined his life.'

'But how can you be the only person who's "worked out" what he's saying.'

And do I believe in what I'm *saying? Am I arguing just to argue, until I've got no arguments left? Why am I doing that?*

'Maybe I'm the only one who's tried,' she said. 'Maybe I'm the only one who's able to put two and two together. Because I made the colour that Banno was singing about.'

'OK.' Tris was sure she'd expected his eyes to at least widen.

'You're not surprised,' she said.

'No. No one else makes colours for the Centre – do they?'

'No. I'm the only one.' She met his eyes. He was surprised at how much like his they were – unexciting brown and hazel. 'It took me a while to put two and two together – that the colour I'd created was unlike anything I'd ever heard of. It would be a complete waste of Sam's time, and mine, to use it for something simple, flat, like maybe a poster of the moon.'

The old song 'It's Only a Paper Moon' came into Tris's head.

'He's not using the paint for any anniversary,' she said. 'Somehow he's worked out a way to get the weight down for as much of it as he needs, and got it on to Surveyor 4. I may have even given him the idea for compressing it. He wouldn't know about that sort of thing. Maybe someone's helped him... Did you hear about the launch?'

Tris thought he had. 'Was that Surveyor? On the news?'

'Yes. Friday. Sam must have worked out a way that the

paint, once it's got to the moon, can be spread over some of the surface. I wouldn't have thought he would know how to do that either, but however it's being done, I think the paint will be spread over Mare Imbrium, the Man's right eye. I mentioned that crater to you once?'

Tris remembered. He pictured the dark grey spot on the moon. Was she saying that Thwaite had figured out a way to give the Man an even 'blacker' eye?

'Do you remember when they said Surveyor's supposed to land, Tris?'

'Just tell me, Francine.'

'Tonight. About 7 o'clock our time. And the "anniversary" celebrations are set for tomorrow. I'm afraid it all fits together.' Tris watched as Francine took a piece of paper out of her pocket. It had a strip of colour on it that was reddish, ambery, almost transparent, sparkling.

'Is that it?' he said.

Francine nodded.

'It's beautiful.'

'Thank you. But painting the moon is not what I wanted the colour to be beautiful for.'

Tris felt a loosening in his heart, as if he'd been playing his cards so close to his chest that he'd hardly taken a deep breath. He wasn't sure exactly how, but he felt that his position of opposition had slipped away. Had he wanted her to be right? Because she was?

'I know.'

'I just wish we had the report,' she said. 'That would be the proof.'

We, he thought. *OK*. 'Would Banno tell us where it is?'

'I don't know if that would happen.' She opened her

mouth wide, like she was giving herself time to think, and Tris had no choice but to stare at her tongue and teeth. 'I should have told you I'd made the colour,' she said. 'Maybe together we would have worked out what was happening, and we could have told NASA. Maybe they could have stopped it…

'You know the Beach Boys song Banno was singing?'

' "In My Room".' Tris said this with what felt like the obedience of a concert pianist's page-turner.

'What's it about?' she said. He felt like they were at the beginning of the Shangri-las' 'Leader of the Pack' and doing some back-and-forth question and answer thing. He didn't want to jump to her every command.

'You know it as well as I do, Francine.' Why was he still being so recalcitrant? Wasn't he on her side now? It was simply something she wanted to know, and she didn't ask things for no reason.

'Just tell me, Tris.'

She tries hard, like a teacher, he thought. 'It's dark and Brian Wilson's alone, but he won't be afraid,' he said.

'Like in "Stand By Me" that Banno sang… And,' she prompted him, 'Brian Wilson's afraid to do what?'

'Tell his secrets?'

'In his room. It's the only clue I can think of. I think Banno is saying that the report is in his room – in Music and Poetry.'

'Why would he put it there.' *Why do I keep chucking obstacles in her path? Be nice, Tristram. Help out. And, if she found the report, that should prove things, one way or the other.*

'Where else, unless he wanted to keep it with him. In his *backpack?* Why would he? I think he wants someone to find it.'

'Maybe he meant his room in the church.'

'I don't think so. I think he got rid of it before he quit.'

'Why?'

'I don't know. But I'm going to have a look.'

'What if someone's there.'

Francine looked at him like she'd had enough of his contrariness, and he thought she might leave then and there.

'There won't be on a Sunday. And I'll just be getting some stuff I need to look at at home.'

'Where are you going to look?'

'I'm not sure. But if it's there, I want to find it.'

'Even if nothing can be done.'

'Even if nothing can be done.'

She cocked her head towards his briefcase. 'Can I borrow that?'

He nodded. 'Should I come with you?'

She pursed her lips and shook her head – 'No no. Wait here. I'll phone you.'

THIRTY

She walked quickly to the Centre. There was a sunless wind, and even though it wasn't solid cold, some people had winter hats on and it would have been hard to recognize them even if she had been walking more slowly.

At the door, she could see the square piece of cardboard hanging inside by two pieces of string:

NASA THWAITE MOON CENTRE
74 Goodmews Way
GOodmews 20897

Founded September 1965
Open Mon–Sat, 9–5

The Moon, Geology, and Local History
Visitors Welcome

The worry poked its head above the ground like a mole: *what if nothing's there*; and she knew the thought could easily take her head down a rabbit hole.

No. She unlocked the front door, pushed slowly through the revolving glass and made her way down the corridor and into Songs and Poetry. It wasn't likely, because it was at the back – but if someone saw someone in the room, and phoned Sam…

She stayed away from the window. It was closed, and she could hear nothing outside.

The room looked the same as Friday. She went over to the desk and opened both drawers and rummaged through them, then walked over to Poetry Corner and turned back round. The tick of the clock in the still of the room made her stop to feel her heart. She scanned the framed lyric sheets and photographs on the wall. Was there anywhere to hide something where no one would look for it?

She could feel some carpet sticking up under her shoe, and looked down. She must have accidentally dragged the corner up. She pushed it down with her shoe, but it didn't stay. She pushed it down again, but it curled up. Was that how it had been before? She knelt down, facing the corner of the room, and gripped the edge of the carpet to see if it would peel towards her. It did; and it kept coming. Had it lost its glue? She looked round the back of the carpet. Nothing. She got up and stood on the corner to flatten it, as much as she could, and looked around the room again.

A line from 'Four until Late', the Cream song she'd been hearing lately, came into her head. Something about a woman being like a dresser and a man going through her drawers. She darted back to the desk, with the same sort of compulsion, she felt, that a squirrel might have that couldn't resist having another go at a bird-feeder.

She opened the top drawer and methodically went through the folders, labelled VISITOR COMMENTS SHEETS.

Just forms. She opened the bottom drawer and went through more folders, with other Centre forms. But as she was closing the drawer, she saw another folder at the back, and pulled it out. It was unlabelled. She opened it and saw a sheaf of paper inside and began to leaf through it. Moon facts. Her heart began to thump. She remembered – *the ones Banno had studied for the quiz? Had he put them there? Tried to hide them there? Why would he do that – if that's what he did. There wasn't anything... secret?*

'*Do you want to know a secret...?*' she said to herself. She rifled through the pages until she came to a sheet with a word in red across the top: EMBARGOED. Below that was The Red Report. She felt giddy, but glued to the floor, as she flipped to the end. Thwaite's signature.

She scanned through the report, her heart in her throat.

It was in the past tense, as if the events had already happened. Kennington Varnen – she'd come across his name somewhere – a NASA engineer, had created a 'moonstick' and had disguised it as a temperature gauge. It had been attached to Surveyor 4 and had carried an explosive mixture of paint, Goodmews Gold, to the moon.

She felt it in her stomach.

It was detonated over Mare Imbrium tonight,

She stopped reading and stared at the phrase, then looked at the rest of the sentence.

spreading the colour over its entirety, for all the world to see.

And the paint would be permanent. She went back to the report's first page, with the date:

July 16th. *Today*: just after 8 P.M. Eastern Standard Time – *or 7 here*. She hadn't wanted to be right, but she was. What could she do? NASA could abort Surveyor, up to a few minutes before it touched down. She could fax them the report. But even if she got it to them, and they accepted it as genuine, would they decide that saving the moon from being painted was more important than landing this mission? Or would they choose to keep their programme on target, and accept this 'stigmata' on the moonscape as a price worth paying?

Would they even *hear* a fax?

She took her notebook out of her bag and made sure she still had the number.

She wrote her message.

This is an emergency communication from Francine Robb, Associate Director and Colour Scientist at the NASA Thwaite Moon Centre, Goodmews, South Dakota.

Five minutes ago, I discovered a secret report to do with Surveyor 4, prepared by my boss, Samuel Thwaite. The report details the contents of a small rocket affixed to Surveyor 4 by your engineer, Kennington Varnen, said to contain a temperature gauge. There is no gauge in this attached rocket. What is inside is a golden paint mixed with chemicals. When Surveyor touches down, this paint will explode out onto the lunar surface, staining the moon. It will be visible to everyone on earth, and it will be permanent.

I know this sounds fantastic, and I have no explanation for why two of your employees have decided to 'paint' the moon. But I am sure – from my knowledge of the colour and from what appears to be the clear science at the basis of this report – that a massive explosion of colour over the moon will occur if Surveyor achieves its soft touchdown tonight.

I implore you to respond immediately, so that I can fax you the report.

I am aware of the importance of this mission, but I am also aware of the irreversible damage to the moon that this paint will cause.

I am in the NASA Moon Centre, and I can see NASA's motto on the wall: 'For the Benefit of All'.

This promise to the world must be kept.

Francine checked that the machine was connected to the phone line, and turned it on. She dialled NASA's number and fed her page in.

She looked at her watch. It had been half an hour since she'd found the report.

When her message had gone, Francine noticed the complete quiet around her. It was all up to NASA now.

She heard a clacking noise and saw the machine spring into action. A message was coming through.

Send report immediately. Please understand we cannot respond further.

Francine fed each of the ten pages into the machine. What would they think, to get a report like this, hours before touchdown? At least they had told her to send it. And they were used to last-minute snafus, *weren't* they? They had happened on other flights; some of them hadn't even taken off.

There was nothing else she could do now. She put the moon facts back into the drawer and closed it, and stuffed the report and her message into Tris's briefcase. When she got outside she saw no one, and locked the revolving doors.

Back at the church, Francine sat down at her dressing table and stared at herself in the mirror. Mother's nose-tic. Would they crash it?

She got up to phone Tris, but she wanted to finish the thought that was troubling her most: why had she taken so long to work out what was happening? Hadn't it been staring her in the face? Sam's pushiness for a colour that seemed impossible should have been a red flag, not to mention his story about an 'anniversary'. But she hadn't had the confidence to question him. She'd trusted him too much. She'd wanted to please him because he'd given her the perfect job. And why *should* she have had to question him? He'd asked her to make all sorts of colours. She enjoyed doing it. Why should she have to worry about making *this* colour?

Was there another thought? She sat down again, to see if that made it come back to her. The moonstick. That was it. They must have got the name from her leaflet. Maybe painting the moon was just a notch on Thwaite's stick, and the Moon Centre had been the first. Though so what. Who cared where he'd got the name from.

'A red flag,' she thought again. Would the paint *be* permanent, though, like the report said? Wouldn't it 'erode', at least fade, even though she'd tried to make it as 'unfadeable' as possible? Wasn't it true that if a flag, for instance, was planted on the moon, it would turn white within a few years?

She dialled.

'Hello?' he answered.

'Tris…'

'Hi Francine.'

'I've got it.'

'The report?'

'Yes. And I've faxed it to NASA.' That catch in Francine's voice that Tris had always liked sounded like it was *gripping* her throat. It made him think for a moment about *John Lennon's* voice and its strangulated urgency.

'Really?'

'Yes. I told them I found it, that one of their engineers is involved—'

'Gee.'

'— and they told me to send it.'

'Wow. You've read it.'

'Enough of it. It's Thwaite's plan, to paint the moon. It's supposed to happen when Surveyor touches down, at 7.'

'Jeez. What do you think NASA will do?'

'I don't know. I hope they'll abort the flight.'

'It's not too late?'

'They can do it if they want,' she said.

'If they do, what will happen to the paint?'

'It will remain inside Surveyor.'

'That would be great.'

'Yeah.'

'When will we know?'

'Maybe not until it lands, or doesn't.'

Tris paused for a moment. 'How did you find it?'

'It was in a drawer. Stuck inside those moon facts.'

'Like you thought.'

'You *men*tioned them. I didn't know. I hoped it was somewhere… I'll show it to you.'

'Do you think Thwaite knows that someone got their hands on it?'

'I think he has to.'

'What will happen to him? And that engineer.'

'I don't know. Do you want to come over in a couple of hours, around 6.30? I'll show you the report. There's nothing we can do but wait till 7 and see what they say on the news.'

'Sure.'

*

Banno could tell the day was ending. He'd spent it playing his guitar, eating the cashews and raspberries Tris had left. He scrabbled around in his backpack until he found his transistor.

He was grateful that the battery hadn't run out, and moved the dial to Goodmews Radio. He turned the volume up just enough to hear the music better.

*

Tris walked up Crescent Crescent and along Copernicus Broadway. The darkening buildings and trees stood out against the early twilight in a Magritte sky.

After a while, who would really care about a coloured moon? If it happens, won't most people marvel at it anyway, then just forget about it? There's so much going on, down here on earth – television, dinner, worries.

He felt suddenly alone. *How lonely life can be. It must be overwhelmingly lonely for Banno, to be alone, to have nobody. Though maybe he's not lonely up there.*

Tris recalled how he himself often didn't feel lonely when he was playing his game, but when he went out, life intruded, and when he'd get back to his flat he'd feel lonely. Was that why Banno had shut him out? Because he was so afraid of feeling lonely after having some contact, and he had to protect himself? *Should I have tried harder to get through to him, tried harder to understand?*

He went up the concrete steps. The door was unlocked. *I'm lucky. I have someone I can talk to.*

As he got inside, he could see the back of Francine's head from her seat on a pew. It looked like she was staring straight ahead.

She turned around.

'Tris.'

He came and sat next to her. She had some papers in her hands.

'It that the report?'

She turned it over and he saw EMBARGOED at the top.

'Do you want to have a look?'

He flipped through it, seeing enough to satisfy himself that this was it, was what Francine had predicted.

'Do you think NASA would ever make this public, whatever happens?' he said.

'I'm not sure if *they* would, but *someone* will. *I* will, if no one else does.'

'People would know you made the paint.'

She looked down.

'Francine?'

She looked back up. Her eyes were clear.

She glanced at her watch. 'Goodmews Radio is monitoring NASA. I'm sure it will be announced soon.'

She picked up her transistor and turned it on. '96 Tears' was playing. Tris loved the song. Suddenly, at 'Too many teardrops for one heart,' the song faded out.

'We interrupt your Sunday evening listening to bring you this live announcement from NASA.'

Tris could feel his heart beating.

'This is NASA control, in Cape Canaveral Florida.' The voice sounded robotic. Tris met Francine's eyes. They were steady, but they were more walls than windows to her thoughts. Her mouth was closed, and Tris knew she was holding her breath.

'Surveyor 4, the latest unmanned NASA spacecraft to be sent to the moon, was due to land safely on the lunar surface five minutes ago. However, based on new information which emerged earlier today, NASA took the decision to deliberately crash the spacecraft into the moon.'

Francine's mouth had opened slightly.

'Surveyor 4 was carrying cargo that was placed in it just before launch, without NASA's knowledge. A paint mixture was hidden on board, and if Surveyor had touched down as expected, the paint would have exploded over Mare Imbrium, the crater that many see as the Man in the Moon's right eye. The crater would have been stained forever.

'By crashing the rocket, we have insured that the paint will remain inside Surveyor, and the moon will remain white.

'Until another mission photographs Surveyor on the moon, we won't have definitive proof that it has crashed, but we are convinced that this is what has occurred.

'The perpetrators of this foiled plot – two NASA employees – have been apprised of the evidence that NASA obtained today, and have been arrested – charged with unauthorized use of government property for private ends. Their plan, which they detailed in a ten-page document, will be released in full to the public tomorrow.

'NASA had a difficult decision to make. We could allow Surveyor to land as planned, and hope that the paint wouldn't be released. We had, of course, many important experiments on board, not to mention the need to insure a soft landing for future moon missions. However, we were not willing to take the chance that the moon might be defiled. It belongs to all humanity. It is For the Benefit of All.

'Finally, we want to assure the American public that NASA's commitment to get a man to the moon by the end of the decade remains firm. We have had setbacks before, and there may be others, but they will not alter our course.'

The DJ came back on and began to speak. Francine turned the radio off. She was smiling.

'You did it, Francine!'

'*They* did it. *We* did it… We need to tell Banno. He won't know what's happened.'

'If he still cares. He won't be happy to see me again.'

'Maybe not. But from his words we worked it out.'

Tris heard this in the rhythm of 'from your beam you made my dream', like Banno had sung outside his hovel.

'I'll go, Francine.' He heard his words come out husky, finding their way through his heart in his mouth.

*

Banno slung his backpack over his shoulder and picked up his guitar, then was through the stile and walking in the freshest, clearest, evening air, with the white moon shining above. He bristled in anticipation, as softly as bamboo, and sang: 'Jimmy crack corn, and I don't care.'

He was sure he'd heard right. Someone had got the report to NASA and the moon had been saved. It had to be Francine. She was the only one who would have keys to the place besides Thwaite. How had she found it? Had she worked it out from what he'd sung? From Tris?

There'd probably been other ways he could have told people what was happening, but he'd done what he could. He wasn't perfect. No one was. What was that line of Dylan's? That it's a lie that 'life is black and white'? Nothing was, not even an oath when there was something more important.

He'd left Francine in the lurch when he quit, and he'd locked Tris out of his life. But they hadn't given up on him.

When Banno reached the lime trees straddling the long lane littered with their little lemon-coloured leaves, he knew he was home.

ACKNOWLEDGEMENTS

Thank you
to all those without whom
this book would not have been.

Thank you also to

The M.C. Escher Company for M.C. Escher's quote © 2022
The M.C. Escher Company – the Netherlands.
All rights reserved. Used by permission. www.mcescher.com

and

Faber and Faber Ltd
for the *Church Going* extract
from *The Complete Poems* by Philip Larkin.

But my last word on thanks,
for the many things,
and the quiet and space,
goes to my wife, Roslyn.

REVIEWS OF *BACHELOR BUTTERFLIES*, JEFF PROBST'S FIRST NOVEL

'A strangely compelling narrative'
THE SUNDAY TIMES

'An atmosphere of anomie with a dash of hope'
JOHN HEGLEY, POET

'Very wonderfully written… It held and intrigued me.
The characters pulled me into their lives'
TONY PEAKE, NOVELIST

ABOUT THE AUTHOR

Jeff is American and has lived in London
since 1990 with his South African wife.

CONTACT JEFF

www.jeffprobst.co.uk

This book is printed on paper from sustainable sources managed under the Forest Stewardship Council (FSC) scheme.

It has been printed in the UK to reduce transportation miles and their impact upon the environment.

For every new title that Matador publishes, we plant a tree to offset CO_2, partnering with the More Trees scheme.

For more about how Matador offsets its environmental impact, see www.troubador.co.uk/about/